CAPTAIN II

by Earl E. Rogers

Barabara Press

Barabara Press
www.barabarapress.com

ISBN 0-9719097-1-7

First Printing August 2004

Printed in the United States of America

To

Sir Charles Evans Boswell

Noble not by inheritance but by deeds

Preflight

This book is a continuation of the letter that Captain Reynard has written to be given to his grandson when he is 18. In the wake of the September 11, 2001 terrorist attacks, Reynard has written the letter in case something should happen to him while he continues his career as an airline captain. All fiction has some basis in real human experience, but to attempt to see either *Captain* or *Captain II* as accurate histories of actual persons or organizations would be incorrect. Reference has been made to some accounts drawn from public records, but, apart from these, all similarities of characters, organizations, and events in *Captain* or *Captain II* to real persons, organizations, and events are purely coincidental.

E. Rogers

Contents

I

An Invitation

by Stephanie Blasini

My Dear Grandson,
before our company begins the busy Christmas flying schedule, I am going to try to finish the letter to you that I started a few months ago. There are moments when I still feel an overwhelming sadness over 9/11, but I am firmly convinced that, over time, those who value democracy and individual freedom will eventually overcome terrorism.

Preston, I told you about the road I followed to become an airline captain. Change the dates and names a little and you have the story of many pilots who worked their way up through the ranks of commercial aviation. My story is not unique, nor probably will it ever be. I think as long as people fly airplanes, young aspiring pilots will have to "pay their dues." The military route is very different, of course, but young military pilots pay their dues too. Often in a much more dangerous and demanding way.

Pilots often are portrayed as steadfast, emotionless individuals by the media. Some even try to fool themselves into thinking they match some kind of popular image. In spite of the attractive uniforms and carefully crushed hats, we still remain very ordinary human beings. We have fears. We have our flaws. We laugh. We cry. We have dreams and aspirations. We marry and have children. Often we get divorces. We get old. Perhaps if there is one characteristic of an airline pilot that does stand out, it is the strong awareness that every day he has lives to protect. The overwhelming majority respond to this awareness with very strong responsibility. They study. They learn. They try to do things right. Flying for them is not a game.

3

If you had the opportunity to watch an airline crew in action you might get the impression they are having fun. They probably are. Pilots love flying, or they wouldn't be there in the first place. But underneath outward appearances, there is a very serious attention to what they are doing. They know they are there to protect the safety of everyone on board the aircraft. Flying at times may become routine, but the stakes are always high. And every pilot knows that if an emergency occurs he or she cannot simply hand the problem to someone else.

When I get into an airplane, I am always looking for the perfect flight. I think most pilots feel the same way. There is nothing more satisfying in flying than to complete a trip knowing you and your crew have worked well together to make a safe and, one hopes, comfortable trip for those on board.

You did your preflight preparations properly. You planned your strategy as to how you would handle the particular weather conditions for that trip. Are there thunderstorms? Will the runways have snow on them? Are there strong crosswinds at the destination? Will fog be present? Or windshear? You checked your aircraft's condition and noted any inoperable items that might cause you to change your plan in any way. Passengers often feel that a smooth flight in smooth air meant that the pilots did a good job. They probably did. But on the days when the air is not smooth and the weather is bad is when the pilots work their hardest.

Because it is something one is always trying to perfect, I have come to see flying as an art form. It is an art form that always has the potential for serious consequences when mistakes are made. But flying also has its beauty. Each trip is a unique creation. Like a dance, the creation only exists in that moment. When the flight is over, or the dance is over, it can never be repeated in exactly the same way. And no corrections can be made. A dancer or a singer will try to hone his skills over many performances. If that jump was not

4

graceful or that high note not sung with elegance, the artist will work on perfecting it. A pilot will also be self-critical and will always think about how he could do everything just a little bit better. What makes flying such a serious art is that if a major error is made, as when the dancer falls or the singer screeches a note, the audience can't just go home and chuckle. Once a commercial airliner takes off, the fates of the artist and the public are inextricably entwined until the performance is over.

So, flying is something I try to do well. It is something I try to perfect. As I try to shape this art, I find it shapes me. It forces me to try to do my best. It requires me to learn from my mistakes and the mistakes of others. It makes me look deep inside to see who I really am. Sometimes I am happy with what I find. Sometimes I am not. It prods me to keep learning and studying. I am always happiest when I can shut down the engines at the end of the day and truthfully say to myself, "Not perfect, but very well done."

The actual flying of the airplane is only part of the job. One flight I remember that gave me a great deal of satisfaction occurred only a month ago. Marcos Rivero and I were getting ready to fly from Chicago to Orlando. As we were doing our cockpit setup in preparation for the flight, a father asked if his little girl could see the cockpit and meet the pilots. She was about eight years old and terrified to be, for her very first time, on an airplane. Even the thought of Disney World and Mickey Mouse waiting for her in Florida was not enough to keep her from trembling. Marcos and I could both see that she had demonstrated great courage just by stepping on board. She was frightened, but she was also determined to make the flight in spite of her fear.

I got up, and we sat her in the captain seat. We began to show her the various controls and switches.

"You see, Kylie, this is the yoke. If I pull back on it, the airplane goes up. If I push forward, the airplane goes down. If I turn it left, the airplane will turn to the left. If I turn it right, the airplane turns right."

I let her move the controls.

"That instrument right in front of you tells us if the nose of the airplane is up or down and if the wings of the airplane are turning us left or right. These two big levers over here are connected to the engines. When I push forward on them, the engines create more power and we go faster. When I pull the levers back, the airplane slows down. That instrument you see on the left side of the panel in front of you tells us how fast we are going while we are flying. This instrument over here always shows us how high we are."

She was not shaking anymore and started to ask us questions.

"What does that lever do?"

"Makes the wheels go up and down."

"What is this for?"

"That is how we tune the radios to receive signals from the ground."

"How can you tell where we are when we are up there?"

"We use radio signals and this computer to tell us our position."

The questions went on for a little longer, and then Kylie said she didn't feel so scared now and that she was ready to go sit with her daddy.

Once everyone was on board and seated, the doors were closed, and we started the engines. Just before we began our taxi, I called back to Elena Moore, our senior flight attendant that day, to ask her how Kylie was doing.

"Oh, she's fine. She's just sitting and chatting with her father."

We taxied out to the runway and received our clearance for takeoff. Chicago was under an overcast sky that morning. On the ground, the day looked very gloomy. Once we were airborne, however, and had climbed about 5,000 feet, we broke out of the clouds into the beautiful bright sunshine. Nothing but clear blue skies ahead for now as far as the eye could see.

We climbed up to altitude and set up cruise at 37,000 feet. The aircraft carried us steadily toward Orlando. Eventually, the cloud cover below us began to break up, and we could start to see the ground. Houses, farms, roads, and cities passed beneath us. The air was fairly smooth. I was able to turn off the seat belt sign and allow the passengers to move around in the cabin.

I called the senior again on the interphone to ask once more how Kylie was doing. She replied that Kylie was happily coloring some pictures.

As we came into the Orlando area, there were some cumulus clouds and light shower activity around the airport. This meant that it would be a little bumpy as we made our approach. We went in and out of clouds while we were being vectored and, occasionally, we got a pretty good bump. The landing was not my best, but it was still pretty good. A few passengers could be heard clapping.

While we had been at cruise, I had written a note to Kylie on the back of a company postcard:

Dear Kylie,
This is your Official Certificate of Courage. Today you did something you were afraid to do. That is called courage. You have shown today

7

just how brave you can be. Everyone can be afraid from time to time. Whenever you find yourself frightened of something again, I hope you will remember how brave you were today.

Captain Reynard

I asked the senior to give Kylie the card after we landed. As the passengers left the airplane, Kylie and her father came up to the cockpit. She thanked me for the postcard and handed me a picture she had colored. On it she had written me a thank you. She gave me a hug. She turned to Marcos and gave him one, too.

Life is not a question of living without risk. It is more a question of risking to live. One can even learn from a child.

As I told you before, Preston, I started writing this account of my life in aviation for you in case something should happen to me. I am hoping to share a little of my world with you. I would like you to see some of the places I have been (physically, mentally, emotionally, morally, and spiritually), and I would like you to meet some of the people I have known. Let's travel just a little further together. Come fly with me some more, Grandson.

Malta

Early spring of 1987, International Air Transport negotiated a wet lease agreement with Air Malta. The contract stipulated that one of our B727s be based on the island of Malta in the Mediterranean, just south of Sicily, from May to September. IAT crews would be assigned to fly it for the whole busy summer tourist season under Air Malta colors. The aircraft had already been repainted. The flying would take us all over Europe and even to Egypt.

This was going to be a new experience for me. My international flying was limited to countries in the Western hemisphere, except for the one trip I had made some years before as a copilot on the Lockheed Electra. In order to better prepare for the flying I would do, I obtained a complete set of the departure plates, approach plates, and enroute charts for Europe. For two weeks prior to going over to Malta, I spread out charts and plates across a large table and attempted to gain a familiarity with the airways we would be using, the navigation aids that formed them, ATC (air traffic control) frequencies to be expected, and the approach and departure procedures that we might be assigned at the different airports where we would be flying. I also studied carefully the ground layout and taxiways for each airport.

There was a lot to be learned. For example, the altitude at which aircraft use a standard altimeter setting (29.92 inches or 1013 millibars of mercury) is usually lower in Europe. (Remember that the altimeter is the instrument that tells the pilot how high the aircraft is flying). Often the altimeter setting will change from a local setting to a standard setting at lower altitudes of 6,000 to 9,000 feet. In the United States the standard setting is not used until 18,000 feet. After takeoff, during the climb, the altitude at which the altimeter is reset to the standard setting is called the transition altitude. It can be found on the approach chart and may be different for different airports. Below the transition altitude, ATC assigns altitudes to be maintained. Above the transition altitude flight levels are assigned. Coming back down from the higher altitudes to the lower altitudes, the altimeters will be reset to a local altimeter setting after passing what is called the transition level. The transition level is not always a fixed level. The approach chart may say "Transition Level by ATC." In this case, the air traffic controller will assign an altitude sometime during descent instead of a flight level, and he will also state the local altimeter setting to be used.

Why is all this setting of altimeters so important? In order to keep aircraft separated from each other, it is important that they all use the same reference. Two aircraft in close proximity to each other but assigned different altitudes could collide if their altimeters are set incorrectly.

Another difference that I noticed was the crowded appearance of some approach plates, departure plates, and arrival plates. Many times several different departure routes or arrival routes would be crammed onto the same plate. Each route could have a number of applicable notes concerning altitudes, speed restrictions, or alternate navigation aids.

Weather report formats and Notices to Airmen formats were also different. Visibilities reported in meters, not miles. Altimeters set to millibars, not inches. Of course, the accents of the controllers would be different from country to country. English is the international language of aviation, and all controllers speak English. However, not all have the same command of pronunciation. I knew there would be times when we would be required to request clarification of instructions received from air traffic control. Knowing ahead of time which frequencies to expect and what instructions would probably be given by the controllers at different stages of the flight would help to avoid confusion at a critical moment. I made a mental note to make sure that all crewmembers, including the flight engineer, be especially alert to all radio communications.

All these preparations did pay off. Our B727 flew all over Europe that summer. I am looking at my logbook now, and here is a list of the cities we flew to: Glasgow in Scotland, Amsterdam in the Netherlands, Lyon in France, Rome in Italy, Cairo in Egypt, Manchester, London, Birmingham, and Cardiff in England, Geneva in Switzerland, and Cologne, Dusseldorf, Frankfurt, Hamburg, and Munich in Germany. Each airport had its own different procedures and challenges. We eventually became very familiar with all these airports.

I still remember well the very first time we went into Geneva. The area was covered with clouds, and the ATC controllers were vectoring us for the ILS approach. We were still in clear skies for the initial part of the approach, but, all around below us, we could see jagged mountain peaks popping up out of the clouds. When the controller finally cleared us to a lower altitude, it took a great deal of faith to descend into the cloud cover. We didn't depend just on faith, of course. I had the first officer keep the terrain chart out where we both could see it, and, using VOR and DME signals, we continuously monitored our position in relation to the terrain while we complied with the different headings and altitudes assigned to us by the approach controller. We knew there were mountains all around us, but, of course, we could see nothing outside the airplane because of the cloud cover that enveloped us.

Passengers sitting in the back, comfortably reading their magazines or listening to music, are usually completely unaware of all the activity that is going on in the cockpit during an approach to an airport. Radios are being tuned, charts are being consulted, controller instructions are being followed, airplane instruments are monitored, the flying pilot is continuously making adjustments to pitch, heading, altitude, and speed. Even if the pilot is using the autopilot, that autopilot requires human input to function. All may be calm in the cabin, but there are times when, up front in the cockpit, the adrenaline is flowing. Passengers often judge a pilot by the last two feet of the flight; in other words, the touchdown. If it's smooth, they say, "Good pilot." If it's not, they may not think so. But all pilots make "greasers" and "thumpers." The passengers don't normally see the real work and all the skill, decision making, and coordination of effort that gets them to the point where the airplane is in a position to make that touchdown.

Flying for Air Malta taught us many lessons. For one thing, we all became more concerned with aircraft security because so many hijackings had occurred in Europe. Just 18 months before, an Egypt Air B737 on its way from Athens to Cairo had been hijacked to Malta. The hijackers' intention was to refuel and fly on to Libya. When their refueling demands were not met, the hijackers threatened they would execute a passenger every 15 minutes until they obtained fuel for the aircraft. They actually did shoot five passengers in the back of the head and throw them down the stairway that was at the front door of the plane. Egyptian commandos, sent by President Hosni Mubarak to Malta, stormed the aircraft. By the time the battle was over, 60 passengers were dead and 38 more were injured.

We learned a little about Egyptian airport security on the first trip we did to Cairo for Air Malta. Once parked on the ramp at Cairo, the aircraft was immediately surrounded by military vehicles. One had a machine gun mounted to its roof, and it was trained directly at the cockpit. "Not to worry," the airline representative assured us, "Just routine." Routine or not, I asked him to get somebody to turn the machine gun in a direction away from us. No results. The soldiers and their weapons remained in position.

Flying in Europe also involved adherence to slot times. Today we see more "wheels up" times issued to pilots in the U.S. when they receive their ATC clearance. The purpose of a "wheels up" time is to hold an aircraft on the ground if it is destined for an overly congested airport. The air traffic is metered into the congested airports so that holding and airspace saturation can be avoided. The "wheels up" time is much more common in Europe because of the tremendous airspace congestion. In Europe, this is called a slot time. Flying out of Frankfurt to Malta, for example, an aircraft will be issued a slot time for takeoff. If the aircraft is not at the end of the runway within 15 minutes of this time, there is a possibility that the flight's slot time may be cancelled, and it could take up to two hours to obtain another one.

Another difference in the Europe flying was the existence of strict noise abatement procedures at certain airports. Noise monitors are placed along departure paths, and if pilots do not adhere to very precise departure corridors they may find themselves subject to a noise violation. Procedures like this are more common in the U.S. today than they were then.

We mastered the new procedures, landed at unfamiliar airports, coped with difficult accents, and remained alert to the possibility of terrorist attacks. For all of us, that summer, the flying represented a stimulating and exciting challenge.

For me it was a great pleasure to have the opportunity to spend time in Europe again. I had joined the Air Force when I was 17 years old, and during my enlistment, I had spent three years in Toledo, Spain. The years in Spain gave me the opportunity to make friends with many people from many different countries. Since then, I have always tried to cultivate an appreciation for different cultures and languages. In addition to being an American, I consider myself a citizen of the world, and although I am sure I won't see it in my lifetime, Preston, I hope that in yours you may see a time when the world can come together in peace and prosperity for everyone. The resources are there.

Malta turned out to be a fascinating place to spend three months. The island has a long and very unique history. At one time, thousands of years ago, Malta was part of a land bridge that stretched from Europe to Africa. Today, the skeletons of small elephants found on the island can be seen on display in the natural history museum. Also on the island are some of the oldest ruins of ancient temples known to man. One of the most interesting was discovered by workmen doing repairs to a house in an ordinary Maltese residential neighborhood. While digging in the basement, they discovered a series of underground chambers that were actually an underground temple. The ancient temple had lain there, forgotten and undisturbed for thousands of years.

In about 1000 B.C. the Phoenicians invaded the island and made it a colony. They were followed by the Greeks in 736 B.C. The Carthaginians later took over, but, eventually, the Romans wrested it from them. The Apostle St. Paul lived on the island while it was a Roman colony. Some scholars believe the Vandals and the Goths occupied the islands after the fall of the Roman Empire. The Arabs invaded in 870 A.D. as part of the Muslim expansion of power. The Normans defeated the Arabs in 1090. Spanish rule under Aragon and Castile followed in the 15th century. In 1530, the island was given to the Knights of St. John by Holy Roman Emperor Charles V. The knights successfully defended the island against the Ottoman Turks in 1565. Napoleon invades in 1798 and expels the Knights of St. John. The British defeat the French in 1800, and Malta remains under British rule until 1964, when it becomes an independent state.

During World War II, the Maltese islands were mercilessly bombed by the Germans and Italians in a furious attempt to destroy the British bases there and gain control of the Mediterranean shipping lanes. The Germans and Italians needed unhampered shipping to be able to supply their troops in Africa. The Maltese never surrendered, and this was a major factor in the defeat of Hitler and Mussolini in North Africa.

As a result of its long and varied history, the island is covered with walled cities, beautiful churches, medieval and renaissance architecture, museums, temples, and, of course, hundreds of hotels and restaurants to accommodate all the thousands of tourists who visit there each year. It was a joy to make friends with the Maltese, who I found to be a very friendly, generous people. They very much liked to sing, dance, and celebrate life. Each city had its own week-long festa during the summer. Every night, somewhere on the island, one could see a fireworks display in the sky.

The IAT crewmembers and mechanics quickly adapted to being on Malta. A few just wanted to work three weeks and go home, but almost all the rest enjoyed being on the island so completely that they decided to stay the whole summer. I was fortunate enough to be able to bring your mother, your Aunt Rose, your Uncle David (they were all little children then, of course), and your Grandma Catherine with me. Other IAT employees brought their wives and families, or girlfriends. The company had rented most of a large, almost empty tourist apartment facility for the IAT employees, and there was plenty of room for everyone. The apartment complex even included a large swimming pool that hadn't been used for years. In the month before I arrived, all the Americans had gotten together with some of the British guests and cleaned out the swimming pool. In a week they had it completely clean, full of fresh water, and in useable condition. The children, and half the adults, spent almost their whole summer running around in bathing suits and jumping in and out of the pool.

The crewmembers and mechanics, over time, started to feel like a family. We spent a lot of time together and got to know each other fairly well. I still have great memories of the evenings when we would light candles, break out the guitars, and everyone, adults and children, would sing until late at night. Some of our Maltese friends would join us at these parties. It was definitely a summer of great comradeship and good will. I think many will remember that summer always as one of their best. Having my children there certainly made it one of the best for me.

I was to establish that summer a special link with the Maltese through an avenue I never expected. It was in Malta, that summer, that I received my black belt in Kempo karate after years of what had been a somewhat uncommon and sometimes solitary journey in the martial arts.

I am 55 years old and almost every day I do certain exercises from the karate training that I started when I was 17. In order to explain to you, Preston, the importance that martial arts training has had in my life, I need to go back to when I was a child.

Growing up in the working class areas of Chicago made it inevitable that from time to time a boy would get into a fight situation. I was never very big or strong for my age, and if anything, my nature tended more to the shy and timid side than to the warrior personality. However, I did have a temper, and when it was aroused, I was able to hold my own in a battle. More often than not, however, I tried to avoid conflict. By the time I reached my teens I had been in a number of fights. A few I won, a few I lost. Most were fought to a draw, and almost all were for stupid reasons. Usually I would end up being good friends with whomever it was I had fought.

In our neighborhood was a boy a little older than the rest of us. He was sort of our natural leader, but he did like to get us fighting with each other just for sport. Tony would go to one of us and say, "I don't think Jerry is very tough. I bet he could be beat easy in a fight." You would say something like, "Yeah, you're probably right. He probably looks tougher than he really is." Having roped you in, Tony would now go to Jerry and say, "Hey, you know what Rich Reynard said about you? He says he could probably beat you up." And so on back and forth until two boys who had never thought of fighting each other were suddenly rolling around on the grass trying to punch each other out. After this had happened to several of us, we all finally caught on that we were being duped. About that time Tony got to be the center of attention in a fight.

Tony's brother Billy liked to talk about how Tony had beat up Bryan Jones in a fight on the school playground. The talk reached Bryan Jones, and he decided to come over to our part of town and set Tony straight. It was now two years later, and during that time Bryan had been lifting weights and practicing boxing with a friend on a regular basis. It only took about two minutes, and Tony had a big black eye and a cut, bleeding lip. He decided he had had enough. Bryan and Tony shook hands, and Bryan went home. Tony never got any of us to battle each other again.

All this stupid fighting and trying to act tough led me to two conclusions:

1) It was not right to fight with anybody unless it was for true self-defense or the defense of someone else.

2) It would be a good idea to learn how to properly defend myself.

Judo was popular in the U.S. about that time in the early 1960s, but karate was just starting to become known. I became interested in both. Many years in and out of different martial arts schools followed. The military, school, and different jobs caused me to constantly leave one area and go to another. This meant having to find another school and another instructor. Sometimes I would just train and learn on my own or with friends. Over the years I probably took class or worked out in more than 25 different schools. Because of differences in styles and school rules, I went back to the rank of white belt several times. One would think that, with all this training over such a long period of time, I would be most expert, but actually I don't think that my fighting skills have ever been at a very high level at any point in my life. I have participated in a number of tournaments, but I have never brought home any trophies. Only once, on a Chicago street, have I had to fight off an attacker.

19

In spite of a lack of natural talent, I have always loved martial arts. And through the pursuit of learning them, I have made many friends and met many people that I never would have met otherwise. Sometimes on layovers, when I was younger, I would take my uniform with me to any nearby school and spar with the advanced students and maybe even an instructor. My goal was never to prove anything. I wanted only to meet new people and attempt to add to my knowledge. For safety reasons, normally only light contact is allowed in sparring matches. Once in a while I would take a hit to the torso or face and go home a little bruised, but there was always a good lesson attached to it. And the injury, I don't believe, was ever intentional. Through all of these efforts, over the years I was able to compare a lot of instructors and a lot of different styles. One thing I became certain of was that no particular style of martial arts is really superior to another, and that the biggest differences among martial artists is a result of individual ability and how well they train. If one goes to any open-style tournament, no one style consistently dominates all the others.

My love for the martial arts has remained strong within me, even into middle age, because I gained the most important thing from them that I think they have to offer: They gave me a personal point of reference. At times of crisis in my life, the active meditation of executing the forms, or *katas* as they are called in Japanese, has faithfully enabled me to again find my center and renew my spirit.

The katas, I should explain, are a series of pre-arranged movements that resemble a dance. The martial artist performs a wide variety of moves in combinations that simulate an ideal combat situation against a number of enemies. I say ideal combat situation because the katas do not really resemble what happens in an actual fight. Nevertheless, they provide good exercise for the mind, body, and spirit. Some schools insist that they be performed in exactly a certain way, but other schools and masters believe that there is much room for interpretation in the way that a particular martial artist

20

will bring a kata to life. And bring a kata to life is exactly what a martial artist does when he performs one. During the kata he blocks, punches, kicks, and perhaps even jumps and turns in the air, all the time attempting to visualize his opponents. Although it may take only one to two minutes, a well performed kata executed at maximum effort can be quite exhausting. Sometimes the same kata can be performed very slowly, as a pure concentration exercise. If one were to look at all the different styles of martial arts, one could easily come up with more than 200 katas, or forms. Some are ancient, and some are of recent origin and are the result of enlightened instructors' efforts to make training more effective and efficient.

Although I do not practice Shotokan karate, my favorite katas come from that style. I regularly practice the five Heians, Tekki Shodan, Bassai-Dai, Kanku-Dai, Unsu, and also a Sanchin breathing kata from the Uechi-Ryu style. The practice of these katas over the years has added something very beautiful to my life. That practice has even helped me, on occasion, to remain focused at difficult moments while flying.

Since we were going to spend the whole summer on Malta, I decided to seek out a martial arts school where I could practice. I had been a brown belt for several years at that point. In the next town over from where we were staying was a school where jiu-jitsu and judo were being taught, but the school owner/chief instructor wanted someone to do karate instruction. He asked me if I would teach over the summer. In return, he would give me a key, and I could use the studio whenever I wished. I began teaching, and my classes quickly became quite popular. After about three weeks went by Anthony Boyanzis, the chief instructor, asked me why I had never obtained my black belt. He liked the way I ran my classes, and he proposed that at the end of the summer we arrange a black belt test so that I could attain the rank of Shodan. He felt on the basis of my teaching ability that I deserved it, and he said that he would personally sponsor me to the British Martial Association.

So I taught all summer when I wasn't flying, and I prepared for the black belt test by teaching and practicing with my students. They wanted to see me get my black belt, too. Malta was very hot that summer. When the wind blew from the south, from Africa, temperatures easily reached 100 degrees Fahrenheit. I would practice basics, combinations, and katas during the day, and in the evening I taught class. Of course there was still the flying to do. The time remaining allowed for a number of family excursions to Valleta, Mdina, the natural history museum, two ancient temples, and several of the many towns that cover the island.

Near the end of the summer, I took my test and was awarded the rank of Shodan. When the test was over I wished I had been challenged with more sparring, but it was extremely warm in the dojo. Nobody wanted to overdo things. I did have to spar with our chief instructor, Anthony, who taught me some very good lessons during our match. After bowing to each other, we took up fighting stances and began to circle for openings. No heavy contact allowed, and we wore protective equipment. Suddenly Anthony attacked. He feinted with a low kick to the knee and then launched a looping, right punch to the head. I easily saw it coming and initiated a left high block. I was ready to follow it up with a left side kick to his exposed midsection. The looping right punch was a trick! As soon as I blocked it, Anthony twisted his punching hand around and grabbed my blocking arm. At the same time, he pulled my arm forward and dropped to the ground. With his right foot, he kicked my forward foot out from under me. When I hit the floor, Anthony tried to lock me in an arm bar, but I was able to kick myself free. We both stood up and circled again. Anthony quickly threw a roundhouse kick. I blocked it and moved in for a clean front snap kick to his groin. Point. Next time, I attacked. I faked a backfist, then punched. Anthony parried the punch, took a half step back, and rear kicked me in the stomach. Perfect shot. I tried another attack. Left jab, right punch, left front kick. Anthony slipped, parried, blocked, and now it was his turn to make a point with a kick to the groin area. We circled again. The heat in the dojo was intense, and we both were breathing heavily and dripping with sweat. The judge stopped us. He never expected me to beat our chief instructor. He just wanted to see if I could fight after I had demonstrated all the basics and the required katas.

The British Martial Association awarded me my black belt. I was 42 years old as I knelt before a row of three black belts who were also kneeling. I untied my brown belt and passed it to them, and they passed a black belt to me. I tied it around my waist and bowed by touching my forehead to the floor. They returned the bow. The school took me out to dinner that night, and all my students thanked me for the teaching I had done that summer. Chief Instructor Boyanzis presented me a trophy (the only one I have received in my whole life). I believe my very worn-out brown belt is still hanging in the school, along with the belts of other students who obtained their 1st Dan there. My road to black belt was perhaps a little unorthodox. But the essence of the martial arts, I believe, is really about each individual learning to seek his own unique Way through life.

With the summer at an end, the contract drew to a close. All the IAT people packed up their belongings and brought them to the airplane for the ferry flight that would take us back home. Some of our Maltese friends had decided to come along with us for the ride back to America. Rich Bonhomme (flight engineer), Dave Tagget (copilot), and I flew the first leg of the journey home. We were to take the airplane as far as Shannon, near the west coast of Ireland, while the other two crews rested in the back. Captain Ron Getz, First Officer Al Cicone, and Flight Engineer Joe Waren would take over in Shannon to fly us across the Atlantic to Gander, Newfoundland. From Gander to Indianapolis, it would be Captain Bob Scott, FO Michael Chovitz, and FE Steve Valente.

Since security was not an issue with no commercial passengers on board, we left the cockpit door open so the children could sit in the jumpseats and view the scenery. When he wasn't busy talking to air traffic control on the radio, Dave Tagget kept up a running commentary on the sights below us for the children:

23

"This is Sicily we are flying over. That big mountain way to the right with the smoke coming from the top is the volcano Mount Etna. If you pass close by it at night, you are able to see red-hot lava running down the sides near the top. Just to our left is Palermo, the capital of Sicily.... There is the western coast of Italy. Look real hard and you can see Rome.... These two giant islands that will pass by on our left are Sardinia and Corsica. Napoleon was born in Corsica. Down there on the right is the tiny Isle of Monte Cristo. Remember Dumas' novel?.... Pisa is way off to the right over there. The Leaning Tower? Too far away to see.... The city up ahead is Genoa. Christopher Columbus came from this region. Over there is Turin. The Shroud of Turin, for a time, was thought to have been the one wrapped around Jesus after his crucifixion.... These mountains are the Swiss Alps. Look! The Matterhorn. Geneva, Switzerland ahead.... Now we are over France.... There! That river is the Seine. Soon we'll see Paris off to our left. If we are lucky we will see the Eiffel Tower. It is easier to pick it out at night.... Down there on the coast is Calais. This is the English Channel. Look far ahead. You can see England in the distance. Those are the White Cliffs of Dover.... That big city down there? Right, London.... This body of water we are crossing now is called the Irish Sea. In 10 minutes we'll be south of Dublin...."

I enjoyed Tagget's comments as much as the children did, since I shared with him a love for history and geography. When we brought the B727 down for a nice landing in Shannon, I couldn't help but feel a sense of fulfillment and satisfaction. My part of our summer flying adventure was over. In Shannon, Getz, Cicone, and Waren would relieve us and fly the next leg. We three could now go back to the cabin and relax the rest of the way home.

After fueling of the aircraft was completed, the fresh crew flew us from Shannon across the Atlantic to Gander. As we got closer to the Canadian shores, we could see numerous icebergs in the water below us. At Gander, just as at Shannon, we stayed on the ground only long enough to refuel and obtain a new flight plan. Scott,

Chovitz, and Valente flew the final leg to Indianapolis. Every one of us felt proud of how we had all worked well together as a team that summer. We flew safe flights. We kept the schedule. We learned to fly to numerous unfamiliar destinations. We had become friends with each other, and we also had made friends with many of the Maltese. There will be times in your life, Preston, when you will know you have faced a challenge well. It's not wrong to pause for a moment to reflect on your triumph. During that same moment, it is also not a bad idea to reflect with humility on your place in the universe and allow your spirit to give thanks for all the gifts life has given you.

The Leader

"**W**e need a union." It was Captain Mark Levitz speaking, and he was going to try to get my support. I had just flown from Zihuatanejo, in Mexico, back to Chicago. Mark had met me in the crew room, and he had asked if we could speak in private. I had been back from Malta only about two weeks. Being in Malta all summer had put me a little out of touch with the political situation within the company. A group of pilots were evidently trying to gain support for a union drive.

"Mark, I really don't think a union is necessary at this company. What makes you feel so strongly that we need one?"

"Rich, just look around you. Our pay is lower than that of almost everybody who is flying airplanes like ours. We have no work rules other than whatever the company decides. Since we have no contract, you or I could be let go, at any time, for any reason at all, with no legal recourse. Our schedules are often very unfair. The company guarantees us certain days off each month, but, on the days we are available to crew scheduling, they can do anything they want with us as long as they don't violate FAA duty and rest requirements. Take, for example, the tail-end ferries that we do. You have done them, and so have I. We fly all night to get the airplane to Europe or some other faraway place, and then the company finds the airplane is needed somewhere else. We are tired and over duty as far as the FAA is concerned, and we are supposed to have some rest. What happens instead? The company declares that since now there are no passengers on board, we don't need any rest by FAA rules. We move the airplane under private owner rules instead. It doesn't matter that we may be dead tired. They may even have us bring the aircraft all the way back from Europe. Or what about the fact that crew scheduling can change your schedule at any time. Remember your trip last Thanksgiving? You were supposed to have the holiday off, but, after you had been with family all day, IAT called you that evening to fly a trip that would keep you up most of the night. Do you remember why that happened when you checked into it? It was because that trip was assigned to our flight manager, and he wanted to get out of it at the last minute. You felt like a zombie all night. Was that fair to you? Was that fair to the passengers on board?"

Mark was really going, and I had to admit that he was right about what he was saying, but I had a different perspective, and it was my turn to get to say something.

"Mark, I do agree with you that we could use better pay and better work rules. As a company, we need improvements in many areas. There are occasional bad situations. But that is not the norm. Most of the time, my schedule is pretty good. Management is trying to hire more people so that the company won't need to change our schedules on short notice. Also, you know as well as I, that this is a small, relatively new company. We have all heard the owner of IAT promise us that someday we will be a major airline. He has asked us to sacrifice and work with him to make this company grow. And he has promised that we will share in the rewards. I believe in what he says. And I believe in our management. Almost all of them are pilots just like us. I trust them to try to do what is best for all of us, and I am willing to do what I can to see that IAT grows and prospers. I think if we just keep doing our best, things around here are gradually going to get much better."

"Rich, nothing here is going to change. As this company prospers, the top people in management are going to make a lot of money. They will continue to pay us as little as possible and try to get as much work out of us as they can. You will work here 20 years, and, in the end, you will have nothing, and they will have everything. As the company gets more and more successful, they will all forget about when they really needed us to get things started. The signs are all around us now. We just need to open our eyes."

"Mark, if anyone else but Jurig Ritter were the sole owner of this company, I might tend to join you. I have worked in some places where management really did abuse people. That is not the case here. Look at Jurig's background. I think he is a man who can be trusted. I say give him a chance to make good on his word."

In the summer of 1939, Gerhard Ritter was a very worried man. From all indications it appeared that Poland might soon be at war with Germany. Although Gerhard was German, he had lived in Poland more than six years. He had married Anna Marie Wosniak in the fall of 1924. They were both medical students in Berlin when they met. Anna's father was a doctor in Warsaw. He ran his own clinic, and his dream was that someday Anna would take it over from him. He had been disappointed that, because of her marriage to Gerhard Ritter, she had decided to stay in Berlin. When Adolf Hitler became chancellor of Germany in January of 1933, Gerhard and Anna Marie made immediate plans to move to Warsaw. There, they would be able to practice medicine in Dr. Wosniak's clinic. Their son, Jurig, had just been born.

"This man will ruin Germany someday," Gerhard predicted. He had watched how the Nazi Party had grown from a small group of misfits and brawlers into the political party that held the most seats in the Reichstag. At one point, it had seemed the Nazi movement would die out, but then the German economy suffered a severe blow. The depression in the United States had caused huge amounts of investment funds to be withdrawn from Germany, and that, along with the general decline in world trade, had left the German economy in shambles. As more and more people became unemployed, and more and more people saw their economic situation deteriorate, the Nazi party gained strength. Many Germans of the middle and upper classes feared the Communists might gain enough strength to take over.

Adolf Hitler promised the fearful everything they wanted to hear. He would stop political rioting and restore order to the streets. He would build a strong economy. Everyone would have work. Germany would be returned to its former status as a great power in Europe. He would punish those responsible for the corruption of German ideals.

Once, out of fearful curiosity, Gerhard had gone to a Nazi rally to hear Hitler speak. He watched Hitler start his speech quietly, calmly. Among his opening remarks, Hitler even used a little ironic humor to gently chide those Germans who still refused to see that he was offering the only sensible solutions to Germany's many woes. Slowly, Hitler picked up the pace. He began accusing his usual list of scapegoats for all of Germany's problems. He raised his voice louder and louder, he waved his hands, and, at times, he moved his whole body to emphasize his arguments. Each gesture, each word was skillfully calculated to excite the anger and indignation of his listeners. He occasionally paused at just the right moments to give his followers an opportunity to applaud and shout their approval. Then he would resume his tirade and work their emotions up to an even more feverish pitch. Hitler's words clawed their way into the frightened, angry, and confused parts of his listeners' psyches. He gave them hope for their fear. He told them who to hate. He got them to shout their anger. And he took away their confusion by giving them easy answers to complex problems.

Gerhard watched the people around him at the rally roar their support for Hitler. It frightened him that even he found it difficult to not get caught up in the frenzy. The excitement that Hitler had created in the crowd was almost overwhelming. He saw a master manipulator, a fanatic who could tap into the unconscious and sinister forces that every human carries within him but that normally remain quiet and under control. Hitler, he could see, had the ability to reach deep into people's souls and use the best and the worst in them for his own purposes. There was no doubt in Gerhard's mind that Hitler saw himself as some kind of messiah meant by destiny to lead Germany out of its disastrous state into a new world of Order, Strength, and German Virtue. Hitler's greatest danger was that he believed in himself, and now, ever growing numbers of Germans were willing to believe in him too.

Four weeks after Hitler became chancellor, he suspended freedom of speech, freedom of the press, and freedom of assembly—all for the protection of the German people. Less than one month after that, the Reichstag voted him dictatorial powers. Over the next two years, he would consolidate his power and destroy all those who might oppose him.

Gerhard was right. Hitler would be the ruin of Germany. But before facing destruction, Germany would create incredible suffering and devastation all over Europe. From the other side of the Polish-German border, Gerhard had watched the growth of Hitler's power. He had seen the senseless persecution of Jews, the enormous build-up of the German military machine, the taking of the Rhineland, the annexation of Austria, the demands made for territory in the Sudetenland, and finally the occupation of Prague and the rest of Czechoslovakia. Gerhard had no doubt that a war was coming soon. He had actually read *Mein Kampf,* in which Hitler described the need to gain more living space for the growth of German culture. That living space would be created in the East. Gerhard was sure that Poland and Russia would eventually be Hitler's next targets. He began to correspond with his father's brother, who lived in a place called Michigan, about migration to America.

Before Gerhard had made any real progress on his plans to go to America, Hitler attacked Poland. Hitler trumped up a border incident to justify his attack on the Poles. Many others in Poland had watched Hitler's rise to power, and they too feared a German attack. What they never suspected was that Hitler had secretly divided Poland up with Joseph Stalin.

On September 1, 1939, Hitler attacked from the West. The Russians stood by as the Germans overwhelmed the Polish forces. Perhaps the Poles could have regrouped until England joined the war, but on September 17, the Russians occupied eastern Poland. With their antiquated equipment and ill-prepared troops, the Poles could not combat two large military machines. Germany and Russia partitioned the prostrate nation along pre-negotiated boundaries. Poland, as a political entity, ceased to exist. Later, Hitler would betray Stalin and march through the Russian-occupied lands of Poland to invade Russia.

Gerhard, Anna, and young Jurig had survived the bombing of Warsaw. Anna's father had not. Under the Germans, Gerhard and Maria were allowed to continue to operate the clinic. They both hated the Nazis and everything that they stood for. Occasionally they aided the underground. It wasn't until January of 1945, with only a few months to go before the defeat of Germany, that the Gestapo arrested Gerhard and Anna. Both were brutally interrogated and, eventually, shot. Jurig was sent to a refugee center in Germany where he remained until the end of the war.

With the war over, Europe was in chaos. Refugees and ex-combatants criss-crossed the continent trying to find relatives and somehow reestablish their lives. Jurig was now 12 years old. By that time he had seen the bombing of Warsaw, the death of his grandfather, the disappearance of his parents, and the hardships of living in a camp with other children who also did not have parents. He was never mistreated in the camp, but it was still not an easy life. Jurig was small for his age. He had to learn to defend himself with his intelligence, not his fists. He had to learn to negotiate. When rations became scarce in the camp, a larger boy once tried to take away his food. Jurig fought as hard as he could to keep this from happening. He took a beating, but kept his ration. Jurig went to another boy who was even bigger and made him an offer.

"If you can keep Schleicher away from me, I'll give you a share of my bread."

Jurig never had trouble with Schleicher again.

After the war, Bertholdt Ritter, Gerhard's uncle in America, learned about the execution of Jurig's parents. He also learned that Jurig had been sent to a camp somewhere in Germany. Bertholdt made himself a promise to find him. It took him over a year, but he finally located Jurig in a refugee camp near Berlin. As Jurig's closest surviving relative, he eventually was able to bring him to America.

Jurig adapted quickly to life in America. It didn't take long for him to learn English, and he did well with his studies in school. His uncle and his aunt gave him the love they would have given their own child if they had been able to have children. Bertholdt and Mary were more than 60 years old, but they were determined to do everything they could for this young boy who had seen so much suffering and who had lost so much. His whole life, Jurig would never forget their kindness and love.

Jurig continued through high school, and went on to college. He studied business, and he honed his communication skills. He found the best way to influence people was to first listen to what they had to say. He was careful to demonstrate his interest in their values, their thoughts, their desires. He also learned that in order to get what he wanted, he had to concentrate on what they wanted.

But Jurig's spirit was plagued with a hidden burden. In spite of all the love and kindness he received from his aunt and uncle, there still existed many scars on his heart and soul. Underneath all his affability, he carried, deep down, an ever-present smoldering rage. That smoldering rage would take many years to ease, but it would

35

also provide him the energy that he would need to attain the economic success and power over his own destiny that he so strongly craved. He had been completely powerless as a child. As he saw himself moving into adulthood, he promised himself that someday he would reach the point where nobody could ever make him feel powerless again.

Jurig was making excellent grades, and he would probably have completed his university studies except for one thought that continued to haunt him. When he was a boy in the refugee camps, he used to watch the many airplanes overhead that filled the skies of Europe. Often, he had wished for wings of his own that might carry him far away from the sadness and misery he saw all around him.

At the age of 20, Jurig decided to learn to fly. Like many aspiring pilots, he began to wash airplanes at the local flying school on weekends. When he had washed enough airplanes, the owner of the school would give him an hour of flight instruction. Slowly the hours accumulated. Jurig obtained his private pilot license. He continued up the familiar path for credentials. Commercial license. Instrument rating. Instructor rating. Multi-engine rating. He quit college. He knew he was now following his real dream.

He began to fly some charters at the flight school. He went on to a night freight job where he flew alone in old airplanes in all types of weather. A big break came for him one night while he was pre-flighting his airplane. Someone wanted to talk to him.

"Hi, I am Jim Walsh. I'm a mechanic for Jet Charter Express. I'm sure you've seen our airplanes in the hangar."

He showed Jurig his I.D. card. Jet Charter Express.

"We have a Learjet that just broke down in Kansas City. It's too late now to get a commercial flight there, and we need the airplane ready

36

to fly in the morning for an important charter. It's a simple fix. I've got a few parts with me, and if you could let me ride along with you to Kansas City, I would consider it a great favor."

Jurig knew an opportunity when he saw one. He also knew it was against the rules to take along any riders. Insurance problems. He could get fired if he let the mechanic ride along. The mechanic knew it, too.

"There is a lot of weather tonight between here and Kansas City. These planes don't have any radar, but, if you think you want to go, I'll take you with me."

They hopped into the old Beech 18 and took off into the darkness. The highest they would fly all night would be at an altitude of 8,000 feet. There were plenty of storms just as Jurig had predicted to Walsh. A line of dark, menacing cumulonimbi stretched all the way across Missouri, and the ceiling and visibility were low at Kansas City. Most of the time, the aircraft was enveloped in clouds and they could see nothing outside except the position lights on the wingtips, and, occasionally, the eerie glow of electrical static discharge that formed a ghostly blue ring around each propellor. Several times during the flight, the aircraft was violently tossed around in turbulence as lightning flashed around them. But the radar vectoring of the controllers helped them to avoid the worst parts of the storms. The cloud cover at Kansas City extended right down to 200 feet above the ground, and the visibility was reported to be less than one-half mile. It's possible that Jurig descended a little lower than the decision height authorized on the approach plate before he was able to make out the approach lights leading to the runway threshold.

Once the aircraft was parked at the ramp, the mechanic was grateful to be back on the ground and that the ordeal was over. A few times during the flight, Walsh had felt as if he were going to vomit. Before he left, he thanked Jurig for the ride and handed him a business card. On the back of the card he had written a name and a number.

"Why not call our chief pilot on Monday? Tell the secretary I told you to call him."

Jurig called the number and gave his name. The secretary put him right through to Chief Pilot Don Kramer.

"Heard you got us out of a tight spot the other night. Jim Walsh says you're a pretty good pilot too. We are going to be looking for another copilot in a few weeks. Would you like to come in for an interview?"

Jurig didn't even have to think about his response. Of course he would like to come in for an interview.

As Jurig expected, he got the job. He was going to fly Learjets. He flew as a copilot for a little over two years, and then a captain slot opened up. Another two years as a captain and Jurig now had four years experience flying jet aircraft. Another job became available. Copilot on a B707 for a travel club. Jurig worked as a copilot again for three more years. During that time he flew to many vacation spots in Europe and learned how to cross the Atlantic in MNPS airspace. Jurig upgraded to captain. His career was in full swing now. The big airlines began to do some hiring. Jurig, by this time, had solid qualifications that would have made him an ideal candidate at any airline. It was at this moment in his career that he was to make a decision that would change his life forever: Instead of applying for a pilot position at a major airline, he decided to look for backers to start his own company.

One bank was willing to take a chance on the persuasive young man who, with enthusiasm, effectively communicated his vision of the future to its officers:

"I am going to give people good service at a low price. The charter market is about to break wide open with deregulation of the airlines coming. By having a travel club in place when deregulation occurs, we'll be positioned to take advantage of the new opportunities. I need one airplane to start. In three years I will have enough business for two."

Jurig went on explaining his business plan. He got his loan.

Now the hard work began. Jurig hired a few other pilots, and he leased an old B707 with an option to buy. He gave talks to a variety of groups and organizations to publicize his travel club. People responded. They wanted cheap travel. Jurig found business for his plane. He flew it wherever people wanted to go. Many times, he himself, along with other crewmembers, would unload the bags from the airplane and take them to the hotel. He kept the books, and he made sure all the bills got paid. At the different airports that he flew into, he gained a reputation for being a fair and honest operator who paid his bills on time. He made it a point to try to get to know personally the people whose job it was at the different airports to fuel the aircraft, bring the food to the airplane, service the lavatories, and clear out the trash from the galleys. When appropriate, he knew how to show appreciation with a tip. He called his fledgling company International Air Transport. And what he had told the bankers came true. When deregulation of the airlines occurred, Jurig was in a position to rapidly expand his business.

He bought more airplanes and hired more pilots, more mechanics, and even some office personnel to relieve him of the duty of keeping the books. He kept close personal contact with his employees. He insisted that nobody ever call him Mr. Ritter. He always wanted to be Jurig to everyone that worked for him. He was quick to help out an employee if he were in trouble. Once he kept a dying employee, one of his first captains, on full pay until the end came. The family never forgot his generosity. He asked his employees to work hard with him to build up a good company. He asked for their loyalty, and he got it.

His employees had nothing but respect and admiration for him. They knew his history, and they were proud that they could be part of his achievement of the American Dream.

Jurig was now gaining the power over his own destiny that he had always so desperately desired. Under his guiding hand, the reputation and size of International Air Transport continued to grow each year. Jurig looked ahead to the future and felt confident in his heart that, no matter what obstacles lay ahead, he would be able to overcome them.

IV

1988

Regardless of the political situation at IAT, it was still good to be back home flying in familiar territory. Most of us were too busy enjoying our flying to get mixed up in a union battle. The effort that Mark Levitz and others were involved in quietly died for lack of interest. Most of us had decided to put our faith in Jurig Ritter. That faith seemed to be justified because the company kept growing. More airplanes were acquired, and more flight crews were constantly being hired. Even a seemingly major disaster a few years earlier had turned into a windfall for the company.

The company had a DC10 that it wanted to sell, but no airline showed any interest in buying it. The airplane simply wasn't being flown at a profit. Then Fortune smiled in the strangest of ways. Some oxygen canisters were being transported in the aft cargo compartment on a ferry flight. At least one of the oxygen canisters activated and began to generate oxygen. The chemical reaction in the canister releases a great amount of heat. It was believed that the heat and the oxygen-rich environment in the cargo hold began a fire in the aft compartment. Firefighters were unable to contain the fire, and the aircraft fuselage became engulfed in flames. Luckily, there were no passengers on board, and the crew had left the aircraft in time to avoid injury. The aircraft was destroyed in the fire. The resulting insurance money helped the company through some financial difficulties. The captain of the flight used to joke that he was forced into an office manager's position, and out of the cockpit, because he had tried to put out the fire.

One trip I flew this year stands out more than others in my mind. We were scheduled for a trip to Montego Bay. All the passengers had

43

boarded the airplane except for one man and a woman who was traveling with him. At the door of the aircraft, the man said that he had suddenly changed his mind and now did not wish to travel. He told the boarding agent that he had a fear of flying. He had thought that he could overcome his fear to make the flight, but now at the doorway of the plane, he found himself unable to get on the aircraft. He wanted his girlfriend to go on without him. He didn't want to ruin her vacation.

I decided to have a talk with him. But before speaking with him, I asked that the company try to obtain a background check on the two passengers. The reason I was suspicious was that, not too long before, in London, an Arab man had decided to not board a flight at the last minute. He told his pregnant girlfriend to go on without him. When the girlfriend went through security, they found that her boyfriend had slipped a bomb into her handbag.

I spoke with the gentleman in private, and he did seem genuinely frightened to get on the aircraft. The question I had in my mind was, "Why?" The gate agent interrupted our conversation and asked to speak with me. She said that the background check indicated the man was a Libyan traveling on a Lebanese passport, and that the woman was a chemist. That was enough to make both the FBI and me very suspicious. We took a two-hour delay to deplane the aircraft and perform a thorough search of the aircraft and the baggage utilizing "sniff" dogs. The man and the woman were questioned by the FBI and their luggage was searched.

In the end it was determined that the man and woman were legitimate passengers, and that there was nothing dangerous about them. It was all a matter of coincidence. We put all the passengers back on board and proceeded without incident to complete our flight. I apologized about the delay to the passengers, but I did not for an instant regret the fact that we had been overly cautious. Evidently the passengers felt the same way, because not a single person complained. In fact, a few expressed satisfaction that we were being so careful about their safety.

For me, this was a good year of steady experience building. Yes, there were a few minor mechanical problems and a few weather delays, but the flying was fairly routine, and I was slowly gaining confidence in my role as a captain with IAT. We flew the B727 to most of the usual vacation spots: Cancun, Aruba, Manzanillo, St. Maarten, San Juan, and Puerto Plata. Plenty of sunshine and plenty of tanned happy passengers. We also made a few trips into Toronto and Montreal. One new destination was Bahias de Huatulco, in the south of Mexico on the Pacific coast. It was here that Mark Levitz, as a fairly new captain, had a close call with danger under very unusual circumstances.

Levitz had brought his 727 into Bahias de Huatulco just before dark. By the time the aircraft was refueled and loaded up for the return trip to Chicago, night had fallen. They started up their engines and taxied out to the runway for takeoff. After receiving takeoff clearance, they pushed the throttles forward and spooled up the power. Upon reaching about 120 knots, they thought they saw something moving on the runway just ahead. It was too dark to tell if they had seen anything for sure. Just a few seconds later, the lights of the aircraft illuminated clearly what was ahead of them. A herd of cows had somehow gotten past the aircraft fence, and several of them were clustered together ahead on the runway. Levitz had no choice at that point but to continue the takeoff and try to get airborne. He pulled back on the control yoke. As the aircraft rotated, they felt an impact on the right side of the airplane. It felt like something had slammed very hard into the right landing gear. Levitz maintained directional control of the aircraft and managed to get it into the air.

The whole crew agreed it would be best to leave the landing gear down. Mark was afraid that if he tried to raise what he suspected was damaged landing gear, he might not be able to extend it later.

45

With animals on the runway, there was never a thought to going back and trying to land the damaged aircraft at Huatulco. They flew with the gear down over the mountains to nearby Oaxaca and made an emergency landing. Inspection of the aircraft after landing showed that the right main gear had, indeed, impacted with a large animal. They were all very lucky that the aircraft had suffered no major damage. Also, none of the engines had ingested any large chunks of animal parts. That could have caused an engine flame-out or severe damage to compressor blades with possible engine disintegration.

The encounter with the cows did not make the news, for which Mark was grateful. But there were two events that year that everyone involved in aviation at that time will always remember. The first was the explosive decompression of an Aloha B737 due to structural failure. The second was the senseless taking of lives by the bombing of a Pan Am B747 over Scotland.

The Aloha B737 was on a short, routine shuttle flight from Hilo to Honolulu and just leveling off at 24,000 feet when, suddenly, with an explosive sound, a large portion of the roof and skin of the forward passenger compartment, starting at a point just aft of the forward door to a point 18 feet rearward, separated from the airplane. Passengers in the forward part of the aircraft were suddenly exposed to lack of oxygen, freezing temperatures, and high velocity winds whipping around them. When the explosive decompression occurred, the lead flight attendant was thrown out of the aircraft into the sea. She was never found. The other flight attendants were thrown to the floor. One was struck on the head by flying debris and fell seriously injured. The captain closed the throttles, extended the speed brakes, and lowered the nose of the aircraft for a rapid emergency descent while the first officer selected the emergency code of 7700 on the transponder and attempted to declare the emergency over the radio. The noise level was so loud in the cockpit that she couldn't tell if her radio calls were being acknowledged by ATC. The pilot and copilot had put on their oxygen masks right away

46

when the depressurization occurred, but it was essential to quickly get the passengers down to an altitude where they too would have adequate oxygen to breathe.

The pilots diverted to Maui. Once below 10,000 feet, they were able to remove their oxygen masks. As they began to slow for the approach, noise levels in the cockpit decreased, and they were able to communicate better with ATC. They requested that emergency assistance for the passengers be ready on the ground. As the captain asked the first officer to extend the flaps for the approach, he found that the aircraft became less controllable. He decided he would make the landing at a higher speed and use the flaps 5 position instead of flaps 30 position for landing. When the landing gear was lowered, the nose gear light did not illuminate to indicate the nose gear was down and locked. The crew tried another attempt to lower the gear. Still, the nose gear indicator showed no green light. Knowing that there were probable serious injuries on board, the captain decided to land right away even if the nose gear was not extended.

The runway was coming closer now. The captain increased the power on the engines to make the landing only to find that the left engine was not responding to the throttle movement. The engine refused to spool up from idle. The captain would have to land with only one engine producing useable power. He must have been feeling a tremendous amount of pressure at this point. Structural integrity of the aircraft was in doubt. Seriously injured people were in the back of the airplane. The aircraft was difficult to control. The nose gear might collapse on landing. One engine was, for all practical purposes, inoperative. They would be making the landing at higher than normal speed. The runway at Maui is 7,000 feet long, adequate distance for a normal landing, but not so long as to leave a large margin for error when landing at high speed. If the brakes were to fail, or if a tire were to blow, the aircraft could easily run off the end of the runway with disastrous consequences. The captain and the copilot knew they had to do it right. And they did. The captain made a good landing, the nose gear did not collapse, the first officer lowered the flaps to full after touchdown, and the brakes brought the airplane to a safe stop. The captain and copilot completed their shutdown procedures and then proceeded to evacuate the aircraft. One fatality. Eight serious injuries. Fifty-seven minor injuries. Twenty-nine uninjured.

As a fellow pilot, I have a great amount of respect for how this crew handled a very difficult situation. They were faced with several simultaneous emergencies, and they handled the situation incredibly well. The captain was faced with quite a few difficult decisions and had to quickly weigh a great many factors. There is no doubt he drew heavily on the years of training and experience he had accrued up until that time to bring his passengers to safety.

When the explosive decompression occurred, at first the captain and the first officer must have experienced a few seconds of shock. Pilots train for explosive decompressions often on their simulator checkrides, but few have actually experienced one. The pilots quickly recovered and began to take action. They put on their oxygen masks. Time of useful consciousness without supplemental oxygen in the rarified air at 24,000 feet is about three to five minutes. The captain closed the throttles and initiated an emergency descent. He had to decide whether to slow the aircraft to a very slow speed because of the structural damage or descend at a higher speed and be able to get down to a lower altitude more quickly. Although the National Transportation and Safety Board (NTSB) made a comment on the accident report that the captain had failed to follow company procedure, as stated on the checklist, by not slowing the aircraft to minimum speed, I feel he made the correct decision by getting the airplane down quickly. Most pilots would probably agree. He had to balance the possibility of more damage occurring with the high speed descent against the fact that his passengers and flight attendants were experiencing extreme cold and lack of oxygen. In simulator training, pilots are taught that in cases of suspected structural damage, the airplane should be put into a descent at a speed not exceeding the existing speed of the aircraft. That is exactly what he did. He got the airplane down quickly to an altitude where the occupants of the aircraft could breathe again.

When the captain attempted to lower the flaps and slow the aircraft for landing, he found the aircraft became more difficult to control. He had to decide whether to fly the approach at the normal slow airspeed and land with an airplane that was difficult to control, or to fly the aircraft at the higher speed. He knew it would be very dangerous to fly an unstable aircraft, but he also knew that landing at a higher speed would require more runway and would take more distance to stop once on the ground. He elected to maintain the higher speed, which gave him better control in the air.

When the crew could not obtain the indication that the nose gear was down and locked, the captain had to decide whether it would be better to get his injured people on the ground right away or spend more time circling to try to get the nose gear to extend and lock properly. He weighed the danger that a collapsed nose gear might create against the fact that he probably had seriously injured people on board who needed immediate medical attention. He elected to land, knowing that, perhaps, the aircraft would slide on the nose for the last part of the landing. Although this would create a shower of sparks, he probably knew that this had been done safely in other aircraft. He probably also mentally prepared himself for the remote possibility of fire breaking out.

When the left engine did not respond to throttle input, the captain now faced an extremely difficult situation. He of course tried to regain power, but was unable. (Later investigation showed that cables going to the engine controls had been damaged by the explosive depressurization.) A single-engine landing is a serious situation in any circumstances, but the factors that the captain now had to evaluate were many. First, a two-engine airplane flying on only one engine has very reduced performance. The additional drag created by the missing portion of the airplane skin around the

49

forward passenger compartment would further reduce performance. If anything went wrong during the approach, a go-around and climb might not have been possible. He knew he would probably get only one chance to make the landing. He had to consider carefully his speed, point of touchdown on the runway, and available stopping distance.

During the approach, the first officer offered the idea that putting the flaps to full just before landing would help get the airplane stopped. The captain agreed that full flaps might shorten the landing roll. He asked her to apply full flaps after touchdown. It should be noted that the captain and first officer worked together very well during the whole emergency. The cockpit voice recorder tape shows that each crewmember took care of his/her area of responsibility well while still monitoring the actions of the other. The captain had to make the final decisions, but the first officer acted as a good team member by providing all requested assistance and offering her input from time to time when she thought it would be helpful. It is obvious from the cockpit voice recorder tape that she was a very experienced first officer because she kept her input to a minimum and did not overload the captain with unnecessary distractions, concerns, or suggestions. She evidently stuck to her job, monitored the captain's actions, and provided him with good backup.

The Aloha incident took skill and good decision making to bring a severely crippled aircraft to a safe landing. The Pan Am disaster was very different. All the years of experience and expertise of the Pan Am 103 crew were negated once a bomb exploded on the airplane.

There seems to be a lot of controversy in the press about who the guilty parties were in the crash of Pan Am 103. Perhaps someday all the controversy will be resolved to everyone's satisfaction. But some facts are clear: On December 21, 1988, a Pan Am B747 came apart in mid air, and 259 passengers plus 11 people on the ground were killed. The evidence points to a terrorist bomb. It was a tragic destruction and waste of human life. I would only like to tell you the effect the crash had on me from a pilot's standpoint.

As a captain, I see my job as protecting the safety of my passengers and my fellow crewmembers. I am well aware there always exists the possibility that I can make an error. In fact, it is the knowledge of my imperfections that spurs me to study and review operating procedures on a regular basis. As I have told you before, Preston, most pilots do the same. We try to be ready for the unexpected, the unthinkable. But when a bomb causes the breakup of an aircraft in flight, we know that all the crewmembers' skill, experience, conscientiousness, and training is immediately rendered useless.

I always feel a vague sense of betrayal when I hear of the crash of a sabotaged airplane. To me it seems like a dastardly act performed by cowards who take advantage of the fact that people wish to live in free societies and not be unnecessarily hampered by government intrusions on their liberties and actions. Terrorists actually use our freedom against us. I also feel sad that commercial airliners become the targets of terrorist groups, because airplanes help promote understanding across cultural barriers by bringing people from all different countries, all different religions, and all different languages closer together.

A friend of mine once asked me, "Why as pilots don't you do something for world peace, since you go to so many different countries and meet so many different people?"

At the time I didn't have a ready answer, but after pondering the question, I think I could give him an answer today: "Just by what they do, commercial pilots contribute to world peace. By helping people to easily visit faraway places, air travel offers a greater number of humans the opportunity to form personal relationships and understand each other."

So the year 1988 finished for me with sadness, but also with a sense that perhaps my work does help a little to bring the world together by giving people of diverse cultures the opportunity to better know each other. I also faced the chilling realization that this was at least one of the reasons why extremists, who wish to tear the world apart, attack airliners and defenseless passengers.

V

My Islam

Preston, by the summer of 1989, it was apparent my marriage to your Grandma Catherine was over. I'm not going to tell you much about the divorce. Let me only say that, sometimes in a marriage, people make mistakes. There were mistakes on both sides in our case. When love leaves, it is often better to move on. Meeting your life partner can be like many other things in life. You don't necessarily get it right the first time. What is important is to try to learn from your mistakes and to be honest with yourself about your errors and shortcomings.

In aviation, there is probably nothing more common than a pilot who has had a divorce. Pilots in the early stages of their careers, when they are also usually building families, have poor schedules. They spend many nights away from home, at times thousands of miles away from their families. Often, they may fly at night and need to sleep during the day. They may commute hundreds of miles to their jobs so that their families can continue to enjoy living in one place and not have to move from city to city. They do the traveling so their wives and children can have friends, familiar surroundings, and some stability. Quite a few of their days off are spent just getting back and forth to work.

For a pilot living in hotel rooms in different cities all month, the loneliness can sometimes be unbearable. Pilots often spend a lot of time hanging around in the bars at the hotels. Of course there are temptations. Some succumb. Some don't. Some wish they had. Some wish they hadn't. Given all these pressures, which the families back at home feel too, love doesn't just vanish all at once. But when the effects of too many lonely nights apart, too many birthdays missed, too many anniversary celebrations bypassed, too many conversations lost, and too many meant-to-be shared experiences that never got shared slowly combine over the years, an imperceptible indifference and distance begins to set in. It happens so gradually that couples are often surprised to wake up one morning only to realize they have very little in common. Worse yet, they don't really care. He no longer cares about pleasing her. She doesn't care if she is attractive to him. I would never wish that you find yourself in a divorce situation, but, if someday you do, consider this: Once the relationship is over, put aside all hate and bitterness so that you can love again. Find someone who really loves you, and try to make it work. Forget about the past, and live in the present. Life is really very short, and to spend it in bitterness and blaming is to waste a precious gift.

Our company had obtained another wet lease that summer. This time we sent a B727 to work for a Turkish charter airline out of Antalya. My knowledge of Turkey was limited. I knew the United Nations Turkish units had been our fierce allies in the Korean conflict back in the 1950s. From having spent time on Malta, I was aware that in 1565, the Ottoman Empire had attempted to gain control of the Mediterranean for an eventual expansion into Europe. I also knew that the Islamic Ottoman capital, Istanbul, had once been a great center of learning and relative religious tolerance compared to the Christian capitals of that time. The dark side of Turkish history, of course, was the officially denied, attempted extermination of its Armenian population during and after World War I. I had also read about Kemal Ataturk's struggle to transform Turkey from an Islamic state to a secular republic.

Our job required us to fly two types of trips. On the first type, we carried tourists from Europe to Istanbul and Antalya. Although we did a few trips to Italy, the great majority of our flights were to cities in Germany. Common destinations were Dusseldorf, Hamburg, Stuttgart, Bremen, and Nuremberg. On the second type, we provided transportation for Turkish workers back and forth to

Germany. These trips could originate out of Antalya, Ankara, or Istanbul. Two completely different kinds of flights. On the first type, our passengers were happy Europeans on holiday searching for fun and sun. On the second, the airplane was full of uneducated, unskilled Turkish laborers willing to brave the uncertainties and isolation of life in a far-off foreign culture in order to find better paying jobs than the ones they could find in their villages.

For all flights to Germany, standard routing from Turkey would take us over Istanbul and across Bulgaria. We'd speak with Sofia Control until approaching Yugoslavia, where we would check in with Belgrade. After Belgrade, Zagreb Control, Wien Control, Rhein Control, then on to the destination city.

As we regularly traversed the Balkans that summer at 31,000 to 37,000 feet, it was hard to imagine, from the tranquility of a jet cockpit, the tensions that existed below because of conflicting customs, ethnicity, and religions. But of course they existed, as the whole world would see a few years later when the region would explode with "ethnic cleansing" all across Bosnia.

Turkey had also had a period of "ethnic cleansing." At one time, over two million Armenians lived in Turkey. During World War I, the Turkish government made a concerted effort to destroy its Armenian population. It carried out this effort by mass deportations of Armenian families into desert regions, where they were left to die without food and water. Massacres also took place. Men, women, and children were sometimes killed with swords by gangs of thugs secretly organized by the ruling Committee of Union and Progress, the *Ittihad ve Terakki Jemiyeti.*

By the time I came to Turkey in 1989, it was quite different from the Moslem countries around it. One of the prime reasons that so much change had taken place can be attributed to Kemal Ataturk. Ataturk ruled as president of a newly formed republic from 1923 to 1938.

57

Under Ataturk, the provision declaring Turkey to be an Islamist state was dropped from the constitution, women's rights were established, coeducation was promoted, Arabic script was exchanged for the Latin alphabet, and religious laws were abolished. Civil code based on the Swiss model was adopted. A penal code based on the Italian model was established, and a business code based on the German model was instituted. In many aspects the country became secularized, but there is no doubt that, even today, outside of major urban areas religious tradition still dominates in many ways.

This was not going to be my first opportunity to stay for an extended time in a Moslem country. When I was much younger, and still in the Air Force, I volunteered for temporary assignment to Tehran, the capital of Iran. The Shah was in power then, and, from what my Iranian friends told me, he was a ruthless dictator who used a team of secret police to maintain his rule through the imprisonment and torture of dissidents. My friends predicted that someday the Shah would be dethroned by an angry populace. They predicted too that the Americans would also be hated, because they were associated with helping to keep the Shah in power. They were right. It is unfortunate that the Islamist regime that replaced the Shah's government turned out to be even more repressive and ruthless than the Pahlavi monarchy. Revolutions can create great changes in a society, but that doesn't necessarily mean they will create respect for the rights of individuals. Be careful of the causes you support, Preston. The Bolsheviks, the Nazis, the followers of Khomeini, the Taliban all promised their people a better life. Read what kind of societies they created. Notice they all valued blind commitment to an ideology over a commitment to individual freedoms.

While in Iran, I was invited to the home of some friends for dinner. There were about 10 men and women present, mostly from the same family. A few women had babies with them. The hospitality and congeniality of the Iranians left me with an unforgettable impression. We began dinner in the early afternoon. Over dinner there was the usual getting-to-know-you small talk. After dinner there was

58

discussion of politics, religion, and the differences in customs among different peoples. Later, the hosts brought out blankets, and we all took a nap on the floor. After the nap we ate a light meal. Musical instruments appeared. We sat on large pillows on the floor, and we spent the next three hours singing and making our own music. Experiences like this always rekindle my faith in the universality of the human spirit and help keep the hope alive within me that people of good will in all countries will someday live free and in harmony.

And how do I reconcile my positive experiences among those Iranian friends with the repression of freedom and often barbaric punishments exhibited by the Islamic state of Iran today? I can only say that I believe there is no such thing as the existence of a bad people or a good people. But there are bad governments and bad systems that can bring out the worst in many. Governments controlled by religion almost always bring repression. Westerners need look no further than the history of Christian theocracies to find examples of equally barbaric punishments and ruthless repression of liberty.

Since 1923, Turkey had been following the path of secularization that Kemal Ataturk had begun. The country was much more Westernized than Iran. It reminded me a little of the Spain I had known in the 1960s. The Turks were very friendly to foreigners, family ties were close, and in much of the country lived a rural population with strong traditions and not a great amount of formal education. There was quite a bit of poverty.

Antalya is located on the southern coast of Turkey in one of the most beautiful areas of the country. The blue waters of the Mediterranean, the clear sky, the beaches, rolling hills, and mountains all combine in elegance. Tourists were enjoying themselves everywhere, swimming, boating, tanning, camping, horseback riding, dining, dancing, and purchasing souvenirs—especially Turkish rugs.

One cannot visit Turkey without being tempted to buy a carpet. Stores displaying beautiful hand-made carpets may be seen everywhere. The store owners will often invite the prospective buyer into the store for tea. He will display his carpets and even give a few tips on how to recognize a good carpet from one of lesser quality. I quickly learned how ignorant I was about Turkish rugs. The type of materials used, from wool to silk, the types of natural dyes used, the amount of knots per square meter, as well as the intricacy of the design, all contribute to the value of a rug. The design of the rug may contain certain symbols that express something about the life of the woman who wove it.

Flying kept us all busy, but there was plenty of free time to relax and enjoy what the area had to offer. I leased a motorcycle for the summer and managed to visit some of the Greek ruins in the area. I can't help but feel a sense of humility when I sit in a Greek amphitheater that is thousands of years old and ponder the people who had sat there and watched plays—very insightful plays, dealing with human psychology—long before the beginnings of my own culture. How unfortunate that our human evolution has never kept pace with our technological evolution. In our modern world we still struggle with exactly the same human limitations, flaws, and uncontrolled passions.

Turkey presented a constant feast of new sights and experiences. Antalya had many shops and restaurants. The old section of town looked as if it hadn't changed much for hundreds of years. There was a large mosque located at the edge of the Old Town with a high minaret from which the faithful were called to prayer. Once in awhile, a small caravan, composed of a flatbed truck blaring its horn and followed by a few cars, would rush by. On the truck would be a young boy accompanied by his male relatives joyously celebrating the day of the boy's circumcision. For the occasion, the boy would usually wear a white, princely looking uniform complete with small sword.

I asked my friend Ishmael, from whom I was regularly taking horseback riding lessons, if the circumcision was performed under anesthesia. He said no. When he was circumcised, he was about 10 years old. The uniform was exchanged for a white robe and then he was held down by a close family friend while the operation was completed. He said he was in great pain during the traditional celebration that followed, but the family kept him occupied with presents to distract him.

Visitors were naturally drawn to the Old Town. Many boats, available for charter, were docked there. One could dine in a great number of restaurants. A rich mix of deliciously tempting aromas constantly assaulted the senses. Of course there were street vendors selling everything from jewelry to t-shirts. Almost everyone bought puzzle rings at some time during their stay. One had the choice of several places to dance, but there were also quieter places where one could hear a little Turkish music and drink tea or coffee.

One of the Turkish flight attendants took me to a music shop one day, where she bought me a gift. It was a collection of Sephardic songs by Jak and Janet Esim. Jak and Janet are descendants of the Jews who were forced out of Catholic Spain in 1492, when the monarchs, Ferdinand and Isabella, used religious fervor to unite Spain and consolidate their power. Muslims and Jews either had to convert to Catholicism or leave. The Ottoman Empire was much more tolerant of other religions, so many Jews went to live in Turkey. The collection of songs quickly became one of my favorite albums. The most enchanting song for me was the lament of a young Jewish woman who had come from a rich family but now found herself reduced to servitude after being expelled from her country because of political and religious intolerance:

"Yo era nina de casa alta, yo no sabia de sufrir...."
(I was once a young girl—highborn, to suffering yet a stranger....)

One of my best experiences was attending the wedding of Ali and Gulfem. Ali was the assistant manager at the hotel where the crews were staying. Gulfem was one of our Turkish flight attendants. The wedding was a joyous affair with more than a hundred people in attendance. Ali and Gulfem sat at a flower-covered raised table at the edge of the dance floor. For dinner we ate lamb and rice. At one point a Muslim cleric appeared in a purple robe. He carried a large book, which Ali and Gulfem signed to seal their marriage before Allah.

The musicians began to play Middle Eastern music after dinner. Most of the young single women went to the area of the dance floor in front of the main table and began to dance seductively for the enjoyment of everyone but especially, I believe, for the groom.

After a time, the musicians suddenly stopped playing.

As if on command, the women stopped dancing and promptly lined up along the sides of the dance area. Now the bride rose from her chair and went to stand in front of the main table. Alone in the silence, and facing Ali, she proudly stood several moments before him—her left foot and shoulder slightly forward, her hands on her hips, her back straight with her head and breasts held high, her gaze fixed intently on Ali's eyes.

Now the music started up again, this time slower and with a more sensuous rhythm than before. Gulfem raised her arms above her head and began to move her hips with the music in slow, controlled circles. Still gazing intently into Ali's eyes, she began to use her hands and arms to elegantly weave flowing, subtle invitations to love. As the tempo of the music quickened, Gulfem's movements became stronger and freer. She thrust her hips forward and rocked them from side to side. When she shook her shoulders, her long, black, silky hair moved about her upper body in waves. She pivoted on one foot as the music played even faster. She loosened the white scarf that she wore around her waist and drew it across her face.

62

Then she waved it high above her in the air. Her face glistened with tiny beads of sweat as she moved very close to the banquet table where Ali sat. For one brief, hypnotic moment, she leaned far, far forward and stretched both arms towards him, allowing the natural perfume of her body to reach out to him, envelop him. Suddenly she backed onto the dance floor and began to trace a large circle, as if claiming her territory and fiercely challenging any intruders. As she completed her circle, the music gradually became quieter, slower, slower. She slowed her steps with the diminishing rhythms.

When the music finally stopped, Gulfem once again stood motionless, surrounded by silence. This time she stood with her feet together, head bowed, her eyes down, her arms at her sides. Very, very slowly she drew up her back and raised her head to once again focus her dark, black, shining eyes directly into Ali's. It was apparent that all Ali saw in the room at that moment was Gulfem. In triumph and applause she gracefully, regally returned to the main table to take her place at the side of her husband.

Now it was everyone's turn to dance. The music began again. A large circle was formed. Everyone made a few steps in one direction, kicked, and then moved one step in the other. Someone began singing. Others joined in. I hummed along as I tried to keep in step with everyone else. The dancing went on all evening. Sometime during the celebration, Ali and Gulfem slipped away unseen to share the pleasures of their love.

In this tourist environment, however, all was not paradise. One can go almost everywhere in the world and find people of good will and generosity, but every society has its individuals who will do violence to others to obtain whatever it is they want. Early on a beautiful Sunday morning, one of the young German tourists staying at our hotel was brutally raped. She had made the tragic mistake of jogging alone along the same path outside of the hotel at approximately the same time every day. There was a building under construction near the path where she jogged. Each day the young workers watched her run by in her shorts and t-shirt, long blonde pony tail flowing in the wind. After a week of watching her, one of the young men knew exactly when and where he would wait for her. As she passed a lonely area with many trees and shrubs, the young man jumped out of the bushes and blocked the narrow path. At knife point he motioned her to take off all of her clothes, including her shoes and socks. He bundled the clothes and shoes together and threw them as far away as he could. When for a moment it appeared she might resist him, he struck her across the face with his empty hand, then he forced her down on her hands and knees. After raping her, he quickly ran off. The physical rape was over in minutes, but the trauma of the deep emotional rape he inflicted would, for a long time, awaken her in the middle of the night. It would take several years of therapy and, later, the attentions of a gentle husband to heal her wounded spirit.

The Turkish police did not take very long to come up with the rapist. They questioned the men at the work site. At first no one admitted to knowing anything. When the police threatened to take all of them to the police station for questioning, the workers told them who they thought it had been. The man was arrested, and the woman was called to the police station to identify him.

At the station, the woman could hear the police interrogating the suspect. They were beating him, and the screams that came from the next room were so terrible that at last she begged the police to leave the man alone. This they did, but she still had to make an identification. Two policemen brought the trembling and terrified young man to where she could see him. He was about eighteen, dressed only in his underwear. His pants were wet and urine dripped down his legs. Although he may have looked powerful and terrifying to the woman only hours before, he didn't look powerful now. He was shaking so badly the two policemen had to hold him up. He had bruises on his face, arms, and legs. Tears rolled down his cheeks. His hands were holding his groin, and it was obvious he was in great pain. The two interrogators holding him up seemed proud of their work.

"Is this the man who attacked you? I think you should know he has already told us everything."

The detective had asked the question very, very gently, and with much sympathy. He was an older man with large, sad eyes. He probably had daughters her age, maybe even a few young grandchildren.

The small, blond German woman looked at the tall, shaking young man. According to the Turkish woman employee from the hotel who had accompanied the young woman to the police station, everyone present felt she recognized him immediately. But something quite unexpected happened at that moment. The German woman looked directly into the pleading eyes of the young man in front of her for several seconds and hesitated to say anything. It is possible she was feeling pity for her attacker and was imagining what his life would be like the many years he might spend in prison. Perhaps she was thinking he had already suffered enough.

The detective seemed to understand the woman's hesitation to identify her attacker. Perhaps he even admired her compassion. But he had seen too much in his years as a policeman. Very softly, he said, "If he goes free, it might encourage others. What happened to you might happen to someone else."

The woman looked one more time into her attackers eyes, then she lowered her gaze to the floor. "Yes, that is him," she whispered. Uncontrollable sobs began to shake her body.

A single violent act had changed the destinies of two human beings. For many years, one would work to overcome her emotional trauma; the other would learn much about the consequences of causing suffering in others.

All of our spirits were dampened by the attack on the German girl, but, even in the face of tragedy, life still goes on. Our flying helped

65

us put the sadness of the experience aside. We still had a job to do. The flights continued every day to Germany, and the crews were working hard to keep the operation running well. The maintenance crews, the unsung heroes of aviation, deserved much of the credit for the fact that we did not miss any flights. As soon as the aircraft would come in from a trip, they would start working on any discrepancies we might have written up in the logbook. They would work all night, if they had to, in order to have the airplane ready to fly again in the morning.

There were aviation lessons to be learned in Turkey, too. Several crashes we learned about, once again, made it clear that no matter what part of the world you fly in, proper procedure is always important.

Turkish pilots from the airline that was chartering our services often flew with us in our cockpits. They were in training. All had been pilots in the Turkish military, but none had any airline experience. They rode along with us back and forth to Europe to get an understanding of airline operations and familiarity with the procedures at the different airports where they would soon be flying.

Coming into Antalya one night, Mehemet, one of our observers, pointed out a spot to us and said that about 13 years ago, below, right ahead of our position, a B727 belonging to a Turkish airline had slammed into a mountain, killing everybody on board. What had happened? Although they were descending at night in mountainous terrain, they abandoned the instrument procedure descent and elected to make a visual approach. Unfortunately they had not identified the airport properly, and they were much farther north of the airport than they thought they were. It was too dark to see the mountain ahead.

He also told us about a German B737 that crashed at Izmir. The investigation concluded that the pilots were well outside the usable limits of the localizer signal when they lowered down on instruments

66

to the glide slope intercept altitude. Once again an aircraft flew into mountainous terrain.

The same day I flew one of our trips from Ankara, a Turkish B727 was involved in an accident at that airport. It is believed that the aircraft was loaded too heavily with passengers and baggage for the runway available. After using the full length of the pavement to get airborne, they collided with the ILS approach light system at the departure end of the runway. The pilot was able to fly the airplane back to the airport and make an emergency landing. No one was hurt, but the aircraft was damaged beyond repair.

We fortunately flew all of our trips with no mishaps. For three months, all of our group worked hard and played hard. The summer in Turkey passed quickly. Suddenly, it was time to say goodbye to friends, pack up everyone on the airplane, and fly home. From Turkey we made our last trip across the Balkans, up through Austria, over Germany on our now very familiar routing, and then across the English Channel to land east of London at Luton. It would be necessary to take the northern route over Iceland to cross the Atlantic. (Winds were too strong from the west to make it non-stop from Shannon to Gander and still have adequate fuel reserves.) After refueling at Luton, we flew on to Keflavik. From Keflavik over to Gander, then back to home base in the U.S.

We had experienced joy, adventure, and sorrow. Life is always a mixture of these things, and it is foolish to expect to live without encountering sadness or tragedy. But still, we could be proud of our accomplishments—another extended foreign assignment well done. As I focused on the positive aspects of our summer experience, I knew in my heart that here was another opportunity to be grateful for life's gifts.

VI

The Fighter

When I returned from Turkey, I found that Mark Levitz had been having problems over the summer. During a takeoff in the Virgin Islands, at St. Thomas, the B727 he was flying had almost met with disaster.

At first, everything had seemed normal. They had taxied to the far end of the short runway to have as much runway available for the takeoff as possible. The wind was blowing from the northeast. They planned to take off to the east towards the mountains. The engines had spooled up nicely to their maximum power as Mark advanced the throttles. Nothing abnormal occurred during the first part of the takeoff roll, but as the airspeed approached V1, there was a sudden shift in the wind. What had been a partial headwind shifted now to a gusty crosswind. The airspeed indicator suddenly showed a loss of airspeed, but it was too late to reject the takeoff. In a split second, Levitz made the right decision. He continued the takeoff. To try to stop at that point might have put them through the fence at the end of the short runway.

The aircraft was below its normal takeoff speed when it left the ground, and it was farther down the runway than it would have been under normal conditions. But the aircraft was flying, and it was slowly accelerating. Since the takeoff had been unusually long, the aircraft was going to clear the end of the runway at a lower than normal altitude. Just ahead was rapidly rising terrain. Although he was at a very low altitude, Mark banked the aircraft to the right so that the flight path would go through the narrow cleft of low ground between the two hills ahead. As he banked the aircraft to the right, a strong gust suddenly caused the aircraft to overbank. Mark quickly

71

corrected, but the right wing momentarily touched the ground. There was no damage, just a slight scrape, but they had been within inches of cartwheeling the airplane into a ball of fire. His quick application of opposite aileron had saved them.

As Mark got the wings back to level, the aircraft climbed enough to avoid hitting the hills. As they completely cleared the terrain, all three crewmembers gave big sighs of relief. They all knew how close they had come.

Mark had just saved them from disaster, but he was about to make the biggest mistake of his just-beginning career as a captain. He decided to not report the incident. People on the ground had seen the takeoff and had already made a phone call to IAT operations before the crew even arrived back at Chicago later that evening.

Mark had decided not to say anything because the airplane had suffered a very minor scrape. No damage of any kind. But the fact that he didn't report the incident made it appear that he had caused the near-accident and that he was trying to cover it up. He was in his first year as captain. Some management pilots were unfortunately only too eager to attribute the wing scrape to Mark having overcontrolled the airplane rather than the gusty conditions surrounding the takeoff. Their contention was that Mark had panicked when he saw the end of the runway coming up and had abruptly rolled the airplane into a relatively steep bank at low altitude. Mark maintained that, contrary to their belief, he had not created the bad situation, but, instead, had saved everyone on board from disaster.

Mark was taken for a checkride in the simulator, where an attempt was made to recreate the situation. Mark performed well and did not overbank the aircraft in any of the recreated scenarios. He was sent back to the line and continued flying as pilot in command.

The whole incident convinced Mark more than ever that the company needed a union. He had had to undergo all the questions and checkrides without any representation or backup from anyone. He had felt very alone throughout the whole ordeal. He did have to admit to himself, however, that he should have filled out a trip report. That would have saved him a lot of trouble. He also had to admit that the company had been quite charitable. Management could have fired him immediately for not reporting damage to an aircraft, even though it had been very slight. Instead of firing him or demoting him, they had, much to their credit, taken time to fly with him in the simulator to try to determine if he had any problem areas in his flying technique. When they found no deficiencies, they returned him to flying status. They valued him as an employee, and they did everything they could to treat him fairly while at the same time protecting the safety of IAT passengers and crewmembers. At that point, everyone involved could be proud of how they had handled their management responsibilities. That would change.

Mark continued flying, but he also continued his union activism. He teamed up with other cockpit crewmembers to try to drum up enough support for a union vote. He and others had previously attempted this, but they had found little interest in unionization among the crewmembers. The situation was changing. The cockpit crews were seeing that in spite of many requests for better pay and working conditions, they received only promises and excuses.

The company was growing, and since Jurig Ritter was the sole owner, he was getting rich. As the equity in the company increased, his holdings became more and more valuable. A few people at the top were making good salaries and were allowed to make side deals that brought them extra benefits, but the pilots were left with very substandard wages and work rules that definitely favored the desires of management. It was starting to become evident to most that if we ever wanted significant changes, we would have to unionize. This was a very disappointing decision for most of us who had placed so much trust and faith in Jurig Ritter. We all wanted to believe that Jurig intended to come through for us, too.

One event that had helped to change my mind occurred during a company meeting. One of the pilots had asked Jurig in front of everyone about the low pay we were receiving and when that might change.

I watched our kindly "Uncle Jurig" suddenly get agitated and say, "Those who wish to find other jobs can certainly do so. There will always be plenty of 'soldier of fortune' pilot types who will be ready to fill any vacant seats in our cockpits."

Levitz had been right all along. He had seen it all before any of us. We had allowed our loyalty and good faith to blind us. Even the flight attendants had seen the light before we cockpit crewmembers did. They had just voted in a union, and they were now in negotiations for their first contract. Their union battle had been colorful. The company's management had tried everything they could to dissuade the flight attendants from organizing. They made up little "One Team" pins that those who were against the union were supposed to wear. Wearing the button supposedly meant that the loyal wearer was for harmony and working together as opposed to agitating for a union and causing divisiveness and discontent. Management never seemed to realize that the discontent among the flight attendants was really coming from the poor way they were being treated.

The vote was about 50/50 right up until the end of the campaign. What finally swayed the vote was a video that the company made and distributed to all the flight attendants. Management had hired a beautiful, blonde, professional actress to smile and put on an IAT "One Team" button and tell all the flight attendants how wonderful they had it. There was also a suggestion that they could lose all the great gains they had made over the years, such as insurance, separate hotel rooms, and days off if they were to unionize. Everything would have to be negotiated from scratch. The intimidation tactics, subtle as they were, created enough indignation among the flight attendants for a significant number of them to change their minds and vote for the union. I couldn't help but think how ineptly management had handled the whole situation. They had taken the hardest working and most fiercely loyal group of flight attendants in the industry and managed to alienate them.

The sudden realization that we pilots had better start looking out for ourselves did not leave me with bitterness. I have accepted long ago that people tend to look after their own interests first. Jurig had his priorities. We had ours. It would be better, many of us decided, if we had a legally established contract that would spell out clearly the rights and obligations of the parties involved. That would be much better than relying on someone's possible future generosity.

My father used to tell me a story about when he was a young man working as an accounting clerk for a very large appliance store. There was another clerk working in the office. About three months before Christmas, the other clerk took another job. The owner of the company asked my father if he thought he could handle all the work by himself. He said he would rather not hire someone else right at that moment, and, if my father could handle both jobs, the owner would show his appreciation at Christmas time.

My father said he could do it. I was nine. My sisters were seven and five. We didn't see much of our father those months. He usually came home late and exhausted. All the responsibility for handling the store's accounts was on him during the store's busiest season. This was before the days of computers and digital calculators.

Just before Christmas, the store owner asked my father to come see him in his office.

"I want to show my thanks for all the good work you've done the last few months. Business has been good, but I expected it to be much better. We didn't do as well as I thought we would. I thought it was important to show you my appreciation for your excellent work. I know you've put in some long hours."

He held out a large bottle of very fine whiskey to my father. My father didn't even like to drink. Not even beer. This was the Christmas bonus he had worked so hard for. With Christmas only a few days away and a family to support, my father just turned around and left. He never went back.

By now it was spring of 1990. Mark and others worked hard to get a union vote. I supported it too, and I spent quite a bit of time talking to other crewmembers, trying to convince them it was time for change. At a ground school I attended, the chief pilot, Captain Mike Scarlatti, gave us all a speech about how IAT was concerned about our future and how having a union on the property would drive the company into ruin. He characterized those who were backing the union as a small group of agitators who did not have the interests of the great majority of the pilots in mind. He also told us that we should be grateful to have jobs in these times of uncertainty, and he informed us that he had a high stack of resumes from highly qualified pilots on his desk.

I didn't like the undertone of his speech. Even though speaking in public does not come easily to me, after he had finished I stood up to speak. I knew I was branding myself as a troublemaker.

"I am for the union, and I believe that having a union is the only way that we are ever going to attain better pay and fair work rules at this company. Our goal is certainly not to destroy the company, and I don't particularly like being characterized as a person who has that intention just because I support the union. Also I feel insulted that you have implied we can all be easily replaced by referring to the stack of resumes on your desk."

The chief pilot declared that that had not been his intention when he mentioned the resumes on his desk. Perhaps not. But everyone in the room was well aware that the company was headquartered in Indiana and that Indiana was classed as an "at-will" state. This meant that any employee at any time could be asked to leave a company without even being given a reason. In the absence of a contract, no company in Indiana was required by law to justify the firing of any employee. In the fine print of the company policy manual was a notice:

"IAT generally has no contracts of employment with any employee. Neither this Manual or any subsequent revisions constitutes a contract.... Compliance with the policies of this Manual does not necessarily guarantee continuing employment. IAT has the right to change the policies of this Manual at any time."

A few cockpit crewmembers were fired during the period that the union vote was being organized. It is difficult to say if it was an attempt to intimidate people. The pilots involved had violated various company policies. It is possible, as management said, that it was just coincidental that these pilots had been activists for the union.

Mark Levitz was among those who were fired.

Every captain had to take a periodic six-month checkride by FAA regulation. Mark was due for his.

He reported for his checkride, only to be confronted with Captain Harry Bruchbuder. Captain Harry had no business being a check airman, according to most of the people who had had to fly with him. He was a tall, rude, domineering individual who obviously enjoyed holding power over other people. Harry was known to use his check airman status to abuse and humiliate people when he thought he could get away with it. There had been many complaints about him, but he managed a very good friendship with the B727 supervisor and also with the chief pilot at that time, Mike Scarlatti (another individual who enjoyed having power over others). Harry was very careful to treat the people above him nicely.

As soon as Mark sat down for the oral portion of the checkride, Harry set the tone for everything that would follow. "Nobody passes a checkride with me unless they have their act together. I expect good performance. I am very fair. If you fail with me, it's your fault."

Right into the questions. "What is the engine fire procedure? What are the memory items for loss of one generator? What do you do in case of a wheel well fire? Tell me what the minimum altitude is at this point of the approach according to this approach plate?"

All standard questions. It wasn't what was being asked as much as the intimidating and arrogant manner of the person asking the questions that made the experience unpleasant. Harry was making an undisguised attempt to shake Mark's confidence. Mark began to suspect that management had selected him for "special treatment" on this recurrent check, but he held his ground. He answered most of the questions well. A few things he had to look up.

Harry stayed on him. "You need to look that up? That is basic knowledge. How could you forget that?"

By the time the oral exam was over, Mark had used up almost all of his reserves of coolness. Now it was time to go into the simulator and fly.

The usual things. Takeoff. Landing. ILS approach. Engine fire. Wheel well fire. Cargo fire. Depressurization. Runaway trim.

Mark felt tremendous pressure. Harry intentionally kept up a fast pace. They moved quickly from one emergency to the next. Each procedure involved checklists and briefings. Mark gave the copilot control of the aircraft while he briefed for an approach. The copilot got lost. He was feeling pressure too. Harry berated Mark, "The captain should be watching the copilot too while he reads the approach plate! What kind of a captain lets the copilot get lost?!"

Now they did a two-engine, non-precision approach. Mark lowered the flaps to 30 degrees.

"What are you doing?! Our procedure says keep the flaps at 25 until you see the field, then you select flaps 30!"

Mark got angry. He had had enough. They stopped the simulator. Mark pointed out in the manual where it said flaps 30 would be used. Harry showed him where in the manual it said flaps 25 would be used until spotting the field. Harry was right. The procedure had been changed, and Mark should have known that. But, also, one had to admit that there was a conflict in the manual. With a normal check airman the conflict would have been resolved quite easily. All Harry had to say was, "Yes, it appears that the change isn't shown on this page. No problem. Your flaps 30 approach was just fine. Let's just do the approach again, and show me you can descend with flaps 25 until we see the field."

That isn't what Harry did. Instead, he said, "Checkride is over! It's a failure! You'll have to talk this over with your supervisor."

Now Mark had officially failed a simulator checkride. This was a very bad position to be in. He could not fly as captain until he passed another checkride. Under normal circumstances a pilot would be given some extra training if there was a discrepancy that needed attention. Almost no pilot flies an absolutely perfect checkride. There is always something that could be done better. That actually is the reason for recurrent checks: pilot performance can regularly be fine-tuned. The purpose of checkrides was never meant to be a management tool for getting rid of pilots who might fall into disfavor with management. The purpose of a checkride is to discover any errors in procedure a generally competent pilot might be making and then correct them. The goal is safety, and the assumption is that a pilot will come out of his simulator session with just a little more knowledge and skill than he had before he went in. It is supposed to be a win-win situation for pilots as well as for their passengers.

Mark was not going to be handled in the normal way, however. The company maintains to this day that it was just a coincidence that three weeks before Mark failed his checkride with Harry Bruchbuder, Mark had severely embarrassed the company's chief executive officer in a ground school by confronting him about pay and work rules in front of a class of 50 pilots.

Mark was called into the office of the B727 flight manager.

"Mark, you have failed your simulator check, and there are a number of other questions surrounding your performance during your first year as a captain. The check airman who gave you your simulator check describes you as being very excitable and confrontational. There seems to be other evidence to that effect. Impulsive and confrontational behavior can be very dangerous in a cockpit where lives are always at stake. A review of your record will be made, and I will have to ask you to come in again next week for a joint meeting with myself, the chief pilot, and the director of operations. We are going to hold off until then on whether or not it is advisable to give you more training and another checkride."

Mark knew he was being set up, but there was little he could do. With a failed checkride on his record, he had almost no credibility. He was in a very precarious position. Would the company terminate his employment? He didn't know. His record as a flight engineer had been outstanding. He had even performed the duties of a check engineer for three years. Mark knew how a checkride should be conducted because he had given very many during his years as a check flight engineer. He also knew his experience with Harry Bruchbuder had been an example of the abusive way Harry was known to conduct some of his checkrides. He had heard the complaints from other pilots. One of the reasons he was working so hard to establish a union was to do away with the possibility of this kind of abuse happening to anyone. He especially felt that people like Harry should never be allowed to become check airmen in the first place. From the way he heard Harry abused the crews he flew with out on the line, it was apparent to Mark that this kind of individual should never even be promoted to captain.

Mark was left waiting a week while higher powers decided his fate. He used the time at home to review his manuals and procedures. If he were to fly another simulator checkride, he had already decided he would request a different check airman.

When Mark was finally brought in for his meeting with management, there was very little discussion about his record. He was simply told that it was felt by all present it would be better if he were to look elsewhere for employment. Mark knew he had been cheated, but he also knew in that moment there was nothing he could do about it. He left without giving anyone the satisfaction of seeing his anger and frustration.

Mark took the case to court. He felt he had been treated unfairly because of his attempts to establish a union. The company maintained that Mark's attempt to organize the union had nothing to do with the fact they had terminated his employment. They also maintained that there had been no unfairness in the way Captain Bruchbuder had conducted Mark's simulator check. They touted Captain Bruchbuder as a fine, dedicated airman of outstanding ability and integrity. They stated that their only motive had been the safety of IAT's passengers. (Interestingly, Harry Bruchbuder was fired one year after the trial for misusing a company credit card.)

In court, the burden of proof was on Mark to show that his termination was because of union activity. His attorney was unable to present a convincing case. The company spent many thousands of dollars on a team of expensive lawyers to make sure Mark wouldn't be coming back. Mark found another job as a B727 captain, and one year later he was made a check airman. Four years after that he was to become an L1011 captain and check airman in another company. Recently, he successfully organized their first union.

VII

Solidarity and Gentle Waters

If the company managers had terminated Mark's employment to slow down the union effort, they managed to achieve the opposite effect. Many pilots who had thought a union was unnecessary up to that point suddenly became very aware of how easily their employment could be taken away if they fell into displeasure with management. Support for the union grew every day as the pilots realized how unfairly Mark had been treated. The company, for its part, attempted to gain support for its position that Mark had been a very unsafe captain and that it had been their regrettable duty, in the interest of safety, to remove such a dangerous person from the pilot ranks. Those who had worked in the cockpit with Mark knew better. He was generally considered a good pilot by everyone who had flown with him on the line.

Pro-union sentiment grew. The pilot group now had a significant split. On one side were people like myself who felt the union was the only way to secure employment rights and fairness. The other group remained loyal to company management. We were all generally too much friends with each other to allow actual animosities to develop. After all, we had helped build this company together and had shared many flying experiences. Except for an occasional spirited argument, there was a general tolerance for each other's views. Company management realized they had made a strategic error by firing Mark, and they were careful to avoid the image that they were effecting a wave of repression. They didn't want to drive more pilots into the union fold, and they didn't want to give any more credibility to Mark's claims in court that he had been fired for his union activity. No more pilots were fired. This did not mean that those of us who were vocal for the union did not feel exposed to the possibility of losing our jobs. We all felt tremendous pressure during this time because we knew that if any one us were to make a mistake while flying, it would probably be used against us.

In order to try to get Mark his job back, I wrote a letter directly to Jurig Ritter emphasizing why I thought Mark had been treated unfairly. This resulted in a four-hour meeting with one of the top management executives. The results were typical of all our efforts. All my views and objections were politely heard, but in the end, nothing was done to change Mark's situation.

Jurig Ritter tried to use his personal powers of communication to allay the growing union sentiment by inviting all the captains to come and talk with him one-on-one to express their views on what needed to be changed in the company. Over and over he heard the same complaints about low pay, lack of benefits, abusive scheduling policies, potential use of checkrides as a discipline tool, lack of job protection, and no legal rights within the company. The truly sad thing was that after receiving all this information, Jurig did nothing with it.

I was one of the captains who decided to accept the invitation to voice my concerns directly to Jurig. When I went to see him, I couldn't help but like him on a personal level. At the same time, I sensed that behind the charm and friendly informality there sat a very astute negotiator. Jurig looked you right in the eye and sympathized with your complaints. He asked all the right questions to draw out your thoughts. He asked what could be done to improve the company. He even stated that he wasn't really against the pilots having a union if that was what they wanted. He said, in his own case, he had always liked to negotiate his own deals without a middleman. Was this statement meant to be a gentle probe to see if I could be persuaded in the future to put my own interests above that of the group? Jurig knew that making people feel special was a very good way to maintain control over them. Give a man just enough status to make him feel a little important, then you own him. Our conversation together was really quite pleasant, but when I left the meeting I couldn't help remembering an old Spanish prayer, "*Dios, librame de las aguas mansas, de las turbulentas me libro yo.*" (God, save me from gentle waters, from the turbulent ones I will save myself.)

Now that the size of IAT has doubled from the days when the first union was being established, one could ask most of the pilots, "Who is William London?" and hardly anyone would know. But Captain William London was the man who in the end drew all the union supporters together and organized a successful vote.

Bill London had grown up in Indianapolis. He was another boy who liked to go down to the airport and watch the planes landing and taking off. Bill had another side to him. He couldn't stand to see people abused. He was tall, and he was strong. On many occasions in the school yard he would intervene if he saw an older boy picking on a younger one. His mother used to tell him, "If you stand by while someone else is being abused and you could be doing something to stop it, you are just as guilty as the abuser." Bill's mother didn't teach her children religion, but she did teach them values. Bill and all of his brothers and sisters grew up with a very strong sense of right and wrong, fairness and unfairness. She also taught them to not put a lot of value on things that could be bought. "The true treasures in this world," she would tell them, "are the treasures you carry within you—your spirit, your compassion, your strength, and your integrity."

After college, Bill joined the Navy. That is where he got his chance to fly. Bill wanted to fly fighter aircraft, but instead he was assigned to a unit that flew transport planes. His job was to fly VIP officers to meetings at different bases and to different cities all over the world. His job required good planning. When Bill flew one of the top admirals somewhere, there would always be a reception ceremony. Bill had to time all of his flights just right so that the flight didn't arrive too early or too late. If the plane arrived too early, then the arriving VIP would find the band not ready, or the honor guard not in place, or, perhaps, the base officials not yet waiting in position to greet him. If he arrived too late, possibly hundreds of personnel and high-ranking officers on the reception team would be made to wait uncomfortably in formation.

In order to arrive at just the right moment, Bill would plan for his flight to arrive in the area always just a few minutes early, and then he would ask air traffic control to give him a series of turns or a short holding pattern in order to land at precisely the correct moment. His plan usually worked well. He would land the aircraft and, exactly on time, his VIP passenger would step out of the aircraft to a warm and enthusiastic reception from the assembled military personnel.

The first time Bill was assigned to fly a particularly important VIP to a neighboring air station, the high ranking admiral called him the night before. He wanted to make absolutely sure that they did not arrive late at their destination in the morning. He suggested that they move up the departure time for the flight 15 minutes. Bill complied. After takeoff, Bill flew the DC9 as slowly as he could, but he still had to ask the controllers for a longer routing and some extra turns in order to not arrive too early. The next time Bill was assigned to carry the same admiral, he once again received a phone call the night before. The admiral absolutely did not want to be late, so he suggested they move up the departure time 30 minutes. Once again, Bill flew the aircraft slowly. He requested out-of-the-way routing and extra turns when they arrived in the vicinity of the airfield. They arrived exactly on time. The third time Bill flew the same admiral, he once again received a phone call.

"I think we should move up the departure time one hour on this one."

"Aye, aye, Sir."

Bill put extra fuel on the aircraft and planned a flight that would take them on a leisurely tour of the area surrounding their destination. Once again he landed and taxied up to the reception area exactly on time. The admiral looked very unhappy.

When Bill flew the admiral back to his home base later that evening, the admiral pulled him aside for a moment before he got into the waiting staff car. "Son, I don't want to be too critical with you because you seem to be a very fine pilot, but it seems that no matter how early I try to get you to depart, you always get me to the destination with barely seconds to spare."

Bill began thinking that perhaps the military wasn't where he would like to spend his whole flying career. He searched the civilian world for job opportunities. One year later he was flying internationally as a B707 captain at IAT right out of his home town, Indianapolis.

It didn't take Bill long to figure out that Jurig Ritter was building his wealth on the low wages of his employees. Bill's degree was in accounting. Bill saw the need for a union long before everyone else, even before Mark Levitz. He tried to stir up interest among the pilot group, but the group generally remained fiercely loyal to Jurig's communicated vision of a great and prosperous future for everyone in the company. It eventually became apparent that Jurig now had a yacht, a personal jet, a helicopter, a very large home, and quite a few other assets in addition to being the sole owner of the company. Still there were calls for belt-tightening and constant explanations from management that sacrifices would be needed to keep the company growing.

As awareness grew, Bill was able to get more people to listen to him when he proposed a union for the pilots. Mark Levitz was one of those people, and Mark had been one of his best co-activists. When Mark was fired, Bill unsuccessfully tried to get him rehired. Bill felt company management had crossed a line. He knew it was now time to make a maximum effort to get a vote through. He spent all of his free time making phone calls, organizing small meetings, and approaching fellow crewmembers one-on-one. His efforts began to bring results. He slowly built an organization. More and more pilots opened their eyes to what they had to do in order to be able to share more fairly in the success of the company they had helped to build. More and more began speaking out. The company still tried to brand the pro-union pilots as a small group of agitators, but there were too many now to make that argument believable. Bill knew he was risking his job, and he knew that everyone working with him was risking theirs, too. "Watch your six o'clock," he would say. The uncertainty put tremendous pressure on Bill's home life as his wife became afraid that they would lose their house and their lifestyle if Bill were fired. A rift was created that would eventually lead to a divorce. He sadly had to realize that his view of the world and that of his wife were based on very different values.

It is probable that certain people in management would have liked to have removed Bill from the picture at this point, but Bill was no first-year captain. He had solid experience as a U.S. Navy aviator and several years as a captain for IAT. Any attempt to besmirch his reputation would be seen easily for what it was.

Jurig asked Bill to come see him.

"Bill, your activities for the union show that you have excellent organizational skills and the ability to motivate our crewmembers. Your talents could be extremely useful to IAT as we try to find ways to improve working conditions and pay for our pilots. Of course, because of the union drive we are obligated by law to maintain the status quo on wages and company policies. But after this is all over, I look forward to making some real changes that will benefit our crewmembers. We want the best for them too, and we, I, could really use your help. With you alongside us, we could make improvements rapidly instead of being tied up in contract negotiations that could take up to two years to complete. You are free, of course, to organize a union if you like. That is your right, and I fully support your rights. But might it not be better for everyone if we could all work together on the same team rather than split up into adversarial groups? How would you like a chance to make some real changes? You could head up a special committee composed of myself, other executives, and pilots. Of course, your work would merit company executive status because of all the responsibility. Also, a substantial increase in pay would only be fair. Your integrity and vision could do a lot to change IAT."

Bill declined the offer.

Just before the vote was about to take place among the pilots to decide whether or not they wanted representation, Jurig Ritter made one final, valiant stand. He made a videotape and distributed it to all the crewmembers. No professional actors this time. I had to admire his tenacity and his attempt to communicate his position. Jurig stated right up front that if a union were voted in, IAT would learn to work with it. But then he went on to explain his vision of a company that needed no union. He described an environment where everyone would work together for the common good so that all would prosper. Harmony, Prosperity, and Sharing were the major themes. He also told about the dangers that having a union might bring: "You will no longer have the same close relationship you have had with management in the past. Our lawyers will talk to your lawyers. What is finally negotiated may not be what you want. Nobody gets something for nothing. To get some things you will probably have to give up others. Can any union really guarantee you better pay, better policies, or job security?"

As in the tape made to combat the flight attendant representation vote, Jurig's tape attempted to subtly play on people's fears and uncertainties. The pilots were not swayed. In the end they looked at the company's deeds over the prior 10 years rather than its words. Which spoke louder was evidenced by the overwhelming majority of the pilots voting for representation.

Preston, I don't want to make this whole letter a story about the union at IAT. But it is an important part of my story, and someday it could be an important part of yours. You are going to find as you go through life that there will be many people who will claim they have only your best interests at heart. Some will be sincere. Some will not. Some will think they are sincere, but still they are not. They usually elicit your support by asking you to join into some kind of a belief system. In our case it was LOYALTY. When people in our company finally asked just what it was we were being loyal to, we couldn't really find any satisfactory answers. Be wary and remember that what people do is usually more important than what they say.

As a final note on the subject, let me say that it has been more than 10 years since IAT voted in its first union, and things have only gotten better since then. In spite of all the dire predictions, the company continued to grow and prosper. Now we have a completely different, and much more enlightened, management team. The little company we hired on with years ago is now considered a major airline. We have better pay and better working conditions. We have the right to ask that a union observer be present when we take our checkrides. We do not have to face disputes with the company alone. There is always a union representative available to stand with us. No one can be arbitrarily fired on false accusations. There is definitely more dignity surrounding our work. Some things are worth risking.

And Captain Bill London? He remained the president of the union for a few years until he allowed others to take over so that he could go back to what he loves best—flying. He and I will retire in a few years, and since more than half of the pilots in our company have been hired after Bill left his union duties, they will never know how much of a debt they owe him.

VIII

Dignity

Once the union was formed I was asked to head the Professional Standards Committee. The purpose of the PSC is to act as an intermediary between the pilot group and management. Sometimes minor problems or disputes that pilots are having can be solved without getting management involved. Or sometimes the PSC can intervene with management on a pilot's behalf. By the time the union had been voted in, Harry Bruchbuder had had a good run as the terror of the check airman cadre. A number of copilots did not want to fly with him, and almost everyone who got him for a checkride did not look forward to the experience. If for some reason Harry didn't like the particular pilot being checked, he would spend the whole checkride belittling him. Harry liked to intimidate and humiliate people. I had already seen what he had done to Mark Levitz, so I wasn't surprised that as soon as I became head of Professional Standards, I received a great number of complaints about Harry Bruchbuder. Pilots said his overbearing manner in the cockpit created so much tension that it detracted from safety.

If there had been just a few complaints, I would have made an effort to talk with Harry to see if anything could be worked out. That was impossible, though, because as long as Harry felt he had the backing of management, I knew he wasn't going to change his methods. Levitz's trial was still going on, so management felt nothing should be done that might put Harry in a negative light in court. I decided to try to get Harry's boss, Tom Lyons, to have a quiet talk with Harry. Tom Lyons had been the B727 flight manager at IAT for several years. I had worked closely with him when I was a B727 captain back on the Malta assignment. We were friends, and I felt I could speak freely with him.

"Tom, I don't want to mention a name, but I have had many complaints about one of your check airman. Perhaps you know who I am referring to. There are so many negative reports about this individual that I thought you should know that it is not just a few people who would like to have him removed from the check airman position. There are many. I wonder if you could do something to make sure that he tries to treat people a little better."

"I haven't heard any complaints, Richard. And besides, anyone who fails a checkride is bound to be somewhat resentful."

"Tom, these aren't just people who have failed checkrides who are complaining. Quite a few of the people who fly with this person feel that his overbearing demeanor in the cockpit takes away from safety. He evidently enjoys intimidating anyone he can. If you could talk to him it might help keep any kind of formal action on the part of the union from being initiated."

"Rich, as far I know there has been no unfairness on the part of any check airman, and the only people who seem to be having trouble flying with any of our captains are weak copilots who should be trying to learn from the captains they are flying with instead of criticizing them."

"All right, Tom. I was hoping this could all be settled in a very simple and informal way so that no one would be hurt, but I am going to have to take action on these complaints and see what the union can do to remove this individual from check airman status."

"That's fine, Richard. But if you go after any of my people, you better have everything well documented. If you don't, it's going to be your ass that will be in trouble."

"Fair enough, Tom. I'll get the complaints in writing."

I had stuck my neck out pretty far. Even though I had the union behind me, if I didn't present a very strong case, I would be dealt with in some disagreeable way. I was sure of that. Tom knew very well who I was talking about. But he was friends with Harry and he wasn't about to let a line captain, even one associated with the PSC, tell him how to run his department.

I now set out to build a case I could present to management. I tried to find out about specific incidents. Dates. Times. What took place? Why was the situation detrimental to safety? Many people had complained, but when I tried to get them to write up their complaints with the specifics, few were willing to do so. Out of all those who had voiced private complaints, very few were willing to commit their grievance to writing. One thing I insisted on was that all complaints be signed. If someone was going to accuse another of misconduct, he had to be willing to stand by it. No anonymous letters would be accepted. In the end, I wasn't able to get enough written statements to be able to make any substantial charges. While all this was going on, I was stepping on a lot of toes. Management had never before been in a position where they had to be accountable to a union. They resented very much my effort to discredit a check airman who they felt was competent. After all, I wasn't a check airman. What did I know about how a check airman should behave? I was just another line captain with a nice little title given to him by the union. I had already incurred a reputation as an undesirable among several managers when I had tried to help Mark Levitz. I was being seen more and more as just a troublemaker.

Not only management got upset. Many check airman took it as a personal affront that I was conducting what they viewed as a witch hunt. It was common knowledge that I was also attempting to get negotiated into the new contract the right of a pilot, if he wished, to have a union observer present during any checkride. This was bitterly contested by management all through the contract negotiations. Many in the check airman group took this as an insult. They also felt it could expose them to some kind of liability in court.

I had put myself in the middle of a storm. Some of the check airman spoke with me to try to determine what it was I was trying to do. I tried to explain that I was only trying to build safeguards into the system in order to remove the possibility that checkrides could ever be used by management as a disciplinary tool. I said I had seen this happen in other companies, and I wanted to make sure the practice would not be a part of our corporate culture.

My intention had never been to cast aspersions on any of the check airman who were doing a good job in the company. It was only this one individual who was out of control and needed to be reined in.

The final outcome of the whole affair was that the check airmen knew exactly who the troublemaker was in their midst. They had heard the complaints too. They pulled Captain Bruchbuder aside and told him he was making them look bad. Under this kind of pressure from his peers, Bruchbuder, like all bullies when effectively confronted, backed down and made an effort to be more of a gentleman with his fellow workers. I heard he was still not a great pleasure to fly with, but that at least he no longer openly tried to abuse people. As for the contract, the clause about the right to have a union observer present, if desired, on a checkride was eventually included. Management fought to have it kept out right up to the end of the contract negotiations. I fell into disfavor with management over the whole affair. Sometimes you pay when you stand up for something. Some punishments, however, one can willingly bear.

Another area where I incurred the displeasure of management was my opposition to how the drug testing program was being administered.

There are many arguments for and against drug testing for pilots. They could be the subject of a whole other book—many books. From my viewpoint, I will only tell you, Preston, that I believe the American public was duped into believing, through pseudo-scientific studies and hysteria, that random drug testing of the American worker was necessary to protect public safety and also to prevent grave losses to the national economy. I am sure these assumptions will someday be proved to have been false. It will also be interesting to see who has actually reaped the profits from the millions of dollars that are wasted every year on these invasive, humiliating programs. The principle of suspicionless searches is for me quite abhorrent, and I find the drug testing procedure itself degrading and demeaning. I am sure it represents just the beginning of a whole host of invasions of privacy that the government will attempt to impose on citizens as the technology for personal searches and surveillance becomes more sophisticated.

As a pilot, I strongly support any kind of probable-cause testing. If a fellow pilot were ever to show signs of being impaired on the job by drugs, I would want that individual tested immediately. I wouldn't want to be on the airplane with him, either. Random drug testing, however, assumes *everyone* is guilty, and then, through a procedure that assaults one's dignity—namely, collection of a urine specimen— the individual must provide proof that he or she is not taking drugs. It is interesting to note that very few countries in the world have random drug testing programs for their pilots or, for that matter, any of their other citizens. With the United States of America leading the charge away from civil liberties, this is slowly changing. Other countries are slowly adapting suspicionless drug testing.

The whole concept of blanket searches goes very much against our traditions as Americans. All kinds of crimes in this country could be eliminated, and many criminals could be caught if only the government had the power to randomly arrest people or randomly invade people's homes to see what evidence the police might find of wrongdoing. Why not arrest people without suspicion and allow the use of torture to uncover information about any criminal or anti-government activities? By ignoring our basic freedoms and our basic dignity, many of society's problems could be solved. Too many children on welfare? Forced sterilization of women. Men who are violent? Castration. Vagrants? Forced labor camps. Children with disabilities or genetic defects? Euthanasia. Mental illness? Euthanasia again. Political protest? Re-education camps. Racial tension? Gas the minorities.

Everyone knows a strong government with unlimited powers can produce a very ordered society. The problem is that when repression is used to protect freedom and quality of life, it destroys the freedom and the quality of life it is trying to protect. Today in America, even school children wishing to participate in extracurricular activities can be forced to submit to random drug testing. The message to the next generation is that it is acceptable to abuse individual freedom and dignity in order to protect public safety and order. This principle would readily be defended by Adolf Hitler, Benito Mussolini, Joseph Stalin, Fidel Castro, Augusto Pinochet, Pol Pot, Idi Amin, Saddam Hussein, and countless others like them. It is sad that the country that likes to present itself to the world as the beacon of freedom cannot find ways to fight drug abuse without abusing the rights of its citizens.

The battles were fought in court, and in the end the U.S. Supreme Court ruled that under certain circumstances, such as in the case of workers in safety-related occupations, it was not a violation of the Fourth Amendment to require random drug testing. Like it or not, we pilots, and millions of other workers in safety-related occupations would now be subject to random drug testing.

I knew it was useless to try to fight having a program in our company. Management really had no choice in the matter. The FARs (Federal Aviation Regulations) mandated the testing. Where I got involved was the way the program was being administered.

The testing program started out in a frenzy of ignorance. Few people in management took any time to think how this program would impact the morale of the employees who would be required to submit to the degrading testing. Management did nothing to safeguard the dignity of its employees. Instead, the managers placed control of the whole drug testing program under a young nurse.

Carla Robbins started drug testing with a vengeance. If the United States Government felt that America's safety-related workers were in reality drug-crazed addicts who needed to be exposed by Big Brother tactics, she was ready to root out the evil wherever she could find it.

The guidelines for drug testing set out by the FAA provided for a certain amount of dignity while collecting the urine sample. First, direct observation of the urine stream from the person providing the sample to the cup was not a requirement unless there was reason to believe that the person being tested was going to attempt to provide a substituted sample. Next, under FAA guidelines, a person could be allowed to go into a private bathroom to fill the specimen cup while the drug tester waited outside. As a precaution against the possible dilution of the sample with water, water faucets would be taped over and a blue dye put into the toilet water. After filling the cup, the person being tested would give it to the tester. The tester measures the temperature of the urine sample to make sure it is at body temperature. Then the sample is packaged up, some forms are signed, and off goes the sample to a laboratory. This procedure was adopted by most of the airlines from the beginning. Not ours. Instead, our program demonstrated an appalling lack of sensitivity to the feelings of the employees.

Taping up water faucets to protect the dignity and sensibilities of employees was a waste of effort for Carla. Instead, she followed the other procedure allowed by the FAA. In this scenario, the drug tester would put the blue dye in a toilet with a stall around it. Then the tester would stand outside the stall and listen for sounds of urination. Listening for sounds of urination was not really required by the FAA, but Carla insisted this was. Now, employees would be monitored as if they were children while they urinated. Many people felt the process was degrading. Carla insisted there was nothing degrading about it and that the way things were being done was required by the Federal Aviation Regulations. Of course, to refuse a drug test meant automatic termination of employment.

I will never forget the humiliation I felt during my first drug test. From that day I have felt that my right as an American just to be left alone in absence of suspicion for any crime had been taken away. Even as I write this letter to you, Preston, I still feel the same repugnance to this program that I felt when it was first started. America has crossed a threshold with acceptance of random drug testing. I am sure other abuses of human rights in the name of safety and security will someday follow.

As I said, I was well aware that the company was required to have a drug testing program, but I also knew that the regulations allowed for a more dignified way to administer the tests. I made an appointment to see Jim Harmon. Jim was now the CEO of the company, and I felt that if he only knew there was a better way to do things, he would immediately take the initiative on behalf of his employees and do everything he could to defend their sensibilities. I still had memories of the great courtesy he always showed fellow crewmembers long ago when he was one of our best line captains.

I presented to him all the information I had about the drug testing procedures and showed him how the regulations allowed for at least some semblance of dignity by allowing tested employees to use a private bathroom. He completely agreed with me and told me I should contact his assistant to effect some changes. Unfortunately his assistant did not really intend to do anything. Though he gave me no open opposition, neither did he bother to help change the procedures. With no pressure from upper management to change her testing style, Carla ignored any challenges from the rank and file.

The worst example of Carla's complete lack of sensitivity to employees' feelings came about three weeks after I had spoken with Jim Harmon to try to get the procedures changed.

A crew landed at San Francisco, and all five female flight attendants had been selected for random drug testing. There was a women's bathroom on the airport. Each flight attendant would be tested, one at a time. There were three stalls in the bathroom. Only one would be used. Only the tester and one flight attendant at a time would be in the bathroom. The flight attendant would go into the stall and the tester would stand outside the stall and listen for sounds of urination. There was only one problem. The tester was a young male. The flight attendants voiced their protests about having to go into a bathroom with a man. This didn't faze Carla at all. After all, many of the male employees had gone into the bathrooms at other locations and had been monitored by women. Refusal meant termination of employment. One by one the flight attendants went into the bathroom with the official drug tester.

To Carla this was just a medical procedure being carried out by a professional urine specimen collector. Nothing to be excited about. Of course Carla's job description didn't come under the category of "safety-related occupation," so she would never be subject to any of these procedures. To become a professional urine specimen collector, incidentally, meant that an unemployed vagrant could take a two-day course in urine collection and receive his official title. The credentials of the tester is not really the point. Even if a doctor is collecting the specimen, it makes the whole procedure no less degrading.

I protested these procedures and tried to get the company to change to the "private bathroom" scenario. Carla simply didn't want to change her methods. Finally the company made a complete reversal in its policy. Private bathrooms would be used just as other drug testing programs at other airlines had been doing from the start. Was it a result of the campaign I had initiated or the complaint

103

I had made directly to Jurig Ritter? I don't know. What I do know is that when one of the management pilots was sent to a local clinic for a drug test, the nurse in charge wanted him to remove all of his clothing, put on a hospital gown and be led to a toilet down the hall. It was at this point, I think, that management probably started thinking they should take a closer look at how the drug testing program was being administered. (After all, this could happen to them.) I often wonder if Carla's opinion of her methods would have been different if she had had to go into a bathroom with a stranger, possibly male, hike up *her* skirt, drop *her* panties, and produce a urine sample while the monitor listened the whole time for sounds of urination. The same might apply for everyone who is for these types of programs but who will never be subjected to the degradation themselves. Just like any abuse of civil liberties, people accept it easily if it is happening only to the "other guy."

Why should high school students who wish to participate in extra-curricular activities (such as acting in a student play) be forced to submit to drug testing? Justification for this abuse has now been expanded from "We must do this for safety" to "We are doing this for your own good." Perhaps parents, teachers, politicians, school board members, or even Supreme Court judges who favor random drug testing should also be subject to the same testing. Would they be just as enthusiastic about such programs? I don't see them volunteering.

IX

Old Love, New Love

B757
photo by Dennis Chang

For six years now, I had been a captain on the B727. During that time I had watched our company grow from a typical "non-sched" carrier to a small reputable airline that provided not only vacation charters, but also scheduled service to a number of cities from its two main bases, Chicago and Indianapolis. True, we had had to fight a gentlemen's battle with Jurig Ritter to form a union and achieve better pay and working conditions, but none of us could deny that Jurig was one of the most astute businessmen in the industry. He had, at this point, accomplished what many others had tried to do but failed.

I have watched quite a few start-up carriers come and go in the years I have been flying. They all made bad business decisions along the way. Some expanded too quickly. Some tried to get by with minimum maintenance on their airplanes. Some made commitments they couldn't keep. Jurig avoided these mistakes and many others. Sometimes his decisions took a great amount of courage. When he traded the B707s in on a small fleet of L1011s, he was risking everything. If his gamble to be able to effectively utilize wide-bodied aircraft had failed, the whole company would have gone into bankruptcy. He had made the right decision, however. The L1011 became an important revenue-producing addition to the fleet, and it brought us business we never would have had otherwise.

Jurig had also established a reputation for always paying the bills. He didn't run up debts. Companies that did business with IAT knew that Jurig's integrity stood behind any dealings they might have with the company. This translated into good cooperation with airport authorities and service providers. When a captain took an airplane somewhere, he could count on prompt fueling, lavatory servicing, catering, water refill, and passenger handling. This was important because prompt services meant few delays and better passenger satisfaction.

Jurig now made another risky and daring decision. He decided to purchase B757s. Looking to the future, Jurig had seen that noise abatement restrictions and fuel costs would soon render the B727 obsolete. The purchase of the B757 represented a major step forward for IAT. These larger, fuel-efficient aircraft would be state-of-the-art and equipped with sophisticated autopilots and navigation systems. Except for the first few, which were previously owned by other carriers, IAT would buy all these aircraft new from Boeing. IAT had come a long way from the day when Jurig had purchased his first aged B707 to begin his operation. He had plenty to be proud of.

At first, I wanted to continue flying my B727. It was comfortable and familiar. It was also very dependable. It very seldom broke down, so its dispatch reliability was generally excellent. Also, most of us 727 pilots liked to hand fly the aircraft. Normally, we wouldn't click on the autopilot until reaching a cruise altitude. Once the descent began, the autopilot would be disconnected, and we would manually fly the aircraft all the way to touchdown. The new trend in the industry was to use automation to its fullest when flying an aircraft. The B757 was part of that trend. Pilots on aircraft like the B757 were encouraged to take full advantage of the automation available and allow the autopilot to fly the airplane. Of course, without proper programming, the highly sophisticated navigation and autopilot systems would be useless. Most of the training in the B757 would be oriented toward teaching the pilots to program the navigation system and manipulate the autopilot.

I could see that the industry was coming to the end of an era. Basic piloting skills would still always be necessary (what happens when all this fancy stuff stops working?), but, more and more, airline pilots would be expected, in normal operations, to manage electronic systems. Hand flying the aircraft would be reserved for landings and for abnormal situations when the autopilot could not be used for aircraft control. There was another change in the philosophy of how to train pilots. For many years pilots spent quite a bit of time with detailed schematics of different aircraft systems, memorizing pages of nice-to-know but generally useless information. Questions like "How many joules of electrical energy do the engine igniters provide during start? How many during continuous ignition?" would be part of written and oral exams. It became apparent that knowing this kind of information contributed almost nothing to the pilot being able to fly the aircraft or handle an emergency. The new philosophy of pilot training would be oriented toward teaching what a pilot actually needed to know to operate the aircraft. It didn't matter if a pilot knew how many volts it took to operate a particular circuit or if he knew at what temperature the strut overheat light illuminated. What did matter was that if a malfunction occurred, the pilot could evaluate the problem and take the required actions. If an engine fire erupted, for example, it was much less important to know at what temperature the fire signal would be activated than how to put out the fire and make a safe landing.

I began training in the B757 in October of 1990. The entire process from first day of ground school to final line check would take about three months. Looking back today, now that I have been on the aircraft more than 10 years, I don't see the course as being extremely difficult, but, at the time, I struggled greatly with the material. Learning the aircraft and its operation required a great shift in perspective. It was difficult for me to imagine how a mere mortal could program the navigation system to get the aircraft to do all the maneuvers that would be required during flight. I felt sorry for those in the class who had no experience with computers. I had at least done some simple programming at home on my PC. Learning the aircraft systems was also difficult because I always wanted more detail about why a system operated as it did or what happened in an electrical or hydraulic system when a particular switch was activated.

109

B757 Flight Deck

All during ground school I attempted to extract as much information as I could from a manual that apparently had been designed to provide only what was necessary, and nothing more. Gradually, I found that much of the information I was seeking was there; it was just being presented in a different way. I also learned to shift my perspective from the old way of learning aircraft systems to the new way.

By the time I completed ground school, I felt I had gained a good understanding of the aircraft systems and their operation, but I still could not envision how the aircraft would be flown by typing commands into the computer. I decided to take advantage of the break between the end of ground school and the beginning of simulator training to go observe several actual flights from the vantage point of the B757 cockpit jumpseat.

The crews who were experienced on the airplane were only too happy to show me how to enter information into the flight management computer (FMC):

"Suppose you are on a radar vector and wish to intercept a particular course inbound to a fix. Hit the DIR/INTC key, then enter the fix you wish to go to into the scratchpad. Enter that fix into the INTC LEG TO box. When the INTC CRS box replaces the INTC LEG TO box, type in the inbound course. Check to see everything is correct on the FMC. Compare that information with the display on the HSI. Is the white dashed line to the desired fix in the correct position? Once you feel that the FMC is programmed correctly, have the other pilot confirm the accuracy of your entries. If all data is correct, press ENTER on the FMC. The white dashed line will now turn into a solid magenta line. Notice that the symbol for the waypoint you programmed the intercept course to is also shown in magenta, indicating that it is now the active waypoint. Next, go to the Mode Control Panel for the autopilot and select LNAV. LNAV will now show up on the ADI right here in white, indicating it is armed for the intercept. When the aircraft intercepts the course, the LNAV indication on the ADI now moves to the active mode position and turns to green. A green box will appear around the newly activated mode for about 10 seconds to indicate the mode recently became active. See, it's not as hard as it sounds. Did you get it all?"

"Uh . . . , yeah . . . , sure. Thanks, I really appreciate your help."

"Good. Here, you try to set up an intercept leg to a waypoint up to the point where we would activate it."

"Uuuh, maybe you should show me that again."

"Which part?"

"Uuh, maybe all of it?"

There were many more things to learn about the FMC and autopilot, but gradually it all started to make sense to me. Today, I feel very comfortable flying an airplane in this manner. Once again, Preston, new tasks can seem quite daunting to learn, but if you work at them, things that seemed impossible when you first try to learn them often turn out to be much easier than you might have originally thought. The important thing is to not give up easily. Stay focused. Keep trying. Find help if you need it.

The observation flights I made helped quite a bit. Simulator training went well, but there were times when tensions developed. I had been paired with a copilot who liked to jump in with the answer if you got stuck trying to figure out how to make a particular entry into the flight management computer. He didn't realize there were many times that I knew the answer while he was struggling, but that I didn't jump in so that he would have time to think out the problem.

Our instructor, Charlie Steele, took it all in stride if we got stuck. He had trained many pilots in this airplane, and he knew eventually we would understand what we had to do. Sometimes he would try to lessen the tension with a little Southern humor.

"Let's try that entry again. This route would be great if we wanted to go to Madagascar, but I think we'd still like to see if we can get the airplane to land at Chicago."

Sometimes when we really drew a blank on how to solve a particular navigation problem, Charlie would say, "Keep trying. Don't get discouraged. When I was learning this stuff, I often felt like a pig staring at a wristwatch."

Little by little, we learned how to take off and hook up the autopilot, program the FMC so that the airplane would fly in the right direction, and do all the other required maneuvers. We now started to give our commands with more confidence.

"Center autopilot ON. Select heading 300 degrees. Set up an Intercept leg to the IOW VOR, 270 degrees inbound."

Now that we could get the airplane to go where we wanted it to go, it was time to learn how to fly it when things start going wrong.

The first thing we learned about malfunctions on the B757 was that Boeing had declared there were no emergencies on this airplane. At least there were no EMERGENCY procedures. We only had ABNORMAL procedures in our checklists. Lose a generator? Go to the ABNORMAL checklists. Loss of all hydraulics? Find the answer in the ABNORMAL procedures. Engine on fire. No sweat. Just another ABNORMAL procedure. I guess nothing ever shook the guys back on the ground at Boeing who wrote these checklists.

It is true that for most of the things that can go wrong on a B757 there really isn't a lot to get excited about. It is just a matter of doing the right procedure to contain the problem, and then modify the operation as necessary. Land if it is serious. Proceed if it is not. The aircraft has several backup systems in each critical area. If an engine-driven generator fails, there is still another engine-driven generator on the other engine. The auxiliary power unit (APU) in the tail of the aircraft can also be started to drive another generator and restore two-generator operation. In the unlikely event that the left engine-driven generator, the right engine-driven generator, and the APU generator all fail, the hydraulic motor generator (HMG) driven by the left hydraulic system or the right hydraulic system through a power transfer unit (PTU) can still provide electrical power to enough equipment to complete a transatlantic flight. If all of these fail, aircraft batteries can still provide power to basic backup instruments so that the aircraft can be landed safely.

Other systems also have built-in redundancy. There are three separate hydraulic systems, two automatic pressurization controllers, backup fuel pumps, backup flight instruments, backup navigation equipment, and backup radios. We learned how to handle problems that might occur with each system. We also learned how to deal with cargo fires, cabin fires, electrical smoke, fumes in the cockpit, and engine fires. Any kind of fire in an aircraft usually requires an emergency landing. The only exception might by a brief galley fire that has definitely been extinguished. Any doubt about origin or complete extinction of a fire requires an immediate emergency landing.

We also learned how to do the different kinds of approaches. ILS approaches were performed with two engines and with one engine. Go-arounds with holding patterns were also included. I admit that I floundered for several days with all the new procedures, but, as predicted by our instructor, on about the fourth day a shift took place in my mind and everything suddenly fell together. Everything that had seemed so impossible before now appeared quite logical.

It was time now for the simulator checkride with the FAA. Another captain and I would take our checkrides the same evening. The other captain, by virtue of his seniority, insisted on going first. No gentlemanly coin flips with this guy. A check airman would occupy the right seat for both checkrides. After more than two hours the other captain came out of the simulator looking very tired. He had passed. It was now my turn. I was apprehensive.

Although I didn't expect it to be, the sim check somehow turned out to be one of the best I have ever flown. The check airman who had run the simulator wrote me a note the next day congratulating me on the good performance. Sometimes it just works like that. I had gone into the simulator feeling a little nervous and a little tired after waiting for the other captain to complete his ride. I wasn't expecting to do my best, but somehow everything clicked right into place. I've done many sim checks over the years. Sometimes you go in feeling very confident and then you make some mistake you never imagined it would be possible for you to make. It happens to everyone at some time. There is no doubt that flying constantly makes you face up to your flaws. There is good reason the simulator is sometimes called the "humiliator."

But that evening, everything worked out just right. We took off and came back to the field for an NDB approach. At minimums the field was not in sight, so we did a missed approach and entered a holding pattern. We dealt with the loss of a generator and started up the APU. The APU fire alarm sounded. Put out the fire and declare an emergency. Landed using the ILS. Next takeoff. Engine failure below V1. Aborted takeoff. Next takeoff, engine fire just prior to liftoff. Handle the fire. Declare an emergency and back to the airport for a single-engine ILS. Landed. Now some air work. Stalls, unusual attitudes. Visual approach with windshear recovery and go-around. Return to the field. Flap extension problem on final. High speed landing. Left main gear collapses. Emergency evacuation. Now I knew why the other captain had left the sim feeling tired. Somewhere, I don't remember when, among all the other malfunctions, we had also handled a wheel well fire. The FAA check airman was satisfied and signed me off for the next step.

To complete the type rating required a short check a few days later in the aircraft. The FAA inspector watched us each, in turn, perform the takeoffs and landings required by the syllabus and then wrote out our type rating certificates. The only trouble I had with flying this new airplane was that I found the brakes much more sensitive than those on the B727. It took a couple of too-quick stops to find the right amount of toe pressure to apply to the top of the rudder pedals.

With the type rating out of the way it was time to do Initial Operating Experience. This was the familiar route to being checked out in any aircraft. Ground school, simulator training, simulator check, type rating check, and then IOE. For the first flight, we flew from Chicago to Orlando and back using all the electronic navigation equipment. On the following flight, the instructor/check captain completely surprised me. He said, "We're going to forget about all the magic stuff on this leg. I want you to fly the airplane just like you would a B727 and use only raw data from the radio aids to get us from Chicago to Las Vegas."

Captain Charlie Steele had given me a good portion of my simulator training. Now he wanted to make a point. He wanted to show me that, in spite of all the electronic navigation equipment on board and the wonderful capabilities of the autopilot, we were still flying an airplane. This was one of the best things he could have done for me during IOE because it allowed me to connect my previous flight experience with flying this new aircraft. The B757 was just another airplane in spite of all its automation. After being on this airliner more than 10 years I have observed many new copilots get so involved with programming the FMC that they forget the basic fact that they are still just flying an airplane. Unfortunately, this tendency during training to create an overdependence on automation has helped set the scenario for some accidents which I will tell you about later, Preston.

My debut as a B757 captain turned out to be a mini-nightmare. Scheduling called me while I was on reserve waiting for my first trip.

"We have an aircraft broken in Detroit. We need you to take a B757 from Chicago to Detroit, pick up the passengers, and fly them to Atlantic City."

This wasn't a good start for any trip. By the time I would get the airplane to Detroit, the passengers, who were all eager to get to the gambling tables in Atlantic City, would already be delayed five hours. In these kinds of circumstances, the passengers don't usually look at the backup crew as heroes who have saved their vacation. Instead, they want to know why it took you so long to come rescue them. I knew I was going to have a group of disgruntled customers before we even started.

It was bad enough that I would be picking up delayed passengers, but the aircraft I was going to fly had the auxiliary power unit deferred. Without the APU, I would need a ground power cart to provide electrical power on the ground once the engines were stopped, and I would need an air-start unit to be able to start an engine. Normally the APU on the aircraft provides electrical and air. There was another complication. There was no tow bar at Atlantic City. The fact there was no tow bar in Atlantic City would make it necessary to load the tow bar we would use in Detroit into the forward cargo compartment after pushing back from the gate. What made this more difficult is that the B757 is designed so that APU electrical power or external power must be used to electrically open the cargo doors. Power from an engine-driven generator cannot be used to electrically operate a cargo door.

None of these procedures is extremely difficult, but, for a captain on his first time out with the aircraft, just getting both engines started required a little more work than is usually expected. Leaving Detroit, the sequence went like this:

Load the passengers. Use air from the ground air cart to turn the left engine starter and start the engine. (The cargo doors are located on the right side of the aircraft.) Disconnect external power and external air. Obtain pushback clearance over the radio from ramp control. Have the tug driver push the aircraft back from the gate onto the taxiway. Set the brakes at the end of the pushback. Disconnect the tow bar from the aircraft and tug. Pull the electrical cart up to the aircraft and reconnect it. Open the forward cargo door and strap down the tow bar inside. Close the cargo door. Disconnect the external power. Remove all equipment away from the aircraft. Obtain permission for a crossbleed start. Increase the power on the engine that is already running and use bleed air from that engine to turn the starter on the right engine. With both engines now running proceed with the normal Before Taxi checklist. By the time we were ready to taxi we had spent almost 20 minutes from the time we had closed the doors for pushback. The passengers, of course, were not delighted, and, in spite of the fact that I had explained our problem with the APU before pushback, they thought the crew was quite inept to take almost 20 minutes just to get the engines started. All they could see was the time they would be able to spend at the tables becoming shorter and shorter.

We had a good flight to Atlantic City, but we found out on arrival that there would be no electrical power or air-start cart available. An electrical power cart was being brought from Kennedy Airport in New York, but it would not arrive for hours. At least when the electrical cart arrived, we would be able to electrically operate the cargo doors. We still had no air cart for engine start, however, so we would be able to shut down only one engine.

After setting the brakes at the gate in Atlantic City, we shut down the right engine and deplaned passengers from the right side of the airplane. The left engine was kept running. It would be monitored all night by IAT mechanics while the crew went to the hotel. The next morning we loaded the passengers into the aircraft and repeated most of the procedure we had used in Detroit in order to have both engines running and the aircraft prepared for taxi.

After takeoff, the controllers immediately cleared us to a number of navigation aids not on our route. There was no time to reprogram the FMC, so we reverted to flying the airplane VOR to VOR, just like with a B727.

This was my introduction to flying the modern airplane that was supposed to be so enjoyable for pilots to fly. At this point I was wondering what I had gotten myself into. It did turn out that I was just unlucky that first trip. Flights after that went much smoother, and I gradually started to gain a great deal of respect and attachment to the B757. It really turned out to be a great airplane to fly.

X

Atlantic

North Atlantic
by Jeppesen Sanderson

The initial trips I did in the B757 were to familiar places. Basically, the same trips I had been doing in the B727 were being assigned to me in the B757. Las Vegas, Cancun, Montego Bay, Orlando, Aruba, and Zihuatanejo were common destinations. But the B757 had a far greater range than the B727. IAT had plans all along to use the airplane to fly over large expanses of water. A change had occurred recently in the regulations.

In the past, two-engine airplanes were not allowed to carry passengers over water further than one hour of flying time from a suitable emergency airfield. These rules were made at a time when piston engines powered airliners. The dominance of the jet engine in the modern world created a whole new standard of reliability. Jet engines have fewer moving parts than piston engines. Instead of depending on the wildly complex interaction of a crankshaft turning, pistons rapidly going up and down, intake and exhaust valves opening and closing in precise sequence, superchargers ramming air through the carburetors, and spark plugs firing to ignite fuel at just the right moment, the jet engine, in contrast, has two or three turbines that smoothly rotate at high speed while performing the basic functions required of any fuel-burning engine. First, air must be drawn into the engine and tightly compressed. The highly compressed air flows into combustion chambers where fuel is added and the mixture of air and fuel is ignited. The rapidly expanding gases produced by the burning of the fuel rush out the back of the jet engine at very high velocity. Much of this energy is used to drive turbines, which in turn drive the compressors and fan blades. Since a jet engine is less complex than a piston engine, it weighs much less in proportion to the power it can produce. Also, because of the simplicity of its design, it has fewer components that might fail. Jet engines do malfunction from time to time for a variety of reasons, but their reliability is generally much superior to that of complex piston engines.

Because of the general dependability of jet engines, aviation regulatory bodies decided it would be permissible, with certain special limitations, to operate fuel-saving, twin-engined jet aircraft over routes where in the past a minimum of three engines on the aircraft were required. This change of regulations was called ETOPS (Extended range Twin-engine OPerationS). Under these rules, a two-engined aircraft could now be allowed to carry passengers across the Atlantic Ocean if the flight were planned to have available, at any point along its route, a suitable alternate airport to which the aircraft could divert in the event of an engine failure. This alternate airport originally had to be within two hours of flying time, assuming the aircraft is operating on only one engine. Later, the rules allowed the alternate to be within three hours flying time on one engine.

This change in rules would definitely have an impact on my life. Before the B757s were even purchased, IAT had planned to take advantage of the long-range capabilities of the B757 to fly trans-Atlantic flights to Europe and beyond. B757 trips now were being scheduled regularly for trips to Europe that would require Atlantic oceanic crossings under the ETOPS rules.

Oceanic crossings represent additional flying challenges to those encountered while flying in close proximity to land. On an oceanic trip, the aircraft is hundreds of miles away from the nearest landfall. There are no radio navigation aids such as VORs in the middle of the ocean, and the aircraft is for an extended period outside of the range of the VHF (Very High Frequency) communications facilities that are normally used to communicate with the air traffic controllers. Because of these factors, a different set of navigation and communication procedures are used for the oceanic portion of international trips. In the past, long range navigation systems such as the outdated LORAN and Omega systems were used to provide course guidance over large expanses of water. Before that, pilots used celestial navigation and actually fixed their position by star sightings. Today's operations in crowded oceanic airspace require much more accurate navigation capabilities. Aircraft today use very sophisticated INS (Inertial Navigation Systems) in conjunction with GPS (Global Positioning System) signals from satellites to provide accurate determination of position while out of range of conventional navigation aids. It is almost certain that within not too many years, all aircraft will use this type of navigation over land too, and the extensive worldwide system of VORs will be gradually phased out.

The problem of communications over the ocean has long been handled by use of high frequency (HF) radios. HF signals have a long propagation ability because the radio signals can be bounced between the earth and the ionosphere. Very high frequency (VHF) communications require line of sight paths for signals to be received. HF has been around for a long time. It provides communications capabilities over long distances, but it is subject to background noise and variations in signal strength. At times it is very difficult to interpret voice transmissions received from ground stations. When there are many users trying to use the same frequency at the same time, communications with ground stations can become extremely difficult. HF use will no doubt also be phased out completely in the not too distant future, and it will be replaced by satellite communication.

The B757s we fly are equipped with three IRUs (Inertial Reference Units) that can give accurate position information for up to eight hours without position updating from outside navigation signals. Couple that capability with satellite information updating, and you have a very accurate tool for long-range navigation. Like any tool, however, it must be used correctly or catastrophe can result. Errors in navigation over the Atlantic are rarely attributed to navigation equipment errors but are much more likely the result of entering incorrect information when programming the route to be flown into the flight management computer. An error of just one number can easily place an aircraft 60 miles off course. For this reason it is very important that both crewmembers verify the accuracy of inputted data to the computer. Just like any other computer, the FMC will only do as it is told. If it is told to do the wrong thing, it will do the wrong thing. Airlines establish extensive crosscheck procedures to ensure the accuracy of navigation information that is loaded into the computer. During the flight, that information is checked and rechecked many times.

Although the procedural details may change periodically, a typical flight segment along the North Atlantic Track (NAT) system goes something like this: (Let's assume a flight has departed New York for Shannon, Ireland. Its route will take it to the eastern edge of U.S. airspace, across Canadian airspace, and then over the Atlantic.)

As the aircraft nears the eastern coast of Canada the crew will obtain its oceanic clearance on a frequency reserved for that purpose. The oceanic clearance will be composed of a named entry fix, a named exit fix, and a series of latitude/longitude fixes that define one of the routes of the North Atlantic Track system. The North Atlantic Track system is a group of generally parallel routings across the Atlantic separated laterally 60 miles from each other. Each routing can have several different flight levels associated with it. The actual north or south position of the tracks will change regularly to accommodate changes in weather patterns across the Atlantic. Just because an aircraft flies a particular series of coordinates along a designated track on one day does not mean that the same track will be defined by the exact same set of coordinates a few days later. To ensure that pilots will have the correct information about the actual coordinates of a track, a track message describing the coordinates that define each track is compiled periodically and provided to the crew as part of the flight briefing package. If assigned track Yankee, for example, the crew

126

will confirm to the controller that they have the latest track message and, if they haven't already done so, they will program into the FMC the coordinates for the route that will take them across the Atlantic along track Yankee.

After programming the FMC, the route is plotted on a plotting chart. At each reporting point, coordinates and course are checked for accuracy, and the HF radio is used to send a position report to Gander Radio if the aircraft is closer to Canada or to Shanwick Radio if the aircraft is closer to Europe. These radio stations pass on the information to the appropriate air traffic control agency. A typical position report follows the standard format of position, time over reporting point, altitude, estimated time of arrival at next reporting point, and identification of the following fix on the route:

"Gander Radio, IAT123, four five north four zero west at zero six zero five. Flight Level three three zero. Estimate four six north three zero west at zero six five five. Four six north two zero west next."

Ten minutes after giving the position report, the INS position of the aircraft is compared to the plotted course for any discrepancies.

This procedure is continued as the aircraft travels point to point across the Atlantic. Once it nears the coastline of Ireland and is within range of VHF facilities, the flight will revert to use of normal radio navigation aids (VORs) and VHF communication radios. The oceanic crossing part of the trip is over. The flight follows an airway the rest of the way to Shannon.

Shortly after qualifying in the B757, I began flying quite a few Atlantic crossings. My trips regularly took me to Belfast, London, Paris, Shannon, Madrid, Frankfurt, and Dusseldorf. I never really learned to enjoy the eastbound flights. Normally you depart in the early evening and fly until the sun comes up. You finish your trip in full daylight. Since the time at the destination is generally about five or six hours ahead of the time where you took off, you actually lose a night of sleep and need to make it up during the day when you get to your destination. If you have trouble sleeping during the day, that only makes it more difficult to get proper rest before you must fly the return leg. Westbound trips are somewhat easier. Most of the time you leave in daylight and continue with daylight until the destination. Jet lag is a little easier to cope with westbound.

The one dislike that I have never gotten over with oceanic flying is that there are so few places to go in case of an emergency and they are all far away for a good portion of the flight. Once over the Atlantic, a flight experiencing an emergency has only a few options. The flight can divert to Gander or St. John's in Newfoundland. It can divert to Keflavik, Iceland. It can divert to the Azores. It can divert to Shannon. Those are the main choices. There isn't much else. Last option of course is a water ditching. Ditching an airplane in the Atlantic is obviously a very undesirable solution to an emergency. However, with an uncontrollable fire on the aircraft this could be the only solution.

I remember a DC9 that had to make an emergency landing in Cincinnati because someone couldn't wait to have a cigarette until the aircraft landed. The person went to the lavatory to secretly smoke a cigarette. When he finished it, he discarded it into the lavatory waste bin. The cigarette was not completely out. By the time the flight attendants discovered the fire, it was out of control. The whole cabin filled with smoke. Even though the pilots made an expeditious landing, many passengers died. This same scenario over the Atlantic could easily result in the deaths of all on board. There are no emergency landing fields in the middle of the ocean.

With twin-engine airplanes, an engine failure out over the water represents a serious situation. The obvious reason is that you are down to your last engine. In the event of an engine failure it is also unlikely that the aircraft will be able to maintain its assigned altitude. If an engine should fail, the pilots will quickly adjust the other engine to maximum continuous power and then turn the aircraft 90 degrees left or right of the assigned track. Depending on which is closest in point of time, the pilots will eventually divert to one of the mentioned alternate airfields. It is important that the pilots take the aircraft off its assigned track if the aircraft cannot maintain assigned altitude, because there may be other aircraft flying along the same track but assigned to an altitude below them. A radio call will be made on the emergency frequency 121.5 to advise other aircraft of the intentions of the aircraft making the diversion. They will also turn on all their lights in order to be seen better by other aircraft.

After the pilots turn the aircraft off the track, they will take up a course parallel to and 30 miles from each track (tracks are separated by 60 miles). While between the tracks the pilots will descend the aircraft to an altitude that is below the organized track system (below Flight Level 270). At the typical weights a B757-200 flies when crossing the Atlantic, it will be able to maintain an altitude of 18,000 to 21,000 feet while at the same time maintaining a speed of 310 knots. Once the aircraft is below the track structure, the pilots will once again turn toward the alternate airport. Now begins the long wait of up to two hours while the aircraft makes its way towards the alternate on one engine. There is no doubt that in this situation the pilots will be paying a lot of attention to that final remaining engine. They will watch the oil temperature, oil pressure, exhaust gas temperature (EGT), and vibration levels probably as they have never watched an engine in their lives. While all this is going on in the cockpit, the flight attendants will be preparing the cabin for a possible water ditching.

What would go through a captain's mind during this situation?

He will try to analyze the cause of the engine failure. He may have even already attempted to restart the engine during the initial turn away from the track. He will quickly evaluate the status of the whole airplane. As part of the engine shutdown checklist, the APU is started to restore two-generator operation and to provide a backup generator in case the generator on the operating engine fails. If he has no APU, he knows that if his only remaining engine-driven generator fails, he will be dependent on the hydraulic motor generator to provide electrical power. He also knows that if he has to depend on the HMG for electrical power, the capabilities of the aircraft will be reduced. His autopilot will not function, and the aircraft will have to be hand flown by himself without the aid of flight director indications. The copilot's instruments will be inoperative. He knows also that on HMG power one of his three inertial reference units (IRUs) will be inoperative, and he will have only one flight management computer. Normally he will have a functioning APU, so it will be unlikely that he will have to rely on the HMG. Nevertheless he will mentally prepare himself for the possibility of further malfunctions. Is the pressurization functioning correctly? Are the fuel pumps working? Is the crossfeed valve open so that the remaining engine will draw fuel from all fuel tanks? How will the engine failure affect the hydraulic system? Are the electrical hydraulic pumps all working? If it is the left engine that has failed, certain components that are on the left hydraulic system will receive backup pressure from the power transfer unit, which is driven by right hydraulic system pressure. Critical items such as landing gear, flaps, leading edge slats, and nose wheel steering will still operate normally. He may quickly mentally review the alternate procedures for gear and flap extension in case left hydraulic fluid should be completely lost.

After quickly assessing the status of the airplane, the captain will assess his flight conditions. What are the winds? Are there thunderstorms ahead? Is there turbulence at the lower altitude? Will engine or wing anti-ice be required? Use of engine and wing anti-ice will further lower his altitude capability (about 1,000 feet for engine anti-ice and about 3,600 feet for engine and wing anti-ice). He will also burn more fuel.

Satisfied that the aircraft is flying safely toward the alternate, the captain will now want to ensure that ground facilities are aware of the flight's position and course to the alternate. It is important that emergency rescue units have this information in the unlikely event the aircraft should have to ditch. He may even be able to receive information on the position of ships in the area along his route to the alternate. Those positions can be programmed into the FMC as auxiliary waypoints and displayed on the HSI. At some point he will have spoken with the senior flight attendant to explain the problem they are facing and the plan of action. He will make an announcement to the passengers, and he will try to allay their fears without detracting from an awareness of the seriousness of the situation. He will attempt to get new weather information for the alternate airport and will use that information to plan his approach and landing. A single-engine landing will require a Flaps 20 setting instead of a Flaps 30 setting. The approach speed of the aircraft will be about 15 knots higher than normal. Landing distance will be longer. Is the runway now wet, or is it unexpectedly snowing in Keflavik? Will there be strong winds or a crosswind? And finally, even though the aircraft is proceeding nicely towards the alternate, just in case, what are the ditching procedures? For that, there are checklists to be reviewed.

The captain will consider all of these factors, and he won't do it alone. He will continuously have the copilot work with him to attain the information he needs, and he will discuss with the copilot their options and listen for any additional ideas the copilot may have. The captain knows it will be possible that he has forgotten something or may have assessed something incorrectly. Additional input from the copilot may provide critical information or a better perspective on some aspect of the problem they are dealing with. In the end, the captain will have to make the decisions, but it is important for him to draw on the first officer's experience, insights, and concerns while making those decisions.

No B757 has ever ditched in the Atlantic ocean. Given the great care in design and maintenance of today's jet fleet, it is unlikely that one ever will. Nevertheless, any crew that crosses open water will always keep the possibility in mind. It is probably because the possibility is so unlikely that it takes a certain amount of discipline to review diversion procedures on a regular basis. Pilots who fly oceanic crossings do review these procedures, however, because they are well aware that if that rare situation presents itself, they need to have a preliminary plan in place.

One ditching that I know of always reminds me of the need for planning on over-water flights. This accident involved a B727, not a B757. The reason this accident remains in the back of my mind is because I have flown the same route from Keflavik to Gander in a B727 under very similar circumstances.

The Air Malta contract that I told you about earlier was awarded to a successful bidder each summer. Air Malta regularly needed the use of one extra airplane each summer to cover the extra flying they would have during the busy tourist season. The same year that I went through training on the B757, another crew flying a B727 for a Peruvian company disappeared into the Atlantic Ocean off the coast of Newfoundland near Gander. Only the flight crew was on board, and they were returning to Peru after flying all summer the same routes between Malta and Northern Europe that I had flown only a few summers before. I felt and still feel somewhat of a connection to this crew, although I never knew them personally. We had flown the same type airplane on the same routes for the same company under identical circumstances. We had enjoyed being on the island of Malta all summer, and perhaps we even knew some of the same people. After successfully completing their summer assignment for Air Malta, the Peruvian B727 was making its way home from Europe. The flight from Malta to Keflavik was uneventful, but on the Keflavik-Gander leg, the B727 crew sent out a distress signal. They said they were indicating "low fuel." Had they become lost? Had there been a fuel leak? No one will ever really know for sure. They did not give a position report, and they crashed into the sea at some unknown location. They disappeared without a trace.

XI

Traps

In spite of not enjoying traveling great distances over water on two engines, I started to develop a strong respect for the B757 as I flew it more. I found it to be a very well-designed airplane. Each engine is capable of delivering 40,100 pounds of thrust. Maximum takeoff weight is 255,500 pounds, and with 216 passengers on board the fuel tanks may be loaded to the maximum of 75,000 pounds of fuel. Over the course of a normal flight the airplane averages about 8,000 pounds of fuel burn per hour. This gives the airplane a very good range of more than 4,000 miles with reserves. The plane can land on a dry runway in a very short distance—less than 4,000 feet at maximum landing weight. It even performs fairly well on one engine.

The cockpit is comfortable and designed to have a low noise level. In the air, one almost hears more noise from the cooling air being routed behind the instrument panel than one hears from the engines. The aircraft systems are heavily automated. On the B727, it was necessary to have a flight engineer to monitor the various systems of the aircraft. On the B757, the flight engineer is replaced by computerized warning systems that automatically display, in case of a system malfunction, advisory messages on a cathode-ray screen located on the instrument panel. For most malfunctions there is enough backup built into the airplane so that the loss of a generator, a fuel pump, a hydraulic pump, an air conditioning pack, or a navigation computer does not represent a threat to the safety of the flight. Even an engine failure, although serious, only requires an emergency landing at the nearest suitable airport.

The airplane is perfectly capable under normal circumstances of flying on one engine. If the engine failure occurs on takeoff, the climb out might be sluggish, especially at high takeoff weights or on hot days, but even in these circumstances the B757 will perform better than many other types of aircraft.

The Rolls-Royce engines on the B757 are very reliable. Rarely does an engine fail. A pilot may fly his whole career without ever experiencing an engine failure. Most of the malfunctions that do occur on the aircraft are of a minor nature, and rarely do they require that the aircraft land short of its destination. A jet transport pilot will experience many more serious malfunctions in his yearly simulator sessions than he will ever experience flying the actual airplane.

In spite of the great safety built into the airplane, serious accidents have occurred. It could be said that the accident I am going to tell about partly occurred because everything *does* go so well with the aircraft most of the time. Pilots become used to the automation, and when this does not perform in the expected way, a confusing situation may result. Keep in mind, Preston, that what I am about to tell you could be applied to anything in life. Sometimes an overlooked or unexpected small detail can completely change the outcome of an event and lead one into disaster. It is easy for us humans to fall into the trap of seeing what we expect to see.

The accident I am going to describe to you happened in South America. AA965 was being flown by a very professional and experienced crew. Because it demonstrates so clearly the perils of overdependence on automation, the crash of AA965 is well known among B757 pilots.

Except for having departed slightly behind schedule from Miami, the flight to Cali, Colombia had been normal right up until the time of initial descent. Cali is located at an elevation of 3,162 feet in a valley between two ranges of mountains. Approaching the airport from the north, an aircraft will have terrain to the right as high as 6,300 feet. On the left, the aircraft will have much higher terrain. Within about

15 miles from the final approach course, the terrain rises rapidly up to as high as 12,000 feet. At night, the high terrain is not visible.

When operating in these kinds of conditions it is important to conduct a thorough briefing, which includes discussion about terrain elevations, obstacles, what navigation aids will be used to back up the flight computer, and what altitudes and headings will be flown during the approach. It is essential to adhere to the published procedure. Once the aircraft deviates from the prescribed flight tracks and altitudes described on the approach chart, there is no guarantee of vertical separation from obstacles or terrain. Available VORs and NDBs should be tuned to maintain raw data backup of the computerized navigation system. It is always important that the flight crew know where the aircraft is and where it is going at each point along the approach to the airport. The term for this is "situational awareness."

The crew of AA965 had planned to descend toward the airport from the north and then proceed over the airport, execute a descending procedure turn and land back toward the north. Ironically, the weather was good and the wind was calm at the destination airport. It is easy to let one's guard down in these conditions. A nice easy approach to the runway was expected. If there had been storms nearby or low visibility conditions or high winds, the crew most likely would have had a slightly higher adrenaline flow.

Upon its first contact with Cali approach control, AA965 reported it was descending to FL200 (approximately 20,000 feet) and their DME distance was 63 miles north of the Cali VOR. The Cali VOR is about eight miles south of the airport, so at that point the aircraft was about 55 miles north of the airport. The controller issued the flight a clearance to Cali and a descent clearance to 15,000 feet. Following are some of the more important excerpts from the cockpit voice recordings. This is not a complete transcript:

2134:59 **Cali Approach Control:** Roger, is cleared to Cali VOR, uh, descend and maintain one five thousand feet, altimeter three zero zero two....

The captain sets up the flight computer so that it will steer the aircraft direct to the Cali VOR and advises the first officer. (The controller really meant "Cleared to Cali VOR via Tulua VOR," but he did not make that clear.) When the captain programs the flight computer for Cali, the Tulua VOR is dropped from the HSI display.

2135:28 **Captain:** I put direct Cali for you in there.

2135:29 **First Officer:** OK, thank you.

Now begins the rapid chain of events that lead to the accident. The controller will offer a straight in approach to land to the south. The decision to accept the approach to the south runway would not be dangerous in itself, but the aircraft would have to lose altitude much more quickly since the distance to the field would be less. The crew was trying to save time. A leisurely approach was now going to turn into a "we have to get down quick" approach. Less time would be available to program the flight computer and cross check everything as the crew attempted to rapidly descend the airplane.

2136:31 **Cali Approach Control:** Sir, the wind is calm. Are you able to approach runway one niner?

The captain asks the first officer if he would like to land to the south.

2136:36 **Captain:** Would you like to shoot the one nine straight in?

The first officer replies they can do it if they descend quickly.

2136:38 **First Officer:** Uh yeah, we'll have to scramble to get down. We can do it.

The controller clears the flight to descend on the Rozo One Arrival to the airport and the captain accepts the clearance.

2136:43 **Cali Approach Control:** Roger. American nine six five is cleared the VOR DME approach runway one niner. Rozo number one, arrival. Report Tulua VOR.

2136:52 **Captain:** Cleared the VOR DME to one nine, Rozo One Arrival. Will report the VOR. Thank you, sir.

The captain hurriedly searches for the arrival chart. They are now getting very rushed. The first officer is going to use the speed brakes to descend the aircraft faster.

The captain asks the controller if he may proceed direct to the Rozo NDB. The controller has no way of monitoring the aircraft's position, other than the radio reports he receives from the aircraft as it passes over the fixes depicted on the published procedure. Linguistic differences are a factor now. The captain believes that his request to go direct to the Rozo NDB has been approved, but the controller is still asking the flight to report passing Tulua, indicating that he is clearing the flight to follow the published arrival. Following the published arrival, an aircraft will pass first over the Tulua VOR, proceed along the 202 degree radial from Tulua to the Cali 013 radial 21 DME fix, and THEN to the Rozo NDB.

The captain enters the identifier, R, into the flight computer intending to make the aircraft go direct to the Rozo NDB. Unfortunately, in the computer data base the correct identifier for Rozo is ROZO, not the R depicted as the identifier on the arrival chart. The airplane begins to turn to the left, away from Cali, because the incorrect fix that has been entered into the flight computer is an NDB with the identifier R located far to the east near Bogota.

The aircraft is still rapidly descending, but the aircraft is not on a published portion of the procedure. Instead of flying over a valley, it

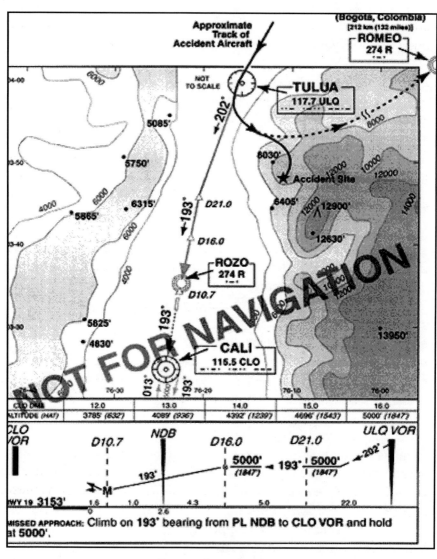

Rozo One Arrival

is over the mountains. At this point they have no protection from obstacles or terrain.

The first officer realizes they are turning away from the airport and comments. The captain diverts his attention from tuning the radios and also sees the aircraft is heading in the wrong direction.

2138:49 **First Officer:** Uh, where are we...

2138:58 **First Officer:** Yeah, where we headed?

Since he doesn't know what the aircraft is trying to do, the first officer says "manual" and disengages the computer from the autopilot. The aircraft rolls from a left turn and a heading of 100 degrees into a right turn as the altitude passes 13,600 feet.

They attempt to correct the course back to the airport. The aircraft is still rapidly descending. Height of terrain below is 8,000 feet.

2139:05 **Captain:** Let's come to the right a little bit.

2139:10 **First Officer:** OK.

2139:10 **Captain:** ...Right now.

2141:15 **Ground Proximity Warning System:** Terrain! Terrain! Whoop! Whoop!...

The crew realized too late that they were rapidly approaching the top of a mountain. Out of the 163 persons on board, only four survived. All crewmembers were killed.

The crew had already planned to do an approach that the captain had done many times before. He had flown into Cali 13 times prior to this trip. Their plan was to cross over the Cali VOR and turn back toward the airport using a procedure turn in order to land to the north. When they accepted a straight-in approach to the south, they put themselves into a situation where they would have to change all their previous plans for the approach. Since they would now fly a much shorter distance to the airport, they would have to hurry the airplane down.

With the aircraft rapidly descending they quickly attempted to look over the new procedure and set up the approach. The wrong fix was entered into the computer and executed apparently without cross checking because the crew was trying to get everything done quickly. By the time the error was discovered, the aircraft had already turned off its course. Instead of arresting the descent of the aircraft while trying to correct the error, the crew concentrated entirely on getting the airplane turned back in the right direction. The whole time they were getting headed back toward the airport, the aircraft was steadily diving toward the top of a mountain. Arresting or perhaps even slowing the descent may have prevented the disaster. Concentrating intently on trying to complete the approach, the captain and the first officer overlooked the possibility of climbing back up to altitude and beginning the whole approach again with more calm and preparation.

We human beings make mistakes. It is important to learn from the experience of others. We must never be arrogant and think, "This could never happen to me." Preston, as you go through life, keep in mind that you are always susceptible to errors no matter how much you know. Keep in mind that gaining experience can increase your confidence and ability, but it can also lead to expectations that everything will work out right just because it did in the past. Remember to keep your options open, and try to not let your thinking get trapped into only one solution to a problem. To any problem of human experience there are usually many answers, not just one.

XII

Walkaround

<Begin at Static Ports

B757 Preflight Inspection
Proceeds in Clockwise Direction

While looking out the window of the terminal, many passengers have observed a flight crewmember making an outside inspection of the aircraft that they are about to board. They see the captain or the first officer walking around the airplane looking at different parts, pausing here and there to take a better look at a particular item. Although it is routine for pilots to inspect their aircraft before a flight, there is a complex and invisible thought process going on in the crewmember. He may do his check quickly, but each item he looks at is important. It would take too long to tell you of every detail, so I'll talk only about the major points. I'd like to describe to you some of the thoughts that go through my mind as I perform the preflight walkaround.

There is usually a recommended procedure for each airplane. Basically the crewmember starts at a given place on the aircraft, walks around it checking each item, and finishes back at the point he started. There are many items to check, and we use the airplane itself as a checklist. Pilots are not expected to perform the same kind of detailed inspections that maintenance personnel make. But by checking the general overall condition of the aircraft on the ground before the flight, a crewmember can do a great deal to avoid problems that could come up in the air.

On the B757, we begin at the left side of the airplane at the static air source ports for the captain and first officer instruments. They must be clean and unobstructed. If they are not, functioning of the airspeed indicators and altimeters could be adversely affected. We move to the nose wheel. What is the condition of the tires? Is there

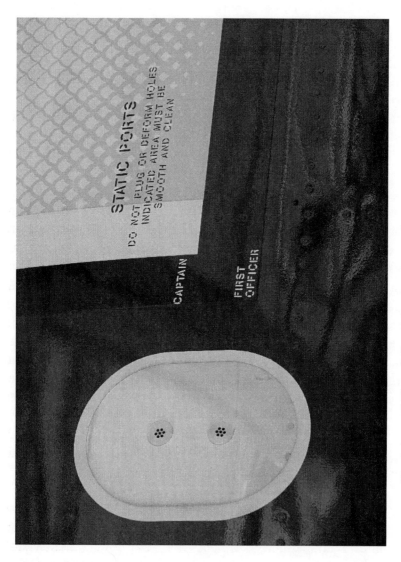

Captain and First Officer Static Ports on Left Side of Fuselage
photo by Rogenio Villarias

146

adequate tread? Are there any apparent defects? Are they inflated properly?

Moving up the nose gear, one looks for any apparent damage or loose nuts or bolts. The nose strut should not be collapsed. There should be some shiny metal visible, indicating that the strut is inflated and will absorb the shocks that will occur during taxi, takeoff, and landing. What is the condition of the hydraulic cylinders and cables that compose the nosewheel steering system? Is there any hydraulic fluid leaking? Complete hydraulic fluid loss from a system can cause all the components on that system to become inoperative.

I once had to deal with loss of a hydraulic system on a flight from Chicago to New York. After takeoff, a hydraulic line on the left system developed a rapid leak. The reason there had been no sign of a leak on the ground was because it was the line for the gear retraction that failed. Once airborne, as we raised the landing gear, all the left hydraulic system fluid spewed overboard through the gear-up line. With no fluid in the left hydraulic system, we had now lost our normal landing gear extension and retraction, normal flap and slat operation, nosewheel steering, left thrust reverser, alternate brakes, some spoilers, part of the inputs to our flight controls, and a few other items. The B757 will fly well with one hydraulic system inoperative because there is adequate system backup from the other two remaining systems. We elected to go on to New York. There would be plenty of airfields with good weather conditions along the way if we were to decide to make a landing before reaching the destination.

Of course, we knew when we arrived at Kennedy we would have to use the alternate flap extension procedure, the alternate gear extension procedure, and that there would be no nosewheel steering. Enroute, there would be adequate time to review all the appropriate procedures. By the time we arrived at Kennedy, airport

147

Pitot Tubes and Stall Warning Vane on Left Side of Fuselage
photo by Rogenio Villarias

personnel were ready for us. The controllers assigned us a separate runway from the other traffic. We requested fire and rescue vehicles to be standing by in the event that an emergency evacuation might be necessary after landing (for example, if a landing gear were to collapse at touchdown). A tow vehicle was waiting to take us off the runway since we would have no steering. With no nosewheel steering, differential braking would have to be used to maintain directional control once the rudder became ineffective during the last part of the landing roll. We landed, the mechanics installed gear pins, and we were towed to the gate without incident.

Back to the preflight walkaround inspection.

While checking the condition of the nose gear, the pilot will look up into the nose wheel well for signs of damage. He checks carefully to make sure the gear pin is removed. Aircraft have points on each landing gear where a pin can be inserted to lock the landing gear in the down position. Maintenance personnel will often install gear pins when they are towing an aircraft that has the hydraulics depressurized. This ensures a gear will not collapse while the aircraft is being moved. It is very important to remove these pins before flight. The pilots cannot retract any landing gear that has a pin in place. Why is this so critical? Because if an engine were to fail on takeoff, the airplane may not be able to clear obstacles in the takeoff path with the gear stuck down and only one engine providing thrust.

The pilot now moves around the front of the airplane. He checks the nose of the aircraft for damage. He looks at the condition of the stall warning vanes and tries to see if the pitot tubes are unobstructed and undamaged. The pitot tubes stick out near the nose of the airplane, forward of and slightly below the captain's and first officer's windows. During takeoff and in flight, ram air effect causes the pressure of the air in these tubes to increase. Comparing this ram air pressure to a static air pressure source makes it possible to determine airspeed. Block the pitot tubes and the pilots will have no accurate airspeed information.

In February 1996, a B757 took off at night from Puerto Plata in the Dominican Republic. Just minutes later, all 189 persons on board were dead.

It is believed the aircraft had sat on the ramp long enough for an insect to try to build a home in the left pitot tube. During the takeoff the pilots observed there was a problem with the captain's airspeed indication. The first officer's airspeed indications apparently were normal. As the aircraft climbed, the obstructed pitot tube caused the captain's air data computer to sense a speed much higher than the actual speed of the aircraft. The autopilot responded by raising the nose of the aircraft and reducing power in an attempt to not overspeed the airplane.

The crew now received conflicting information from the aircraft warning systems:

1) Because excessive speed was being sensed from the captain's airspeed, the loud overspeed warning sounded.

2) Because the actual speed of the aircraft was nearing the stall speed, the stall warning was activated.

The crew disconnected the autopilot and applied thrust to avoid a stall, but their action came too late; the airspeed decreased to stall speed. The wings now were not producing enough lift to sustain flight, and the aircraft crashed into the ocean about five miles off the coast.

As a B757 pilot, I know that it would have been almost impossible to detect, during the walkaround, the presence of a small amount of mud packed into a pitot tube by an insect. But the accident does illustrate the importance of having in the back of one's mind a quick reference between speed and power. If a B757-200, for example, is in level flight with the flaps up and a power setting of about 60 percent of maximum N1 turbine speed on each engine, the airplane will fly at approximately 230 knots, depending on its weight.

With this knowledge the pilots will be able to maintain control of the aircraft and prevent it from stalling, even without a functioning airspeed indicator. They will also be able to configure for an approach and fly an ILS all at about the same power setting with just a few minor adjustments. B757 cockpits now usually have a performance table on a laminated card readily available to the pilots that contains different combinations of pitch and power to be used in the event of inaccurate airspeed indications.

After looking at the pitot tubes, the pilot continues around the right side of the nose gear and inspects it from that side, as he did the left. He looks to see that the total air temperature (TAT) probe is in good condition, and he checks the right static air ports. The static air ports provide an air pressure reference that is not subjected to the effects of ram air, as is the pressure in the pitot tubes. Since air pressure decreases the higher one goes, the static port air pressure can be used to determine the height, or altitude, of the aircraft. As mentioned before, the airspeed indicators require both a dynamic and static pressure source to function. If the static ports become blocked, neither the height nor the speed of the aircraft can be accurately determined by normal means.

Just eight months after the Puerto Plata accident, an Aero Peru flight taking off from Lima also met with tragedy because of erroneous instrument indications. This time it was the static ports that were blocked instead of a pitot tube. Prior to the flight, aircraft mechanics had washed and polished the aircraft. According to proper procedure, they had taped over the static ports to prevent entry of water into the system. They forgot to remove the tape. During the preflight walkaround, the tape over the ports was not discovered. Soon after takeoff, the pilots noted that their altimeters were not

151

showing a climb. Shortly after that, they realized that their airspeed indicators were not functioning properly. Now they found themselves in a very abnormal situation. They knew neither how high they were nor how fast they were going. To make matters even more confusing, a series of alerts went off in the cockpit. At various times during the flight the crew was confronted with system malfunction alerts on the EICAS screen in front of them, the stick shaking of stall alerts, and the loud siren warning them of an overspeed. Attempting to determine the cause of these different alerts distracted them from their primary task, which was to get control of the aircraft. Once again, by setting power and pitch the crew could have established a stable climb and possibly flown to an area where they might have encountered visual meteorological conditions. They also could have made use of their radio altimeter to tell when they were close to the ground to avoid flying into the water.

Instead of concentrating first on stabilizing the flight path, the crew spent time looking for and reading abnormal checklists that would not help their situation. When, for example, the Rudder Ratio message appeared on the EICAS, the crew searched the Quick Reference Handbook (QRH) to find the Rudder Ratio checklist only to read that they must "avoid abrupt inputs" to the rudder. For the problem they were dealing with, this was useless information. After a series of climbs and descents, and alternate airspeed accelerations and decelerations, the aircraft finally flew into the water, killing everyone on board.

Hindsight is always 20/20 as they say, but to try to find a better way to deal with a situation should always be the goal when reading about a crash. Only by doing so can a pilot prepare himself for the day when he might encounter a similar situation.

I don't know if you will ever decide to become a pilot, Preston, but there are a number of lessons to be learned here, and they probably don't apply just to aviation:

1) Identify and concentrate on solving the primary problem. In this case it was to gain positive control of the aircraft. By referring to a chart, the crew could have set climb power and initially about 10 degrees of pitch and the airplane would have been in a safe, stable climb.

2) Try not to get distracted by irrelevant information. In this case, the crew was constantly diverted from their primary task by a number of warnings. As they attempted to sort out and deal with all these conflicting warnings, they were less able to pay attention to the flying of the airplane.

3) Have a good familiarity with all the abnormal checklists. Knowing ahead of time that reading the checklists for all the erroneous alerts they were receiving was not going to help their situation would have allowed them to concentrate on the primary problem of aircraft control. I believe it is very important for pilots to make a periodic review of all their abnormal checklists so that they know what the checklist is going to tell them almost before they even look it up. In this manner, they won't spend time during a critical situation looking up useless information.

4) Don't be in too much of a hurry to land. Most of the time it is best to land as soon as practicable when there is a serious problem. Fire on the aircraft is probably the best example. But in this situation, the airplane had no ongoing hazard that would have required an immediate landing. Fuel was not a problem for the moment, and it was likely the aircraft could have been flown quite safely to a destination where there was good weather.

5) A few times during the emergency, the first officer initiated radio calls, ATC requests, and reading of checklists without conferring with the captain. This seems to only have added to the confusion in the cockpit.

Continuing alongside the fuselage, the pilot will continue checking general condition. Is there any evidence that anything has hit the airplane? Occasionally a de-icing truck, catering truck, or lavatory truck will run into an airplane and do damage. There are several antennas on the bottom of the fuselage. Are any broken? Near the forward cargo door there is a little green plug on the side of the fuselage. If that is missing, it means that the oxygen bottle for the crew thermally discharged because too much pressure had built up in it. Having oxygen in the bottle is extremely important. If the aircraft were to suddenly depressurize at high altitude, the pilots would have only about 30 seconds of useful consciousness before the effects of hypoxia would take over. Pilots are taught to immediately don their oxygen masks if any kind of a pressurization problem occurs above an altitude of 10,000 feet. If, when they don their masks, there is no oxygen supply, they will eventually become incapacitated. Now they will be unable to descend the aircraft to a lower altitude where air is more plentiful.

We are at the right wing. Is the leading edge in good condition? Is there any sign of a fuel leak? Is the engine cowl covering the engine secure and undamaged? Is there oil leaking under the engine? How do the fan blades and turbine blades look on the engine? Are there any nicks on any blades? If a fan blade breaks in flight, it can cause severe engine vibration and damage. The engine will have to be shut down, and an emergency landing will be necessary. Once on a preflight I found that several support struts for the cowl on one engine had broken loose. This grounded the airplane until a repair could be made. We follow the wing around to the tip and see the position lights are working. (Red light on the left wing. Green light on the right wing. White on the trailing wingtip on both wings.) We are working our way along the back of the wing, checking for condition and position of flaps and spoilers.

Now we are at the landing gear. Once again we are checking wheels and tires. We are also checking brake wear indicators to make sure the brakes are not worn down. We need those brakes to stop. But don't touch them. If the airplane has just landed, they are going to be hot. This airplane weighs 198,000 pounds at maximum landing weight. The friction created by the brakes to stop it generates a great deal of heat. We look up into the wheel well. Once again we are looking for general condition and any signs of leaks or something loose. We look to see that here the gear pin is removed, too. A quick check of the strut tells us that it is not collapsed. Just like the nose gear, the main struts have cylinders that are charged with nitrogen. Nitrogen is also used to inflate the tires. Why nitrogen? Because nitrogen will not sustain combustion. On March 31, 1986, a Mexicana B727 took off from Mexico City enroute to Puerto Vallarta. A tire believed to have been serviced with air instead of nitrogen exploded in the wheel well. Hydraulic lines and fuel lines near the tire were ruptured by the explosion. An on-board fire ensued. The airplane crashed in the Sierra Madre of western Mexico.

We continue moving along the right side of the fuselage, past the cargo door, and on to the tail section. Once again, general condition is checked. The horizontal stabilizer, vertical stabilizer, elevators, and rudders must all be free of damage and hydraulic leaks. After checking the tail section the pilot moves around the left side of the airplane. There are a few components on the left side of the aircraft that are different from the right, such as the pressurization outflow valve, but, in general, the pilot checks the same items on the right side of the plane that he did on the left. After checking everything, he is now back at the point where he started his preflight walkaround. Although many thoughts go through his mind while this check is made, the whole process takes only 10 to 15 minutes. These 10 to 15 minutes are some of the most important of the entire flight.

XIII

Takeoffs

"IAT 123, you are cleared onto Runway 4 Right. Position and hold."

We check for traffic, turn on the landing lights so that we can be seen easily, and taxi the 757 into position on the runway. Takeoff clearance will come at any moment. The before takeoff checklist is complete, and I make my own quick final check: engine parameters normal, elevator trim set, speedbrake lever full forward, flaps in the correct position, rudder trim set, radio on correct frequency to receive and transmit, side window closed and secure, a quick scan across the panel to try and find anything that might have been missed. Everything looks good. We'll be ready when the takeoff clearance comes. Directly ahead at about eight miles is the skyline of Chicago. On a clear day the buildings would be easy to see, but today the visibility is only one-half of a mile. We can't even see clearly to the end of the runway. I have my hand on the throttles, ready to advance them to takeoff power.

The tower calls, "IAT 123, cleared for takeoff. Turn right to heading one one zero."

I move the throttles forward to a vertical position and wait for the engines to stabilize.

The first officer calls out, "Engines stable."

"Set max EPR."

The first officer responds by engaging the autothrottles in EPR mode. As the autothrottle control moves the throttles forward, I follow their movement with my hand to make sure that takeoff power is being set, and I look at the engine gauges to see that the engines are responding properly. As each engine spools up to develop more than 40,000 pounds of thrust, the power of the engines can be felt rumbling through the entire airplane, and I can hear their reassuring roar behind me.

I take my feet off the brakes. The airplane begins its takeoff run. We feel the acceleration as we are pushed back slightly in our seats. The airspeed indicators come alive and show the speed is picking up.

"80 knots."

In response to the first officer's call I make a quick check of my airspeed. It also shows 80 knots. Our instruments agree. I call out confirmation.

Now that the aircraft has accelerated beyond 80 knots, there are only a few things that would cause us to reject the takeoff and bring the airplane to a stop on the runway. In the back of my mind I am thinking, "Bells and swerves." Bells meaning fire warnings. Swerves meaning engine failure. Almost anything else is not worth risking the danger of an emergency stop. Once an airplane is moving at high speed down a runway it will take a great deal of braking energy to keep it from running off the end. A predetermined speed, V1, is the highest possible speed at which a rejected takeoff will be possible if the aircraft is taking off at its maximum allowable weight for that runway. For today's weight that speed is 135 knots.

The airplane is still accelerating. As required, five knots below V1 the first officer calls it out. I remove my hand from the throttles. We are now committed to the takeoff. Whatever happens now we keep going. There is not enough runway left to stop without running through the airport fence.

The first officer continues his callouts.

"Rotate." I raise the nose of the aircraft by easing the control yoke toward me.

"V2." We are at flying speed now. The aircraft leaves the ground and begins its climb.

"Positive rate," the first officer calls out, indicating the altimeters are showing that the airplane is climbing.

"Gear up."

The first officer raises the landing gear.

We have barely climbed 400 feet. Then it happens.

There is a loud noise from the left side of the airplane, and the nose of the aircraft suddenly jerks to the left. I push down hard on the right rudder pedal to keep the airplane straight. The first officer yells out that there is an engine failure. The fire bell begins to ring, and the fire warning lights illuminate on the left engine. Obviously the engine has suffered severe damage and is possibly burning.

"Silence the bell." The first officer quickly responds by reaching up to the Master Warning/Caution switch in front of him and pushes on it. The bell stops, but the fire warning lights remain illuminated.

The airplane is climbing, but with power coming from only one engine, it is climbing slowly. We begin the turn to the right in order to not continue toward the buildings in the downtown area of Chicago. We bank the airplane the minimum amount necessary to complete the turn, because the airplane will climb even more slowly when the wings are not level. We want every foot of altitude we can get. There are other tall obstructions in the area.

"Declare the emergency."

"Midway Tower, IAT 123 has an engine failure. Declaring emergency." The first officer also requests to remain on the easterly heading. He advises we will be calling back shortly for vectors to O'Hare airport, where the runways are longer. He asks for fire and rescue equipment to be standing by.

The aircraft has now climbed to 700 feet above the field elevation.

I lower the nose to maintain a 200-foot-per-minute climb. We need to get the flaps up so that the airplane will have less drag and be able to climb better. As the aircraft accelerates, I call for the different flap settings.

"Flaps 5." The first officer moves the flap handle.

"Flaps 1."

"Flaps up."

"Set maximum continuous power. Flight level change. Bug the speed." The first officer accomplishes the requested items. The airplane is now well under control and climbing to 3,000 feet. It is time to take control of the possible fire.

"Engine Fire/Severe Damage memory items."

The first officer turns off the autothrottle switch. He moves his hand down to the throttle of the failed engine. I guard the throttle of the good engine, and we verify he is pulling back the correct throttle. After closing the throttle of the damaged engine, he moves his hand down to close the left fuel control switch. Once again we verify, and I guard the fuel control switch of the good engine with my right hand. We follow the same procedure as he pulls the illuminated left fire switch to the up position. The switch remains illuminated. The fire is still burning. He discharges the fire-fighting chemicals from the first engine fire bottle into the engine. He waits 30 seconds. The switch is still illuminated. He discharges the remaining bottle. He waits. We both wait. The light goes out. The fire is under control. It's time to run the checklists and get vectors for the approach.

"Let's stop there and go on to the next maneuver." It is the simulator instructor speaking.

We have been practicing an engine fire as part of our yearly simulator check. Except for me letting the heading vary a little after liftoff, we were pretty happy with how we had handled the problem. The instructor was satisfied, too.

None of this was a real situation, but it could have been. Every takeoff holds the possibility of an emergency. In spite of that, ever since I made my very first takeoff, there has always been something magical for me about that moment when an airplane racing down a runway to attain flying speed suddenly converts itself from a lumbering ground vehicle into a graceful bird capable of traveling through the sky. What has changed from that first takeoff 30 years ago is that I have a much better understanding of the risks and more respect for the dangers involved. It is my job to keep those risks and dangers to a minimum; and I try to do that every time I fly.

To a passenger sitting in the back of the airplane, the takeoff may be a little frightening. This is especially true for people who don't fly frequently. The engines come up to their takeoff power. They are loud. The airplane trundles down the runway and picks up speed. Suddenly, the nose goes up, and the wheels leave the ground. The passenger hears the thump of the landing gear as it retracts into the

163

wheel wells. Later, after the airplane has gained a little altitude, he hears the whining of the jackscrews as they turn to retract the flaps.

The pilot is aware of all these things, but there are many other things going through his mind. For him the takeoff actually began when the aircraft was sitting back at the gate. There are really two phases to a takeoff. The first is planning. The second is execution.

When a pilot plans a takeoff, he takes into account a number of factors. He knows that this is one of the most critical maneuvers he will perform for each flight, and he has to plan properly so that it will be successful. He has already checked the aircraft logbook and the condition of his airplane. He has decided the airplane is safe for flight. He knows he will have 200 lives in his hands.

Which runway is being used? This is usually determined by the wind. When an airplane takes off into the wind it can get up to flying speed using less runway. Is there a crosswind? When the wind is blowing strongly from the side of the runway, the pilot will have to counteract the effect of the wind in order to keep the airplane straight during the takeoff roll. The airplane will try to turn into the wind when there is a strong crosswind, just like a weathervane. If an engine should fail, he knows it will be even more difficult to control the airplane if the failed engine is on the same side as the wind. He will have to fight both the tendency of the wind to weathervane the aircraft and the tendency of the airplane to turn toward the dead engine.

What is the condition of the runway? Is it raining? Is it slippery? These are factors that will affect controllability and the ability to stop the airplane should something go wrong and the takeoff must be rejected. What is the reported visibility? How far ahead of the airplane will the pilot be able to see as the airplane moves rapidly down the runway to gain flying speed? How quickly will he have to transition to flying solely by instruments after the takeoff? If the visibility is very low, the transition will occur almost immediately after the pilot executes the liftoff. He must be ready for a complete loss of visual contact with the ground to avoid becoming disoriented.

How heavy is the airplane? Because a heavier airplane needs to accelerate to a higher speed before it can fly, it's going to use more runway on the takeoff roll. Appropriate takeoff speeds (V1, Vr, and V2) need to be calculated. Balance is important, too. Passenger and cargo weight must be distributed in the cabin and the cargo holds so that the airplane is neither nose-heavy or tail-heavy. Either situation can cause control problems in the air.

How hot is it outside? Higher temperatures mean the engines develop less power. Less power from the engines will lengthen the takeoff roll, and the aircraft will not climb as well over obstacles as when the air temperature is lower. Longer takeoff rolls also mean the tires will heat up more. Everything is related. Severely overheated tires can be dangerous. They can explode.

By the time the aircraft gets to the end of the runway, the pilot usually has mentally rehearsed the takeoff. He has thought about what he must do to get the aircraft safely into the air, and he tries to anticipate what problems might occur on the takeoff and immediately after the aircraft is airborne. As he rolls the airplane into position, he makes a quick check of the airplane, runway condition, wind, obstacles ahead, and sky condition.

In spite of planning, takeoff accidents do occur. Sometimes they are caused by something being overlooked. At other times there may be mechanical failures. There are other instances when something completely unexpected happens. In the yearly ground schools I have attended over the years, many takeoff accidents have been discussed in order to give the pilots a better awareness of the hazards and pitfalls surrounding this critical maneuver. These are some examples:

A DC9 attempts a takeoff after a lengthy delay during taxi. The crew becomes distracted at the time when they would normally set the flaps to takeoff position. The warning that is designed to sound and alert the crew of an incorrect takeoff flap setting malfunctioned. Shortly after takeoff, the aircraft entered a stall and crashed. Lesson:

Be especially alert when distractions occur and the normal routine and rhythm of events is interrupted. Make a double check of all items. It is a good idea to form the habit of always making a final check (by touching each item) of the elevator trim, speed brake handle position, flap position, rudder trim, and radio setting before taking the runway.

A DC10 has a tire blow out during the takeoff roll. The captain attempts to reject the takeoff. More tires blow, and the airplane is rushing toward the airport fence. The captain swerves the airplane off the runway to try to stop it. A landing gear collapses. Fuel is spilled from the wing and a fire ensues. Lesson: Rejecting a takeoff at very high speed is one of the most dangerous maneuvers a pilot can attempt. Once past about 80 knots, it is best to have a "GO" mentality unless something like engine failure or fire occurs. Now that the industry has had the opportunity to review numerous rejected takeoff accidents, the prevailing wisdom is that, at high speeds, the takeoff should in most cases be continued if the airplane is capable of flight.

A B727 takes off from New Orleans with thundershower activity around the airport. It encounters windshear and a sudden loss of airspeed and altitude. It crashes into a residential area near the airport. Lesson: A phenomenon called microburst can occur unexpectedly when the conditions are right. Severe downdrafts can develop in seconds, and they can easily overpower the ability of the aircraft to climb. We are taught to scan the takeoff path with radar and to visually scan the sky ahead for signs of thunderstorms. Windshear reports from the tower are also taken into account. This captain took additional precautions to combat the possibility of windshear. He planned a higher climb speed to counter any airspeed loss, and, to get a better climb, he planned a higher engine power setting by turning off the air conditioning packs during the takeoff. The weather situation was typical for summer days at the New Orleans airport. The NTSB considered the takeoff decision to have been reasonable for the prevailing conditions at the time of takeoff. The flight was hit by an unexpected microburst directly over the airport while the takeoff was being executed. In a critical situation like this, pilots are taught to trade airspeed for altitude right up to the point of reaching the stickshaker stall warning to try to avoid ground contact. The pilots raised the nose of the airplane, but they could not effectively combat the combined effects of airspeed loss and downdrafts at the very low altitude where the microburst overtook them.

One snowy winter day in 1982, a B737 taking off from Washington National crashed into the Potomac River after stalling out and hitting the 14th Street Bridge. There was snow accumulation on the wings at the time of takeoff, and it was determined that the engines were set at considerably less than full takeoff power. Lesson: A snow contamination check should be made of the wings just prior to takeoff in snowy conditions, and engine anti-ice should be on. The crew had failed to turn on the engine anti-ice. Because the engine anti-ice was off, the probes for the engine pressure ratio (EPR) indications had become obstructed with ice. Since the probes were obstructed, the EPR gauges indicated the engines were developing takeoff power when, in reality, they were not.

Sometimes a crew will find itself facing an emergency that has been thrust on them by others. This was the case with Valuejet 592.

I actually met the captain of Valuejet 592. She was a nice woman who showed up in our 757 cockpit one day to request a jumpseat on a trip I was working from Chicago to Florida. For me, it has always been a pleasure to help a fellow pilot position somewhere by allowing him or her to occupy one of the empty seats in the cockpit. Actually, it is this informal network of pilots helping each other to move about the country that allows them to keep their families in one place and enjoy a relatively stable lifestyle. Pilots often change bases many times during their careers.

I don't really remember what we talked about as we occasionally chatted during the flight. I am sure it was the usual pilot small talk about schedules, bases, airplanes we've flown, and airports we have been into. Jumpseaters, out of courtesy, don't usually get involved in lengthy or deep conversations with the operating crew. When we arrived in Florida, she thanked us for having given her a ride, smiled, shook our hands, and quietly left. At the time, none of us guessed that she would, in the not too distant future, be fighting bravely over the swamps of Florida to save a burning and doomed DC9 from disaster.

Their takeoff from Miami was normal, and the cockpit voice recorder shows the crew completed all their checklists and takeoff procedures in a standard and routine fashion. As the DC9 reached 10,000 feet, signs of trouble began to develop. The following excerpts from the cockpit voice recorder (CVR) show a crew courageously facing death and still doing their best to save the lives of everyone on board:

Sound of chirp heard on cockpit area microphone channel with simultaneous beep on public address/interphone channel.

14:10:07 **Captain:** What was that?

14:10:08 **First Officer:** I don't know.

14:10:12 **Captain:** 'bout to lose a bus?

14:10:15 **Captain:** We got some electrical problem.

14:10:17 **First Officer:** Yeah.

14:10:18 **First Officer:** That battery charger's kickin' in. Ooh, we gotta...

14:10:20 **Captain:** We're losing everything.

14:10:21 **Departure Control:** Critter 592, contact Miami center on 132.45, so long.

14:10:22 **Captain:** We need, we need to go back to Miami.

14:10:23 Sounds of shouting from passenger cabin. Fire! Fire! Fire!

14:10:32 **First Officer:** Uh, 592 needs immediate return to Miami.

14:10:35 **Departure Control:** Critter 592, uh, roger, turn left heading 270. Descend and maintain 7,000.

14:10:39 **First Officer:** Two-seven-zero, seven-thousand, five-ninety-two.

14:10:41 **Departure Control:** What kind of problem are you havin'?

14:10:44 **Captain:** Fire.

14:10:47 **Departure Control:** Roger.

14:11:07 **Departure Control:** Critter 592, when able, turn left heading 250. Descend and maintain 5,000.

14:11:10 Sounds of shouting from passenger cabin.

14:11:11 **First Officer:** Two-five-zero, five-thousand.

169

14:11:38 **First Officer:** Critter 592, we need the, uh, closest airport available...

14:11:42 **Departure Control:** Critter 592, they're going to be standing by for you. You can plan runway one two...

14:11:46 **First Officer:** Need radar vectors.

14:11:49 **Departure Control:** Critter 592 turn left heading one four zero...

14:12:57 Sound similar to loud rushing air. Possibly the cockpit window has been opened at this point to clear smoke from the cockpit.

14:13:18 **Departure Control:** Critter 592 you can, uh, turn left heading one zero zero and join the runway one two localizer at Miami.

14:13:25: End of CVR recording.

Most modern aircraft today do not carry large oxygen tanks to supply passengers with breathable air in the event of a pressurization loss at altitude. Instead, near each seat an oxygen generating canister is located. If the oxygen masks drop from the ceiling because pressurization has been lost in the cabin, a quick pull on the mask activates a firing pin, and the decomposition of a sodium chlorate "candle" produces enough oxygen for the passenger to breathe while the airplane descends to a lower altitude. Contrary to the belief that many passengers have, this oxygen supply system was never designed to provide breathing air in case of smoke or fire in the cabin. The only purpose for a passenger oxygen system on an aircraft is to comply with the FAA requirement that oxygen be made available for the relatively short time period it takes to make an emergency descent.

Because there is a chemical reaction occurring in the canister, the canister can become quite hot. Tests show that typical temperatures are around 400 to 500 degrees Fahrenheit. According to the NTSB report of the accident, a box of supposedly "empty" oxygen canisters were placed in the forward cargo hold of flight 592 along with an aircraft tire. The box was not labeled as hazardous materials, which would have alerted the crew to the fact they might be carrying dangerous cargo. Pilots of commercial aircraft carrying passengers are trained to not accept boxes that are marked as containing hazardous material. It is the responsibility of the shipper to mark such cargo with the appropriate labels.

The NTSB report determined that during taxi or takeoff the canisters in the forward hold were jostled and that one or more of the canisters were activated and began releasing oxygen. The combination of readily available oxygen and a heat source caused a cargo hold fire that spread rapidly through the aircraft and eventually made it impossible for the pilots to keep the aircraft from crashing.

There are other voices in the industry who say that the heat generated by the canisters would have been insufficient to start a fire in the cargo hold. Their contention is that faulty electrical wiring and even the possibility of intentionally bypassed circuit breakers caused a fire to start and spread. Whichever of the two was the real cause, the pilots were suddenly confronted with a severe emergency shortly after departing Miami. Picturing myself in their situation as a fellow pilot, I can appreciate what their feelings must have been when they realized they had an uncontrollable fire on board with multiple failures in the electrical system. This crew made a valiant effort to get the airplane immediately back to the airport, but the fire eventually damaged the cables going to the flight controls. Without flight controls, it became impossible for them to prevent a deadly, high velocity dive into the waters of the swamp.

You can see, Preston, that getting an airplane into the air for a safe flight involves more than pushing the throttles forward and pointing the nose toward the sky. Successful takeoffs involve planning and skill. Perhaps they are a metaphor for other risks that we take in life. If we plan well and execute well, our endeavors have a good chance for success. But also we must remain alert to respond to the unexpected when it occurs. That we try to prepare for, too. In the back of our minds we can't help being aware that, in spite of all our preparations and our attempts to do the best we can, someday it may not be enough.

XIV

Landings

B757 Short Final
photo by Matti Eskelinen

174

We are flying to Sao Paolo. Departed Florida in the afternoon. While the sun was setting we worked our way down the Bahama island chain and across the Caribbean. The islands of Grand Turk, Hispaniola, and Puerto Rico are long behind us now. Our 757 crossed the northern coast of South America near Georgetown. It is night, and we have been dodging a wide grouping of thunderstorms over the Amazon basin. Very little below us but dark, sparsely inhabited rain forest. Winds that weren't supposed to be this strong are slowing our groundspeed and lowering our fuel reserves.

Rob Glaser, the first officer, punches a few keys on the FMC. The computer is telling us we will land at Sao Paolo with a little less than 5,000 pounds of fuel. Less than 45 minutes worth of flying time. If we encounter no more storms. If the winds don't get stronger. If we don't lose pressurization and have to go to a lower altitude. If there is no engine failure. If the weather is good at Sao Paolo and no holding is required. IF, IF, IF. Even IF nothing adverse happens before we arrive over our destination, we still won't arrive with enough fuel to go to the alternate airport and be able to hold for 30 minutes as required by regulations. We have been flying all evening. We are tired. The passengers are tired. They want to get to the destination and get out of the cramped airplane. Some could get irritable if we divert to the closest alternate. Brasilia is an unfamiliar airport for us, but it has good ILS approaches and a long runway. It's raining there, and we will have to do an approach with showers around us. Our time on the ground might be extensive. We will be even more tired when we take off again after having refueled.

"What do you think?" Rob asks. In the dim light of the cockpit, he has been watching me eyeing the fuel gauges and distrustfully looking over the Sao Paolo weather forecasts.

I'm remembering the words of Captain Whitey Ortman from years ago, when I was first training to be a 727 captain. "They don't give out hero buttons...." He was right. None of this is about trying to be a hero in somebody's eyes. It is about safety. All of commercial aviation is based on compromises from the size of the engines on the planes to the length of the runways, but, in the end—even in a world of compromises—it is the captain who is charged with juggling all the factors in a given situation to effect a safe flight. The decisions aren't always easy. The world is seldom painted in black and white. There are, instead, infinite shades of gray.

All the temptations are there to keep going. Everything should be OK. The weather has a good chance of remaining above landing minimums at Sao Paolo. There probably won't be many storms once we get a little farther south. Relatives waiting at the destination are expecting us to arrive on time. Too many late arrivals of our flights and we will see a drop in business. A diversion and extra landing with all the associated costs and fees will erase all the profit the company would have made from this trip.

I give Rob my answer. "I think we should get the company on the radio and tell them we are going to land at Brasilia for fuel." He nods his head in agreement. It is the answer he wants to hear, and I am hoping that I have created enough trust and confidence during all of our interactions over the course of the trip that he would have advocated his viewpoint if I had wanted to continue to Sao Paolo.

We call dispatch and tell them of our situation. They agree to advise the operations people at Brasilia that we are stopping in for fuel. We advise ATC we wish to divert to Brasilia. They issue the amended clearance to the new destination. We turn the aircraft onto the new course and begin a descent to a newly assigned altitude.

The lore of aviation is filled with wise and sometimes darkly humorous quips. They all contain a lesson of some kind. One is: "Takeoffs are optional, landings are obligatory." Landings are probably the part about flying that fascinates people the most. Taking off and leaving the ground thousands of feet below can be exhilarating, but an airplane cannot defy nature forever. It can fly hundreds and hundreds of miles, but there will always be a point where it must give up its freedom and return to earth to once again meekly obey the laws of gravity. And pilots are well aware that unless very special care is exercised, severe penalties may be waiting for those who dare to hurtle through the sky at high speeds far above rivers, mountains, cities, and plains.

Most passengers have a fairly good idea of when a landing ends: They are down on the ground and the airplane has decelerated to a very slow speed. They have already felt the sensation of the airplane descending. They have heard the gear thump down and lock into place. They hear the noise it makes in the slipstream. They have, perhaps, watched as the flaps were extended. And most have at some time or another looked out the window to see the ground coming closer and closer until the airplane finally touches down.

But when does the landing begin? For most pilots it begins back at the departure airport before the airplane has even left the gate. At the same time the crew is planning how to make the takeoff, they are also making a preliminary plan for how they will get the airplane back on the ground.

How much fuel will be needed to get to the destination with adequate reserves in case something goes wrong? Weather can change, especially if the forecast is for marginal visibility or if storms are expected to be in the vicinity of the airport. The pilots make a judgment based on forecasts and their own experience as to what the weather conditions will be at the time of arrival.

How strong will the winds be, and from which direction? Are they gusty? A strong crosswind will make the landing more difficult. Which instrument approach will be used? How long is the active runway? Will the runway be wet? Slippery? Snow or ice on it? What will the visibility be? One mile? One-half mile? One-quarter mile? Are the required radio navigation aids for the different approaches working? What about approach lights and runway lights? Are all the correct charts and approach plates that might be needed for the flight available in the cockpit?

What about high terrain, mountains? Are there obstacles around the airport? Turns may have to be made to avoid them. Washington D.C. National is a good example of an approach designed to avoid obstacles and prohibited airspace. Landing to the south, pilots often fly a localizer approach on a southeasterly course to about 1,000 feet above the ground, and then it is required to visually maneuver the aircraft over the Potomac River up to a point where they must make a close-in, low altitude turn to the right in order to line up with the runway. At Mexico City, pilots make a rather sharp turn to final when landing to the northeast to keep an adequate distance from mountains and buildings. Naples, Italy requires close attention to procedure turn altitudes. There are mountains all around the approach path. Catania, Sicily has a volcano close by. If you approach Kerkira, Greece from the south, about one-half mile from your touchdown point, you will have cliffs on the left and a small island immediately to your right. These are just a few examples. Each airport is different. Some are easier than others. Some runways are longer than others. At some short-field airports or on slippery runways it is better to get the airplane down on the ground a little more aggressively and not try to go for that extra smooth touchdown. If the runway is short, a firmer landing right at the touchdown zone is undeniably more desirable than a smooth touchdown far down the runway.

Sometimes people ask me, "How do you actually make the touchdown?" Here is what the manual says about a normal landing for a 757. Generally, the technique works well, but even a highly experienced pilot will occasionally be surprised with a rougher touchdown than he expected. This technique is called an attitude landing, as opposed to the full-stall landings that are often made in light airplanes:

1) First of all, the aircraft is configured properly with the gear down and flaps in the landing position.

2) The approach is stabilized, meaning that the aircraft is on the proper profile, neither too high nor too low, and the airspeed is at a basic 1.3 times the stall speed with 5 to 20 knots added depending on the headwind. If the airplane weighs 198,000 pounds, for example, and the headwind is 20 knots, the target approach speed will be 132 knots + 10 knots wind correction = 142 knots.

3) After the airplane has crossed the runway threshold and is about 30 feet off the ground, a slight nose-up change in pitch is made (about 3 degrees only). This change in pitch slows the sink rate but doesn't stop it.

4) While holding the same pitch attitude, the power is gradually reduced. Now the pilot waits until the airplane lands itself.

Sounds simple. Making it work all the time is a little harder. I have made many superb touchdowns over the years, and I have made some that made me wish I had stayed home that day. A slight error in timing or pressure on the yoke can make a difference. The important thing is that the landing is a safe one. Meet that requirement, and the rest is really just pride.

One more point on touchdowns. The 757 has very good autobrakes. Once the airplane touches down and the autobrakes begin to take effect, there is a possibility that the nosewheel may land hard even though the main wheels touched down lightly. This will be especially true if a high autobrake setting is used, the airplane landed with a nose-low attitude, and the center of gravity of the aircraft is forward. So with each landing there are actually two landings. The first one gets the main wheels on the ground, the second one gets the nosewheel down. One has to be careful to not relax the yoke and allow the nosewheel to come down too quickly.

One of the most important things to know during any landing is how *not* to land. Every so often the aircraft landing ahead of you may not clear the runway right away. I had this happen recently at Los Angeles, when a B747 landing ahead of us decided to roll all the way to the end of the runway instead of turning off on one of the taxiways.

"IAT, Go-around!" comes the command from the tower. (We have already decided that, anyway.)

Our airplane is only 100 feet off the ground and is almost at the runway threshold. What do you do now?

Add power, raise the nose of the aircraft, retract the flaps to the 20 setting, and start climbing. Once the climb is established, raise the landing gear. Keep climbing until about 1,000 feet above the airport, reduce power, reduce the pitch, and retract the flaps as the airplane accelerates. Level off at the assigned altitude and maintain the flaps-up maneuvering speed.

Although an infinite combination of factors can contribute to an accident, there seem to be several natural hazards that are most associated with landing accidents. Windshear, rain or snow with resultant wet or slippery runways, low visibility, and strong crosswinds can be mortal enemies.

On August 2, 1985, an L1011 was approaching Dallas/Ft. Worth Airport from the north on the ILS for 17L. The aircraft just ahead of it landed safely only minutes before, but storms were in the vicinity of the airport. Although the approach began quite normally, conditions changed very rapidly, and the crew was unable to prevent the aircraft from crashing short of the runway. The selected excerpts from the cockpit voice recorder show how rapidly conditions changed, and how their efforts to arrest the descent of the aircraft proved futile. The first officer is flying the airplane. The captain is handling the radio.

18.02:35 **Approach Control:** Delta 191 heavy is six miles from the marker, turn left heading 180, join the localizer at or above 2,000, cleared for ILS 17 Left approach.

Captain acknowledges the approach clearance.

18.02:43 **Captain:** Delta 191 roger. Got all that. Appreciate it.

18.03:03 **Approach Control:** Delta 191 heavy, reduce your speed to 160, please.

Captain acknowledges speed reduction.

18.03:09 **Captain:** One six zero.

The autopilot locks on to the approach.

18.03:11 **Captain:** Localizer and glideslope captured.

Approach Control advises the wind is changing because of a rain shower near the arrival end of the runway.

18.03:31 **Approach Control:** We're getting some variable winds out there due to a shower out there north end of DFW.

18.03:46 **Approach Control:** Delta 191 heavy, reduce speed to 150, contact tower 126.55.

Captain checks in with the control tower on the new frequency and comments on the shower.

18.03:58 **Captain:** Tower Delta 191 heavy, out here in the rain, feels good.

Tower acknowledges captain's call, clears aircraft to land on runway 17 Left, and gives an advisory that wind is from the east at 5 knots gusting to 15 knots. (These are not particularly difficult or strong winds.)

18.04:01 **Tower:** Delta 191 heavy, Regional Tower, 17 Left cleared to land. Wind zero nine zero at five gusts to one five.

18.04:05 **Captain:** Thank you, sir.

The first officer, who is flying the airplane, calls for the Before Landing checklist to be read.

18.04:07 **First Officer:** Before landing check.

The flight engineer begins reading the checklist.

18.04:08 **Flight Engineer:** Landing gear.

18.04:10 **Captain:** Down, three green.

The first officer notices lightning coming out of a cloud that is ahead.

18.04:18 **First Officer:** Lightning coming out of that one.

18.04:22 **Captain:** Where?

18.04:23 **First Officer:** Right ahead of us.

18.05:20 Sound similar to rain begins and continues to impact.

Evidently a speed loss now occurs, because the captain tells the first officer to push the throttles forward to get more power from the engines.

18.05:26 **Captain:** Push it up, push it way up.

18.05:27 **Captain:** Way up.

18.05:29 Sound of engines revving at high RPM.

18.05:30 **Captain:** That's it.

The **G**round **P**roximity **W**arning **S**ystem now warns the aircraft is getting too close to the ground.

18.05:44 **GPWS:** Whoop! Whoop! Pull up! Whoop! Whoop! Pull up!

Captain calls for the first officer to push throttles up for more power.

18.05:47 **Captain:** Push it way up!

Ground Proximity Warning continues as aircraft gets closer and closer to the ground. It is telling the pilots to raise the nose of the aircraft to stop the descent, but the aircraft, at this point, does not have enough power to fight the severe downdraft they are in.

18.05:48 **GPWS:** Whoop! Whoop! Pull up! Whoop! Whoop! Pull up!

18.05:57 End of recording.

The L1011 had been caught in the windshear of a microburst. As it approached the runway, a sudden severe downdraft emanating from a rain shower in its path caused a rapid loss of airspeed and overpowered the capability of the aircraft to climb. The aircraft struck the ground and obstacles short of the runway.

Windshear does not necessarily happen only in areas of shower activity. I remember on one occasion while on final approach to Guadalajara, Mexico our B757 suddenly encountered a 20-knot loss of airspeed. The tower had issued a windshear alert so we were carrying extra speed. Rapidly adding power allowed us to compensate for the airspeed loss. This all happened instantaneously and in absolutely clear conditions.

If storms, heavy rain, greatly reduced visibility, strong crosswinds, and a wet, slippery runway are all encountered together, the landing can quickly turn into a disaster:

The crew of an MD80 on approach to Little Rock, Arkansas was trying to beat a line of thunderstorms to the airport. This in itself is not unreasonable. Many times pilots will attempt to get the aircraft on the ground before the bad weather moves in. This is a judgment that the crew makes depending on their observation of the situation and their experience.

At first the crew was on vectors to runway 22 Left. They planned to land to the southwest while the storms were still west of the field. While on their vectors to the final approach course, the wind suddenly changed so that it was blowing from a more northerly direction. The crew did not think it prudent to land with a tailwind, so they requested that the controller take them off the approach to runway 22 Left and instead vector them for runway 4 Right. Now things got very hurried in the cockpit. New approach plates had to be quickly reviewed and the approach planned. While being vectored for the new runway, the crew decided to try to keep the airplane close in to the airport and try a visual approach. It might have worked, but they lost sight of the runway.

On the Cockpit Voice Recording, from the first officer is heard:

"There's a cloud between us and the airport. We have just lost the field...."

184

Since the crew has lost sight of the field, the controller now gives the flight radar vectors to the runway 4 Right ILS final approach course:

"You can fly heading 220. I'll take you out for the ILS."

He gives them a few more turns:

"Heading, 270. Heading, 330."

Now come the final turn and the approach clearance:

"...three miles from the marker. Turn right heading zero two zero. Maintain 2,300 feet until established on the localizer. Cleared ILS runway 4 Right approach."

Shortly thereafter the controller gives a wind advisory:

"...wind 350 at 30 gust 45." (These are very strong crosswinds.)

And then the controller gives a windshear alert:

"...shear alert center field wind 350 at 32 knots, gust 45. North boundary wind 310 at 29. Northeast boundary wind 320 at 32."

Now the controller calls out that the visibility has dropped to 1600 RVR, or about one-quarter of a mile. There is heavy rain over the field.

The crew acknowledges the visibility report.

In the cockpit, the crew is facing very strong, gusty crosswinds and greatly reduced visibility conditions. The wipers are turned on. The first officer sees the field ahead and realizes they are right of course. The crosswind is blowing the aircraft to the right of the runway centerline. Several seconds before touchdown, the captain calls

Spoilers Up and Flaps Down MD80
photo by Pekka Lehtinen

out he has the field. They land but the aircraft begins to slide. The captain applies reverse power, but the spoilers are not deployed. Since the spoilers are not up, the wing still has lift, and the weight of the aircraft is not transferred completely to the wheels. The captain desperately tries to get the airplane stopped by applying more reverse thrust. This doesn't help. The aircraft leaves the runway and crashes through the airport fence. The captain and 10 passengers died. There were 105 injuries. The other 24 persons on board escaped injury.

Preston, there is an important lesson here. Sometimes to deal with a really bad situation it might be better to mentally step back from it for a moment and try to gain a shift in perspective. That shift might open up a whole assortment of other possibilities that one may not see while his mind is absorbed in the fury of the fight. It is important to develop your knowledge and skills, but it is just as important to develop the ability to shift to an alternate plan if necessary.

Remember that any of us may sometimes get so overwhelmed by the details of a situation that we can lose sight of the bigger picture. Also, the reverse happens: We may concentrate on the bigger picture and forget important details. It seems to me that if we want our problem solving to be effective, it is important to be able to rapidly shift between both perspectives while at the same time adapting to changes in the situation as the problem evolves. To some people I suppose this comes naturally. For me it takes effort. Try to work on it. It's a skill worth having. Someday it could save your life.

XV

Pacific

North Pacific
by Jeppesen Sanderson

NOT FOR NAVIGATION

It's more than 3,600 nautical miles from Phoenix, Arizona to Honolulu, Hawaii. One of IAT's B757s is out over the Pacific. Honolulu is still almost 900 miles ahead. The sky is almost cloudless. The water below looks tranquil. Winds are light at altitude, and the air is smooth. It should have been a peaceful trip. But even in perfect conditions, the unexpected can be waiting.

Captain John Pierce and his first officer Randy Wilson have just realized they have a serious problem. When they recorded their fuel on board at the last waypoint there existed only a slight fuel imbalance. The left wing tank gauge showed 200 pounds more fuel than the right wing gauge. Perfectly normal. Slight imbalances of fuel often occur as the autothrottles adjust the engines to maintain a constant cruise airspeed. The amount of fuel consumed by each engine is not expected to be exactly the same. On a very long flight a crew may decide to open the crossfeed valve, turn off the fuel pumps on one wing tank, and balance up the fuel by allowing both engines to draw fuel from one tank. When the fuel tank quantities are balanced, the inactivated fuel pumps are turned on, the crossfeed valve is closed, and each engine once again draws fuel from the tank on its side of the airplane.

Although there had been 200 pounds more fuel in the left tank than the right at the last waypoint, in the 15 minutes since the last fuel check, the situation had completely changed. The left wing tank gauge was now indicating that the fuel in the left tank was 500 pounds less than the fuel in the right. This meant that in the last 15 minutes, more than 700 pounds of fuel had been drawn from the left tank than from the right. As Captain Pierce observed the fuel in the left tank decreasing rapidly, he knew right away what he was going to have to do. He was well aware that in the fuel section of the abnormal procedures checklists it stated quite clearly:

"An increase in fuel imbalance of approximately 1,000 pounds or more in 30 minutes should be considered a fuel leak."

The checklist also stated that a visual confirmation of the leak should be made if possible. To confirm the fuel leak he would have to send the first officer back to the cabin to look out one of the passenger windows for signs of fuel spraying from the left engine or strut. Looking at the rate that the fuel quantity was decreasing in the left tank made it clear to the captain that he would have to take immediate action to avoid losing so much fuel from the left tank that they might not be able to make it to the Hawaiian islands.

"Engine Shutdown Checklist, Randy. I'll guard the good engine."

Pierce put his hand up near the right throttle and right fuel control switch to ensure that the wrong engine would not be shut down. Randy had already taken out the Quick Reference Handbook (QRH), which contained the abnormal procedures checklists, and had turned to the correct page. He knew John would probably not waste time sending him back to the cabin to make the visual confirmation.

The first officer began to read the procedure aloud and perform the required items. He ruefully half smiled to himself as he read the first item on the checklist. **"Plan to land at the nearest suitable airport."** The nearest suitable airport was more than 800 miles from their present position. He continued with the checklist:

```
" AUTOTHROTTLE ARM SWITCH . . . . . . . . . . . . . . . . . OFF
  THRUST LEVER . . . . . . . . . . . . . . . . . . . . . . . . . . . . . CLOSED
  FUEL CONTROL SWITCH . . . . . . . . . . . . . . . . . . . . . . CUT OFF
  APU . . . . . . . . . . . . . . . . . . . . . . . . . . . . . . . . . . . . . . START"
```

The engine was now shut down, but there was still plenty to do. Captain Pierce adjusted the power on the remaining good engine to just below the Maximum Continuous Power setting, then he turned the aircraft 90 degrees to the left of course and allowed the airplane to begin a gentle descent. Overwater emergency procedures in the Pacific required him to establish a 25 mile offset from his assigned routing. Once he had his 25 mile offset, he would parallel his original track and begin a rapid descent to below flight level 290 in order to keep his aircraft clear of other airplanes on the Pacific route structure. Flying below the route structure, he would proceed directly to Hilo, the alternate airport. As he initiated the turn to attain the 25 mile offset, he turned on all the landing lights so that other aircraft in the area might see his aircraft better. He also glanced up at the fuel gauges. With the left engine shut down, the left fuel gauge no longer showed a rapid decrease. There had definitely been a leak as he had surmised and, no doubt, it was somewhere on the left engine. He was glad that they had been able to shut down the engine before a possible fire had developed.

With the engine shut down and the flight path under control, Captain Pierce now asked the first officer to send out a Mayday call on the VHF emergency frequency 121.5 so that other aircraft in their vicinity would be aware of the deviation they were making. Randy quickly made a call giving their position, the altitude they were passing, and a short description of their intentions. Randy also checked the weight of the aircraft against the One Engine Inop Altitude Capability chart and determined that at about 300 knots indicated airspeed they would be able to maintain approximately 20,000 feet of altitude. The captain would now be taking the aircraft to Hilo instead of Honolulu because Hilo was closer to their position. After they managed to get an amended clearance from ATC, Randy got the approach plates and airport diagram out for the Hilo airport.

Now that the aircraft was well established on its diversion course and the cockpit was organized, Pierce asked Randy take care of the airplane and the radios. He had to talk to the senior flight attendant.

He was glad Meg Grady was with him today. She had years of experience dealing with tough situations, and he was certain he could count on her to do well if their predicament worsened. He pushed the flight attendant call button. Meg answered on the interphone right away.

"You have an engine shut down, right?"

"Yes we do. Fuel leak. Left side. We are descending to 20,000 feet and we're planning on landing at Hilo. Should take us about two and a half hours. Everything else looks OK for now. Other engine is running fine. I'm going to talk to the passengers and let them know what happened, and then I'll ask that you prepare the cabin for a possible water ditching. If we lose the other engine for some reason, we'll have about 20 minutes after it happens before we all go for a swim."

"Thanks for the words of encouragement."

"Like I said, everything looks OK for now."

Captain Pierce made the announcement to the passengers, and then settled in for the long wait until they would reach the island of Hawaii. Air traffic control had advised them of the position of three ships along their route if the worst case scenario were to develop. They also advised that a Coast Guard C130 would attempt to intercept them as they got closer to the coastline. Although everything looked under control, he knew that if problems were to develop on the remaining engine, they might not make it to Hilo. He opened his manual to review the ditching procedures in order to plan how he would make a water landing if necessary:

"If the surface is smooth, land into the wind. If surface is rough, ditch parallel to the waves or swell. Use flaps 30 and normal approach speeds if possible. The landing gear remains retracted....

194

"Try to make contact with the water at minimum speed and sink rate....

"Enter the water with wings level to the water surface....

"A second or third impact is usually encountered during ditching. To avoid injury, all personnel must remain braced until the aircraft comes to rest....

"The airplane may float for a considerable time if not damaged. Safety dictates that all aboard be evacuated as rapidly possible."

They made it sound easy. Pierce knew, however, there is always a gap between theory and the real world. If the other engine failed and they really did have to ditch, he knew 200 people would be counting on him to accomplish a water landing with minimum damage to the aircraft so that it would float long enough to deploy the life rafts and evacuate the airplane. He noticed his palms were slightly moist and that his heart beat a little faster than normal. He looked out the window at the water below and was thankful that not only were they flying in daylight but that also the winds were light and the sea relatively calm. He checked the instrument indications for the right engine. EPR, still normal. N1, normal. Fuel Flow, normal. Oil Pressure, normal. Oil Temperature, normal. Engine Vibration, normal. Randy was checking the right engine instruments too. Pierce looked at the clock. Still more than two hours before they would reach land....

This story had a happy ending. The Rolls-Royce engine mounted on the right wing continued to run perfectly. The aircraft made it to the alternate airport where Pierce performed a good single-engine approach and landing. Upon inspection of the left engine, it was found that a connector had worked loose on the fuel control unit, causing the serious leak to occur. If the pilots had not shut down the engine when they did, they might not have had enough fuel to make it to the alternate.

I have flown quite a few trips to Hawaii, Preston, along the same route, always to Honolulu or Maui, and I have had the good fortune to not encounter any emergencies like the one Pierce and Wilson had to confront while flying over this long expanse of water. But every time I head out over any ocean and see the coastline receding behind me, I begin to prepare myself mentally for the possibility of being far from land in a crippled airplane. I'm sure all pilots do the same. One cannot allow oneself to be lulled into complacency by cloudless skies, smooth air, and previous successful flights. Each flight is different in its possibilities. Each flight is a new roll of the dice. Because of good aircraft maintenance and good crew training the probabilities for an uneventful ocean crossing are very high, but there is always the chance that on that particular flight on that particular day....

Being aware of the possible dangers does not mean that one succumbs to a fear of them. It only means that if something unexpected were to happen, the captain and the first officer have already given some thought to what they will do. As the aircraft crosses the water, they mark their position on a plotting chart. West Coast-Hawaii plotting charts are different from the Atlantic plotting charts in that one does not have to draw the route. Fixed routes and waypoints are already depicted on the West Coast-Hawaii charts. (The track structure does not shift north and south with the weather and winds as on the Atlantic.) The pilots periodically record the time and fuel on board as they pass over waypoints. They make a position report at each waypoint where it is required. They monitor the engine instruments for signs of trouble. And they keep track of their position relative to the ETP, the Equal Time Point.

The ETP is the point on the route where it takes an equal amount of time to return to the U.S. mainland in case of trouble or continue on to Hawaii. One could think of this as the halfway point distance-wise except for the fact that winds exist at cruise altitude. We used to have to calculate this manually many years ago. Today the computer flight plan does it for us. If a serious malfunction that requires a diversion occurs before arriving at the ETP, the captain turns back to the U.S. mainland. If it happens after the ETP, he diverts to Hilo.

Procedures are quite similar on North Pacific routes. Some years ago, IAT obtained a charter contract to provide service from Seattle to Japan with a stop in Anchorage. I flew these flights regularly for several months. We typically started off in Seattle, flew past Vancouver Island, the Queen Charlotte Islands, the Alexander Archipelago, and eventually landed at Anchorage to take on fuel. After an hour on the ground we continued on to Japan. From Anchorage we headed west to pass by Bethel and then headed out over the Bering Sea. Our routing would normally keep us just outside Russian airspace. An "abeam Shemya" position report was required. Shemya is a large "rock" at the end of the Aleutian Island chain that almost no one has heard of. It has a 10,000-foot airstrip built by the U.S. military, and it can be used as an emergency landing field. Shemya also played an important role during World War II in the battle for the Aleutians. Our route westbound would take us about 160 miles north of the island.

After passing Shemya, the only other place before coming within range of Japan to make an emergency landing would be Petropavlosk on Kamchatka. The long name is really a combination of (Saint) Peter and (Saint) Paul in Russian. The company had issued a briefing package in case we ever had to divert there. None of us ever did. The closest we would come to Petropavlosk on our route would be about 200 miles. During the Cold War, a Korean Air 747 flying over these waters strayed off its flight path into Russian airspace. Fighter jets were scrambled, and the 747 was downed with a missile. That threat no longer existed for us, but maintaining correct track over the water was still just as important on our flights as it had been years ago. Any aircraft off its assigned track is a possible collision hazard for other aircraft in the vicinity.

Once we reached Japan we might land at Sapporo, Misawa, or Tokyo. On the return trip we might fly to Iwakuni and then back to Anchorage.

One of the best parts about this flying for me were the long layovers at a hotel outside of Tokyo. Once on the ground, the crew might spend a whole week until we made a return flight. I used the time to explore the area on a bicycle that the hotel provided for a very small fee, and to study Japanese. Although I never got much farther than simple phrases like, "Good morning," "How are you?," and "I am from America," I did manage to get past some of the dismay Westerners normally experience when confronted with the writing system used in Japan. I also found that the structure of the language was in many ways less complex than European languages. No convoluted verb conjugations and elaborate systems of subject, object, and adjective agreement. Probably if the writing system weren't so difficult to learn, more Westerners would learn Japanese.

What makes Japanese so difficult for Westerners is that words are actually represented in three different ways. Some words are represented by Chinese characters (*kanji*). Although there is a certain logic to how these characters originated, one really must just memorize about 2,000 of them to be literate. Other words that are of Japanese origin are represented by characters that represent 47 syllables (*hiragana*). Words of foreign origin are usually represented by yet another group of characters that represent syllables (*katakana*). Japanese, I was surprised to learn, contains a great number of words borrowed from English. Hamburger, stereo, sports, iced coffee, coin laundry, and chocolate are a few. There is an extensive list.

My bike rides and occasional train trips allowed me to try out my Japanese and to gain a feel and appreciation for everyday life in this country as I saw people go about their routine affairs. Everywhere I went, the people were very polite. When I was hungry, I would sometimes drop into a supermarket to buy some snacks and then eat these in some convenient resting spot. I took plenty of photos of signs in Japanese and put together a small interesting collection of store signs, railroad crossings, hospitals, and offices. I used these photos to study the Japanese symbols. Occasionally, I would ask someone for directions, and I always received a very courteous response. Once, I was able to help a mother and young daughter change a flat tire on their car. I can't say I penetrated the culture as I had, for example, in Spain. My stays weren't long enough to even attempt it. But I did try to learn everything I could by being an aware and polite observer. When I visit any country, I look at the everyday things that make up life. How do adults interact with each other? How do children interact? What clothes do they wear? What movies are playing? What books and magazines are available in the book stores? What is the level of cleanliness? How often do people genuinely smile at one another or extend a small kindness? Observing all the small details around me teaches me much more about a country than going to see all the famous monuments. For me, Japan was one of the most agreeable and civilized countries I have ever visited.

Having flown over Pearl Harbor many times while landing at Honolulu, I also couldn't help but reflect on World War II. A much different, militaristic Japan had existed then. I knew about Nanking, the Bataan Death March, and the slave labor camps in the mines near Iwakuni. Contrasting the Japan of today with the Japan of World War II left me with the same conclusions I come to when I contrast the Germany of World War II with the Germany of today. In any culture, when blind adherence to any philosophy or belief system takes over a government, human values are eventually trampled.

In both Germany and Japan, propaganda machines were established to manipulate the national psychology and suppress any opposing ideas. Repressive regimes seek to use all the good things that exist in a culture for their own purposes. The desire to obey the law and custom, the desire to protect one's family, friends, and country, the pride in one's heritage, personal honor, the traditional songs, the traditional celebrations, and the belief in God all become distorted and are used to make people think they are doing the right thing. Leaders don't usually get very far by telling people they must be evil. Instead they learn to convince people they are being good by following the dictates of the leader.

Whenever I go to either of these countries I meet kind, friendly, responsible, and courteous people. Where were these people during the war? The answer is simple. They were right there all the time. But their leaders encouraged them to see the world in narrow nationalistic terms and lose sight of the fact that we must all find a way to live together on this planet. Seeing the commercial ties, the great friendship, and the respect that America maintains with Japan and Germany today gladdens me and demonstrates to me that former adversaries can find ways to live in harmony together for their mutual benefit. History shows us that after winning a war it is even more important to win the peace. A war plan without an effective peace plan almost equates to no plan at all and will only sow the seeds for the next war.

Preston, it is our great tragedy as a species that good people can be induced to commit bad acts, especially if they are given absolute power over others. People who, under other circumstances, might have lived out quiet, peaceful lives can be led to commit atrocities in the name of whatever cause, philosophy, or religion they espouse. No society, probably almost no person, is immune from this. Flying has given me the opportunity to view the universality of the human spirit in a wide variety of cultures. What I always seem to find no matter where I travel is that, at their core, people are much more alike than they are different. The desire to be happy, free, and treated fairly seems universal. And another observation always seems to ring true wherever I go: Unless they have been taught or brutalized to feel otherwise, most people do not wish others to suffer, nor do they wish to suffer themselves. We must ask ourselves what our behavior teaches children. Does it teach them to love or to hate?

200

XVI

Sex

She is going to be 50 years old next month. Her name is Anne Muscovitz. She has lost her youthful glow. As a young woman she was probably quite beautiful in the way that young women are beautiful. Now her beauty is of a different kind. It is the beauty that comes from a more complete and calm place inside her soul. You see it in the way she moves and the compassion in her eyes. Life has challenged her and strengthened her. She reads, she seeks, she questions. She does not believe in myths. In her voice you feel her experience and wisdom. She is gentle and feminine, yet you very much sense her inner strength and power. Some men might be afraid of a woman like this. I appreciate her maturity of spirit. Women like this are capable of deep love. They make challenging, stimulating partners in, and out, of the bedroom. They have no need for pretenses or charades. They do not live in a world of illusions, waiting for others to make their dreams come true. They have known the joyous freedom of following their hearts and facing life with all its realities.

Next month, Anne will be upgrading to captain. She has been a captain before. Six years at a commuter airline. Before that she was a captain for five years in the corporate and freight world. She has waited four years for her seniority number to allow her to bid a captain slot at our airline. I am happy she will be upgrading soon. She flies the airplane as well as any pilot in the company. Better than some. I like the confident, friendly, relaxed way she goes about doing her job. These thoughts are going through my mind as we fly over a country where the majority of the men would find a woman like this to be a threat to their culture, their religion, and their privileged status. Far below us is Saudi Arabia, where most women, including even wealthy ones, live a life of second-class citizenship. Before I allow myself to become too proud, I remind myself that in my own country women have had the right to vote for fewer than 100 years. I take a moment to reflect on all the abused, enslaved women who exist in the world, and I feel certain in my heart that the continuing struggle for women's equality will be the most important undertaking of this new century. Freedom for women will eventually also bring freedom to men.

Anne and I are on the last leg of a two-day trip we have been doing together. We are over Saudi Arabia, returning to Italy from Diego Garcia.

The trip to Diego Garcia had begun yesterday with an early morning takeoff from an air base in Italy. We climbed up to altitude and continued over to the Ionian Sea. We passed south of Greece and directly over the island of Crete and the ruins of ancient Minoan civilizations. We then monitored the autopilot as it set a course for Cairo. The sky was clear as we flew over the Nile Delta, and it was quite easy to pick out the pyramids at Giza. Near Luxor we turned east and crossed over the Red Sea. After more than an hour of flying over craggy mountains and hot deserts of Saudi Arabia, we continue over Qatar, the United Arab Emirates, and Oman. The Arabian Sea and the Indian Ocean lay ahead of us. Once over the water, our navigation computers faithfully turned us toward Diego Garcia, a small island under British control with an airstrip and military base, part of the Chagos Archipelago in the Indian Ocean hundreds of miles ahead.

Over the Indian Ocean, Bombay Radio is barely intelligible on the HF receiver. We think we hear an altitude change assignment but there is so much interference and static on the frequency we cannot confirm it. Anne suggests we climb up 500 feet just in case another aircraft has been assigned to our altitude on an airway crossing our route. I agree it is a good idea. We climb up and turn on the landing lights to make ourselves more visible. We are actually flying between the airways now. Twenty minutes later we are able to communicate with Bombay Radio clearly enough to hear that we had indeed been assigned a higher altitude. One hundred miles out from Diego Garcia, we are able to make radio contact with the control tower located on the air base. The airstrip appears ahead. Anne makes a nice landing.

We taxied to the parking area and shut down the engines. The accuracy of our inertial reference units has precisely led us to this little dot in the middle of the Indian Ocean. After our passengers deplaned, the military commander came on board to welcome the crew. He gives us little maps of the base. Behind him is a team of drug sniffing dogs. Their handlers run the dogs up and down the cabin. No drugs. That's good. We don't need any complications.

We will spend 12 hours resting until we take the airplane back along the same route we came. I'm exhausted from the long flight, and I decide that before we do the long trip back tomorrow, I am going to get as much sleep as possible. Anne says she needs to take a walk before she can wind down enough to get some sleep. The military puts us up in the visiting officers' quarters. Not luxurious accommodations, but adequate. There aren't many women on this base, and I notice that before the flight attendants have even made it to their rooms, they have already been invited to a barbeque party.

The next morning, Anne was especially quiet. Except for acknowledging my callouts ("Set standard EPR, Gear Up, Heading Select, Climb Power, Flight Level Change," and so on), she barely spoke until we were over Saudi Arabia. I assumed she was tired. I didn't really know her that well. Actually, I had met her for the first time when she introduced herself to me just before the trip. We had talked a little on the flight down to Diego, but the conversation wasn't particularly personal. The usual stuff. Pilot talk. I knew she was feeling me out. I guessed she wanted to know if I was one of those "macho" captains she had had to fly with from time to time in her life before she would allow herself to open up. That was fine with me. I could understand. I knew a few of our captains did not like the idea of women flying airplanes. Some liked to even push them a little to see if they could get them to break down. I knew who these captains were. I had little admiration for them, and I was glad that at IAT we only had a few like that. Those same captains had a history of trying to belittle their male coworkers, too.

Because Anne was so quiet, I decided to find out if everything was OK. "Get enough sleep after your walk?"

She turned her head in my direction, and I could see she was going to confide in me.

"I had an unpleasant experience on the beach."

She then told me what had happened.

After putting her bags in the room assigned to her, Anne had changed into a workout suit and decided to explore the island. She managed to borrow a bicycle. At first she rode around the main base area where most of the buildings were, but finally she headed toward a deserted part of the beach, where she spent some time relaxing and listening to the waves. She didn't notice the four men who had approached her. Now, as the sun was beginning to set, she realized she was not alone.

One man had sat down to her left. Another to her right. Another sat down in front of her, and a fourth was standing behind her. The one in front seemed to be the leader. He displayed a wide and overly friendly smile. They were apparently all contract workers. The base hired quite a few from other countries to take care of the many maintenance jobs. Normally these workers did their jobs and did not cause trouble. They earned salaries that were much higher than what they could have earned in their own countries. At the end of their contract, they could go back home with quite a bit of saved-up money, or they could stay and work longer.

Anne was aware that they had been drinking. The man behind her said something in a language she did not understand, and the two men at her sides giggled just a little.

The man in front of her smiled even wider than before and said, "The beach is very beautiful, yes?"

Anne thought it better to answer. No need to antagonize them by remaining silent. She answered in a pleasant way, "Yes, it is very peaceful." And then to gain back a little of the initiative, she asked her own question, "Do you know what time it is? I have friends waiting for me. I promised them I would be back from the beach before dark."

"He probably knows I am bluffing," she thought. But at least she could see just a flicker of doubt in his eyes.

"Here, we make very nice party. You like drink?" He held out his bottle of wine to her.

"No, thank you. That is a nice offer." She stood up. "I'm sorry, my friends are waiting. They are probably wondering why I am late."

The other three men stood up with her. None of them touched her, but they were all less than an arm's length away. Anne had studied self-defense for years when she was younger, and she had learned enough to know she could not fight off four men. Perhaps if they were very, very drunk. But they had just begun drinking. Their bottles were still fairly full. Perhaps that could work in her favor. They might not have drunk enough yet to lose their control. The man in front of her began tapping his bottle slowly against the side of his leg. He put on a clownish, sad face as he added a mock begging tone to his voice.

207

"I am sorry if you go. Come with us to swim. The water is warm. You will feel ve-e-e-ry nice." Now he smiled the too-wide smile again.

Anne knew it was now or never. Still no one had dared to touch her, but the leader was getting bolder. She knew if he signaled the others to grab her, they would.

"I am very sorry, but I am late. Thank you for your invitation." She turned and walked directly past the man who was standing behind her. Her movement caught him off guard, and he instinctively moved slightly out of her way to allow her to pass.

Their leader stepped forward and grabbed her arm. With her forward momentum she knew she could probably pull him off balance and deliver one kick. If she did that or tried to run, however, she was sure the other three would attack her. They would have her loose clothing off quickly, and, at that point, there would be no turning back for them. They might even kill her and swim her body out to sea.

She did not even try to pull her arm away. She stopped and slowly turned around. In a calm, commanding voice she told her assailant, "Release my arm immediately. I am an officer, and you will spend the next 20 years in jail if you don't let go of my arm right now." She looked directly into his eyes. "Take your bottles, go down the beach, and make your party."

The man looked back into her eyes. What he saw there told him quite clearly that this woman would not submit to them. She would fight them. She would scratch them and leave them marked. It was a small island. She was right. They would be caught. He could see she was giving him a chance to back down. He decided to take it. His hand dropped from her sleeve. Anne walked back to the bicycle, mounted it, and deliberately rode off slowly. She didn't even look back. Only after she had securely locked the door to her room did she break down and cry.

"Anne, did you report this to anyone?"

"No, I don't think I would recognize them if I saw them again, and I didn't want to delay the flight this morning. Besides, they didn't hurt me. They had just been drinking a little, and I was stupid to go to a deserted part of the beach so close to dark. Maybe they thought I was looking for a party."

Anne had decided to be more charitable than I would have been, but it was her decision. They had not forced her. She had offered them the possibility that all would be forgotten.

After Anne related her story, I wanted to hear more about her life. And she felt comfortable telling me. She told me she was born in South Africa. That accounted for the English accent.

"Where I grew up, women didn't go to school to learn a profession. We were all taught to find rich husbands. I wanted to fly airplanes, but that was impossible at the time. Men had the profession firmly in their control, and women were clearly not wanted. I bought a plane ticket and went to America. Once I was in New York, I started to work illegally. The only work I could find was serving drinks in bars. My family would have been scandalized if they had known, but I never told them. They thought I was working in an office. No bar owner ever asked if I was in the country legally. I started taking flying lessons and obtained a student visa. As I accumulated my ratings, I was allowed to work as a flight instructor. Slowly the hours built up in my logbook. I was able to build a lot of time by flying with rich men who owned their own airplanes but who were not very proficient at flying them. My job was to keep them from hurting themselves. They would pay me as an instructor for my time. I was pretty nice looking then. Some wanted more than flight instruction on these trips. I always gently made it clear that I wasn't interested."

"How did you make the transition to more professional flying?"

MU2
photo by Joan Martorell

"A friend of mine was flying cancelled checks from New York to Boston in an MU2. He allowed me to come along and help load the freight, and I would learn how to fly the airplane."

"Did you play the 'girl' card when it came to loading the freight?"

"Not as much as I should have!" she laughed. "It wasn't that bad. I got used to it, and it helped me stay in shape. Today my back hurts once in a while from those days, but it was a good way to build turbine time."

"Did you finally get a freight job?"

"Yes, the friend I was flying with quit and got a job with a commuter airline. I took over his run and began building up multi-engine turbine time flying the MU2 at night. My logbook was filling up quite nicely after two years. I eventually found a corporate job flying the same kind of airplane. No more loading freight. That part was good. On the other hand, I had to put up with arrogant executives who considered me as a sort of well-trained chauffeur. They wanted me to carry their bags from their limos to the airplane. I refused and got away with it because I was a female. I think a male pilot might have gotten fired. Another corporate position came up with a good company. The owner had two pilots. He treated us well and paid us well. I stayed on that job two years."

"Commuters next?"

"Yes," she smiled. "Sounding like a familiar story?"

"Yes."

"I started working as a copilot for one of the largest commuters in the Midwest. We were a feeder airline to TWA. I flew out of St. Louis. Just as I was about to upgrade to pilot in command, I fell in love with one of our captains and got married. This wouldn't have made a big change in my career except for the fact that I got slightly pregnant after being married two years. Six years later I was left with a young son and a divorce. I started flying again back at the same commuter. Made captain one year later and spent several years flying there until I came to IAT. This company was the first place I ever flew jets. Also, until coming here I had no international flying experience. That, as you can guess, changed very quickly."

"Doesn't sound like you've had a very easy climb. It must have been difficult trying to raise a child on your own and build a flying career at the same time."

"I was lucky to get help from my parents. After the divorce, I was able to bring them over from South Africa. They help me with my son quite a bit."

"Still, there must have been times when you became really discouraged."

"Yes, but whenever I started feeling sorry for myself, I thought about what my grandmother and mother had been through during World War II, and I knew my life has actually been pretty good."

"What did they do during World War II? I know my own mother spent her time during the war taking care of her little sister while my grandmother worked in a factory putting ignition harnesses on the engines of American bombers."

"Well, you know I am Jewish, right?"

"I guessed that, since your last name is Russian. You don't look very Slavic, and not too many Russians leave Russia to go live in South Africa."

"My grandmother was a young woman and my mother was 13 when the Germans invaded Lithuania. In Vilnius, the Germans went to the jails and released the common prisoners to commit their atrocities for them. German patrols rounded up groups of Jews and had these criminals club them to death. My grandmother and mother were able to avoid being captured. A Christian family hid them for weeks until it became too unsafe. They were then smuggled to a farm in the country, where another Christian family had the courage to hide them. They lived in a small basement storage cellar and did not dare appear above ground during the day. As the end of the war in Europe approached, they had to leave the farm where they had been hiding. With only three months before the final battles would be fought, they were captured by German soldiers. They were eventually sent to a concentration camp and put to work in a camp factory. My mother said the clothes they were given barely protected them from the severe cold of winter. They became very ill, but they were lucky. The Russians liberated the camp very soon after, and they were freed. Practically on foot, they crossed post-war Europe to Italy and managed to board a leaky steamer to South Africa. My mother met my father there. He belonged to a Jewish family that had emigrated to South Africa from Russia before the Russian Revolution. So you can see, I have had it easy."

I wouldn't say her life has been easy, but I would be willing to say that her grandmother's and mother's sufferings were more than anyone should have to bear.

Although most women pilots I have known do not have quite the astounding family histories that Anne's family has, I have found that most have had to pay their dues, just like the men I find in this profession. I asked Anne if she had ever suffered any discrimination because she was a woman.

"Surprisingly, less than you might think. Most of the men I have worked with have been pretty good and have not treated me any differently then they would treat a male pilot. Of course, I have always treated them with mutual respect, too, and I have tried to leave sex out of my work environment. I like being a woman in my time off, but at work I am a pilot. And I try to be a professional pilot and do my job well. That is how I want to be treated. There have been a few unpleasant incidents. I've flown with a few pilots who just can't seem to see a woman as a fellow professional. They have to make remarks from time to time about women or women pilots. Some use intentionally suggestive language or tell offensive jokes. I'm not a prude, and I can enjoy a good dirty joke as well as anyone. But I don't like it if it is being told just as a crude attempt to embarrass me. I don't get embarrassed, but I wonder sometimes why the individuals who have tried to do this just don't grow up. It would be better for everyone, including themselves. I have women pilot friends at other airlines who have had some bad experiences with overbearing captains, but even they say their experience with most of their male coworkers in the cockpit has been generally good. How about you?"

"How about me? What do you mean?"

"I mean, you have treated me with respect this whole trip, just as I have treated you with respect. I feel we are starting to become friends. But how do you feel about flying with women pilots?"

With frankness and sincerity she had asked the question. Anne deserved an honest answer.

"If you had known me 30 years ago you might have seen a different person. I'll admit that I too was one of those men who thought this was a man's job and women should stay away. But I like to think that I have grown as a person during my 55 years of life. By the way, I still see myself as an unfinished product, both as a professional and as a human being. I know I have a lot more to learn; also I know I am running out of time to learn it. Do I like flying with women? Do I like flying with men? I like flying with *you*. I try to see everyone as an

214

individual, and I am happy to see people living their lives in whatever way makes them feel free and joyous.

"So, what if *I* were the captain and *you* were the copilot?"

"And if you were the captain and I were the copilot? That's a difficult question. I haven't been a copilot for a long time. I have been a captain for many years, and I am used to being in command. But I do suspect that if our roles were reversed and you treated me with the same respect you are treating me with now, it wouldn't take me long to adapt. That's about as honest an answer as I can give you."

Anne smiled. "Good enough for me, Captain."

We continued on to Italy....

XVII

The Bravest Captain of Them All

Whenever I go far away on a flying assignment for a long time, I always like to check in on a good friend of mine when I get back. His name is Captain Dan Blackton. More than any of my friends, Dan has shown me that we shouldn't waste a single day of our lives and that we should be grateful for each day our bodies allow us to enjoy good health.

Dan didn't start out with the intention of following a flying career. He was going to be a musician. His father was a musician, and a good one. He began to teach Dan to play the French horn when he was a little boy. By the time Dan got to high school he was good enough to sit first seat in the school band. He dreamed of being in the Chicago Symphony one day. By the time his senior year in high school ended, Dan had come to an important conclusion: although he very dearly loved music and playing the French horn, he was not one of the gifted. He continued to practice hard every day, and he continued to try to prepare himself for a career as a musician, but by the time he was 21 he knew that after giving himself every chance to be a great French horn player, it was not meant to be. Although he would love music his whole life and would occasionally play in some of the major orchestras in the Chicago area, he knew he would have to look for another profession.

Dan turned to his other love. A very different love. He decided to build a career in aviation. Along with his passion for music, Dan had always had a fascination with airplanes. He used to watch them fly overhead on their way to Chicago O'Hare or Chicago Midway airport when he was a boy. When he was very little, sometimes he would beg his father to take him to the small airport close to their home so that he could watch the small private airplanes land and take off. He promised himself he would get a pilot license someday.

Dan wanted to fly planes, but he also had a very strong curiosity about how they were put together. He decided to start in aviation by earning an airframe and powerplant repair (A&P) license.

He did well in his A&P courses, and in just a few years he was working on large jets for a major airline. While he spent several years maintaining jets, Dan eventually, in his spare time, obtained his private pilot license, then his commercial rating, instructor rating, instrument rating, and multi-engine endorsement. He now had the basic license requirements to apply for a flying job, but he did not have very much flying time. He also had a family. This meant that taking one of the very low-paid, entry level flying jobs to gain experience would not be a practical option for him. There was another possibility. If he were to obtain a jet flight engineer rating, he could apply to a freight carrier or some smaller airline and begin flying in jets right away. True, he wouldn't be at the flight controls, but this was one way to get his foot in the door. He would gain a lot of experience in jet aircraft operations, and he could still build his flying time as an instructor in small airplanes on the side.

Dan went to work for Lyon Air, a small freight outfit with six old B727s that hauled freight in the middle of the night to various parts of the U.S. out of O'Hare airport. As the flight engineer, Dan was responsible for doing the pre-flight inspection of the aircraft, supervising the loading of the freight, getting the proper amount of fuel on board, preparing weight and balance computations, and calculating the performance speeds for each takeoff. Another important part of his job was filling out the aircraft logbook and making sure all the required maintenance inspections had been completed. During flight, it was Dan's job to monitor the electrical, hydraulic, fuel, and pressurization systems of the aircraft, and be prepared to handle any problems with these systems if they came up. "Sitting side-saddle," as the flight engineer seat position was called, was not where Dan actually wanted to be, but he was getting good experience.

After a few years at Lyon Air, Dan was hired by IAT, where I had just become a new B727 captain. Dan and I flew many trips together, and we slowly formed a strong friendship. It always made me feel good when I saw that Dan would be on my schedule for the month, because he not only was an excellent flight engineer who could be counted on to do things right if we ever were to have an emergency, but he also had a good sense of humor and liked to expound on his philosophy of life, which was of a very practical nature and not overly tainted by lofty idealism. He liked to think of himself as a pretty good amateur psychologist, and he enjoyed trying to "figure people out."

One day, as the airplane cruised along at 31,000 feet and each of us sat alone with his thoughts, Dan broke the silence and said, "You know, I'm a little tired of all these radio talk shows where women get to call in with all the problems they are having with their husbands. Maybe I could be a radio talk show host on a program just for men. Guys could call in their problems, and I could tell them how to solve them. I think that I could do just as good a job as anyone else I've heard on WLS."

The copilot turned around and asked, "What would you call your program?"

Dan replied, "I think I would call it 'Dan the Man.' I'd start out each program by saying, "Hi everybody, this is Dan. I'm not a therapist, I'm not a psychologist, I'm not a social worker, I'm just a regular guy. Call in your problems, and we'll work on them together, man to man."

John Stokes, the copilot, was becoming a little intrigued now with the idea of a radio talk show with a "regular guy" male perspective.

"OK, Dan, I'll be a sample caller. Let's see how you do."

"Fine, John, this is Dan the Man. How can I help?"

"Well, Dan, I am newly married, and I would like to know what you think is the most important thing a guy should do in a new marriage to set the ground for a good relationship?"

"Now listen, John. The most important thing of all is to get control of the money right away. If you get control of the money at the beginning, you have a better chance of holding on to that control later in the marriage. If you let that power slip away in the beginning, in five years she will have control of all the finances and you'll never get it back. Every time you want to buy a new fishing rod or have a little beer money, you will have to ask her for it. Get control of the money for a happy marriage. That's the key to everything, big guy."

"Uuuuuh, thanks, Dan, for your, uuuuuh, help. Bye."

John decided to try again and play another caller. "Hi Dan, this is Joe, and I've got a problem."

"Go ahead, Joe. This is Dan the Man ready to help, good buddy."

"Well, Dan, a few months ago I had an affair with a woman at work. We didn't plan anything. It just sort of happened. You know: Christmas party at the office, a few drinks, a back room with no lights where we were looking for more Coca-Cola. In the dark, I bumped into her while she was bending over some boxes. I apologized. She giggled. I giggled. I don't know why I ran my hand up her skirt, I didn't mean to, but she didn't stop me. We closed the door and locked it. My wife found out from a friend of a friend. For weeks now, she's been crying to all her friends about how I run around. Every woman in the neighborhood has heard about how I have cheated on my wife. I hate to take my car out of the garage in the morning to go to work because I feel like all the wives on the street are staring at me with disapproval."

"Joe, listen. Your problem is one of perspective. I had a similar problem when I was married. My wife did the same thing when she found out I had had an innocent little affair like yours."

"Well, did you feel ashamed too?"

"Not really, but, if you feel bad, just wait. It will pass, and things will probably get better. What happened with me was that after a few weeks of my wife's complaining over coffee to her friends and them telling her what a rat I was, I started to get phone calls whenever my wife left the house from several of the neighbor wives suggesting it would be nice if I would come over for coffee while their husbands were at work."

"Gee, thanks, Dan. I never looked at it like that."

"You're welcome, Joe. Have we got another caller?"

I decided to be a sample caller now. "Hi Dan, this is Bob, you've got a wonderful show and I love listening to your great advice. What would you tell someone if he thinks his wife is seeing someone else? What should he say to her?"

"Bob, don't say nothing. You go down to Radio Shack, and, for 50 dollars, you can buy all the equipment you need to tap the phone. I suggest doing it in the basement somewhere where your wife never goes. The little tape recorder you hook up to the phone will give you all the info you need. Because the most important thing you need to do is find out who the guy is and then you've got to get even."

"Well, Dan, I'm not a violent guy. I'm not ready to go *shoot* anyone."

223

"No, no, Bob. That's not how to get even. You'll just end up in jail. The key is to find out everything you can about the guy and then drive him crazy. Look, for example, once you know where he parks his car at night, you go down to the drug store and buy a package of feminine hygiene napkins. Stuff one of these into his gas tank. What happens is this. The napkin floats around in the gas tank. The car will run fine, but every once and a while the napkin will cover up the gas line and the engine will quit. He'll stop the car, the napkin floats away from the gas line, and now he can start the engine. The car may drive two or three days before the napkin floats over the gas line again. He'll spend a lot of money taking the car to mechanics who will charge him a lot of money to change parts, but eventually the engine is going to quit again."

"Well, Dan, I was thinking more about how to solve the problem with my wife."

"Oh yeah, you got to get even with her too—I forgot. One day just go over to your wife's boyfriend's house with a six-pack of beer. Knock on the door. Tell him who you are. He's going to get nervous. You can count on it. He doesn't know if you're carrying a gun. Smile. Be friendly. Tell him you'd like to have a little talk. You sit down together. You open up a beer, and then you thank him! Tell him how grateful you were that he came along so that you can get out of the marriage. Tell him about every little thing you couldn't stand about your wife. Don't sound mean. Just act like you are trying to help. Sort of like when you sell a used car to someone and you tell him about all of its little quirks. Finish your beer. Get up. Shake his hand. Tell him he can call you anytime he needs help. Leave. Get a divorce. Find another woman."

John Stokes and I didn't know how much of what Dan said was meant to be serious and how much he was pulling our legs, but we both agreed that the talk show would probably be an overnight success.

Dan had gone through a divorce. This I knew. It wasn't very amicable, either. After the divorce, Dan had dated a number of women. Finding women was never really difficult for him. He was dark, of Slovakian descent, and quite handsome. When I was between marriages, he and I would sometimes go to discotheques on layovers, where I would spend all night trying to get someone to dance with me while he would take his pick from the girls who would go up to him and ask for a dance. Yet, it was always apparent to me that despite all the attention he got from the opposite sex, his real wish was to find a soulmate. When he met Cheryl, it became obvious to those who knew him that he had met the woman he was looking for.

Cheryl had also left an unhappy marriage. After having had what she didn't want, she set out to have what she did want. When she met Dan, it didn't take long for her to decide that this would be the man to whom she would give her love for the rest of her days. Cheryl and Dan got married. They set out to build a life together. Dan continued flying. Cheryl had a small business of her own that she had been running for several years. They both had been hurt in their previous marriages, but their love for each other gradually healed all the old wounds. They bought a house. They had a son. Cheryl's first child. The child she had always dreamed of having.

In addition to the loving relationship he was building with Cheryl, Dan's career was also beginning to flower. The years he had spent in the flight engineer's seat on the B727 and the extra flying he had done in his free time to build hours eventually allowed him to move into the copilot position on the B727. Now he was doing what he had always wanted to do. He was at the controls of a transport jet aircraft. A few years later, he moved to copilot on the Lockheed L1011. His flying in the large, heavy jet took him all over the world. Dan crossed the Atlantic Ocean more times than he could count. He was becoming quite good at flying the airplane, and his judgment had been seasoned by ice, rain, turbulence, engine failures, and aircraft system problems. A captain position became open. Dan applied for the upgrade and got it. He would begin captain training in three months. His dream was beginning to become true. He felt that he was now, after many years of hard work, enjoying the love and success he had always wished for. He was 43 years old.

Six weeks before his class date for captain school, Dan visited the doctor. He was concerned that he seemed to be getting a lot of colds. The doctor examined him and drew a few blood samples.

"I'll have the results back on these in just a few days. Come see me on Thursday, and we'll see if we can get these colds cleared up."

Thursday was the day that would change Dan's life forever.

"I got the results back on your blood tests. Dan, I am afraid I have something difficult to tell you."

"Just tell me, Doctor." Dan was afraid he already knew what the doctor was going to tell him. Dan knew there was a hereditary disease that ran through his family.

"Dan, you have leukemia. It is one of the more uncommon types. What the disease really is, is a cancer of the bone marrow. The bone marrow is responsible for making new blood cells. When you have leukemia, the bone marrow is producing white blood cells at too rapid a rate. The cells don't go into the bloodstream as well-formed mature cells. They are malformed, and more and more they crowd out the healthy cells. As a result, your immune system becomes less and less able to fight off disease. There are treatments available, and we can start you on chemotherapy . . . ."

The doctor's words seemed to drift off in the distance. Although he was hearing what the doctor was saying, Dan's thoughts were elsewhere. He was thinking about how one of his favorite uncles had died from the same disease. He was also thinking about how everything he had worked for seemed to be slipping away from him.

226

He felt as if some sinister great power had suddenly taken hold of the events of his life and that now he had no control over what would happen next. He thought of Cheryl, and he thought of how her happiness, the happiness they had built together, would turn into a daily and exhausting struggle for life over death. Until the end came.

Dan went home to his wife, and when the seriousness of what he had to tell her really penetrated both of their consciousnesses, they cried together. Dan told her that he didn't want to put this burden on her. He told her he just wanted to die so that she could go on with her life. He wanted to go away so that she could start over with someone else.

Cheryl took both of Dan's hands in hers. Through the tears in her own eyes, she looked straight through the tears in Dan's eyes right into his soul. She willed her heart to send him a message of love on silent golden wings. Then, she spoke the words that Dan would never forget his whole life, the words that would give him the strength to endure everything that he would go through in the coming months.

"Dan, I have loved you almost since we first met. I truly cherish the many gentle, beautiful, wonderful qualities that you have inside of you. Before I met you, there was always something missing from my life. You make me feel complete. You are my lover, my friend, my companion. No matter what happens now, I promise I will be with you at your side. No matter what happens, I promise you will be able to count on my love. And I know, with God's help, we can face all the challenges that lie ahead of us. Dan, I will fight this battle with you. I love you with all my heart."

Dan began his chemotherapy. There was a new experimental drug that the doctor wanted to try. The drugs prevented him from flying from the first pill he took. He experienced nausea, and he endured excruciating pain in his bones. One day, Dan showed me the type of needle that the medical technicians employed to extract periodic bone marrow samples from him. It looked more like a small nail to me than a needle. Dan said that they forced the needle through the bone of his hip until it reached the bone marrow. He said when they actually extract the marrow, the pain is indescribable.

Dan's condition did not improve. He became weaker and weaker. He experienced constant pain. The marrow samples showed the cancer was getting worse.

His doctor told him, "Dan, it doesn't look like we are having much success with the chemotherapy. I think it's time we began thinking about a bone marrow transplant."

There was a special hospital in Houston. Dan went there. After a long series of tests and another round of chemotherapy, the doctors decided that a bone marrow transplant was the best option. Although the chances for a complete cure were low, there was a chance.

The procedure would involve exposing Dan to very high levels of radiation, which would effectively kill all of his bone marrow—healthy as well as cancerous. After all of his own cells were killed, healthy cells from a donor would be transplanted into his body with the hope that the healthy cells would produce new cells that were not cancerous. Dan's oldest son, Daniel, asked to be the donor. After tests, the doctors found that Daniel's marrow was a very good match to that of his father's. That meant there was a good chance that, after the transplant, the doctors would be able to control the tendency of the body to reject tissue that was not its own. Daniel was approved by the medical team to be the bone marrow donor who would save his father's life.

One problem emerged. Daniel was only 15 years old and was under the physical custody of Dan's ex-wife. She agreed to allow Dan's son to undergo the procedure, but she insisted on accompanying him to Houston. Dan and Cheryl would have to pay her expenses.

228

The doctors performed the procedure, and medically it was a success. The son's cells started to grow in the father's body, giving him a new chance for life. The drugs the doctors administered to Dan kept the host-graft reaction in check. Dan was extremely weak by this time. He had lost a great amount of weight, and the combination of illness, drugs, and radiation made him into, as Dan described himself, an old man. He spent a great deal of time in the hospital, and later a recovery facility in Houston, before he would be able to return home to Chicago. During all this time, Cheryl's love kept her true to her pledge. She accompanied Dan through every trial of Dan's illness. This was not easy for her. She still had to run her business, keep up the family finances, care for Dan and Cheryl's son, Christian, and travel by airplane back and forth between Chicago and Houston.

One act of kindness I witnessed I will never forget. The chief pilot of Southwest Airlines in Chicago, upon hearing of the plight of a fellow pilot and the bravery and dedication of that pilot's wife, took the initiative to arrange a special pass so that Cheryl could travel non-revenue back and forth to Houston. The same chief pilot initiated a collection among the Southwest pilots based in Chicago and sent that money over to our airline, IAT, to be added to the money we were collecting to help the couple.

When Dan was finally brought back to Chicago, he was a shell of the man he had been only one year before. He had no strength of his own, and had to be moved in a wheelchair. His spirit was almost broken, but Cheryl assured him of her love and somehow kept him from going into a deep depression. The survival rate for the procedure he had undergone was low. Most people, including Dan, didn't think he was going to make it. Sometime during this period, Jurig Ritter sent Dan a personal letter of encouragement and raised Dan's rank in the company to Honorary Captain. Someone mistakenly put a message on the internet to all the IAT pilots that Dan had died. But Dan didn't die. Although the drugs he was taking to combat the host-graft reaction caused him tremendous

229

discomfort, Dan continued to fight back. He began to look at each new day as a special gift from God. He also began to correspond with others who had undergone the same procedure as himself. He read medical articles and learned as much as he could about his disease. As his knowledge grew, he didn't feel quite so powerless. Slowly, he started to regain his spirit and his strength. He could now move about the house easily, and he could begin to enjoy having visitors.

The doctors watched Dan's blood counts closely. And so did Dan. Although nowhere near normal, there were definite signs of improvement. When Dan passed the 90-day point of his recovery from the radiation therapy, he started to feel like he really had a chance. He and Cheryl, alone one night together, lit a candle and tearfully celebrated that he had made it through the most critical period.

The blood counts improved. Dan became stronger and stronger. He began to have more contact with friends. His weakened legs still made it difficult for him to go up and down stairs, but he was able to, once again, enjoy the freedom of driving his car short distances. In the middle of all this triumph, disaster now again came into his life. The drugs used initially to control the host-graft disease had nearly destroyed the functioning of his kidneys. Most people don't give much thought to their kidneys, but they are very important organs. The kidneys make it possible to control the water levels in the body, which has a direct effect on blood pressure; they maintain a balance of important electrolytes; and they allow the body to rid itself of the unwanted end products of body metabolism. Without properly functioning kidneys, Dan would now be required to be hooked up to an artificial kidney machine three times a week. The only miracle that could free him from this routine would be a kidney transplant.

Dan got himself on the recipient list in case a donor kidney were to become available. He had very little hope that this would ever occur. The doctor explained to him that because of his age and his medical history, he would have low priority on the list of recipients. Dan also had a relatively rare tissue type that could not be easily matched. In spite of this, Dan and Cheryl regularly prayed for a miracle.

Late one night, more than a thousand miles away from Chicago, a young man was driving home alone along a rural highway in Texas. He took a curve too fast. The car left the road and hit a pole. The young man died on the operating table while the doctors struggled to save his life. His driver's license identified him as an organ donor. Dan and Cheryl would never have prayed for this kind of miracle, but nevertheless, for them, a miracle had occurred.

The telephone rang after midnight at the Blackton home. Dan was to go to the hospital right away. The doctor told him about the young man who had died in the automobile accident. His tissue type was almost the same rare type as Dan's. At that moment, one of that young man's kidneys was on a Learjet that was racing for Chicago.

The transplant operation was a success. Because of the donor's youth, the new kidney functioned extremely well. It would be many months before the incision in his abdomen would heal completely, but Dan was now free of the dialysis machine. This freedom opened up a new world of possibilities. For the first time in years he was well enough to take on a full-time job. He began teaching ground school at a commuter airline. He had never lost his love for aviation. One year later, Dan received incredible news. His health had improved so greatly that the FAA had approved his request for a third-class airman medical certificate. He would be able to fly private planes again. Dan is now grateful for each new day that life gives him. He says he finally understands what real love is all about, and he calls himself the most blessed pilot in the world. I always think of him as the most courageous.

XVIII

Pause and Reflection

I will never forget the feeling of joy that came over my spirit when the small training aircraft first left the ground on my introductory flying lesson. I felt as if a whole new world of freedom and adventure was suddenly opening up for me. As the motor churned loudly to turn the propellor that would pull us through the air, the little aircraft lifted the instructor and me higher and higher while the ground slowly dropped away. Down below one could see the cars, roads, stores, houses, and people all appearing to get smaller. I was looking at the world from a perspective I had never had before—the front seat of an airplane. The thought ran through my mind, "We must look very small to God." We climbed to almost 3,000 feet above the ground! That seemed very high to me at the time. All around us we had clear skies. Far above us there were just a few scattered clouds. My instructor handed me the controls and began to show me how I could make the aircraft turn, climb and descend. The aircraft responded quickly to my touch, and the sense of freedom I was feeling was almost intoxicating.

Like all freedoms, flight also brought responsibilities. My wonderful instructor, Jack Rossolla, allowed me to enjoy for a while the pleasure I was experiencing in my innocence, but he knew that there was much more that he was going to have to teach me if I were to become a pilot. Almost anyone can be taught to control an aircraft. Controlling it with skill and precision is a little more difficult. And controlling it in accordance with the applicable regulations, procedures, and good operating practices is more difficult yet. But over the years I learned all these things. Or, it is better to say, at least I have tried as best I could. As I near the 20,000 hour mark in my flying career I sometimes wonder where all the time has gone.

235

Has it really been 30 years since I made that first introductory flight? Many of the people I have met along the way have passed on, just as not too many years from now so will I. Cycle of life. I am grateful that I have been able to do the kind of work that many dream of— the kind of work that I dreamed of. It took effort to get here, but I don't regret a single moment of the journey. It has all molded me in some way, the good moments and the bad moments. I have doubts about my abilities occasionally, but I have also come to the conclusion that having doubts about oneself is much better than not having any.

I realize when I take these few moments of reflection that I have been forced through my profession to see the world in a very unique way. The sky for me, perhaps, is still a place where I feel a wondrous amount of freedom, but it is also a place where I feel a tremendous amount of responsibility. Where a non-pilot may see a clear empty sky, I see airways that crisscross each other all over the globe. I see regulations that must be complied with and procedures that must be followed. And I also see the possibilities for disaster that exist if these procedures are not followed and these regulations not complied with. Where some might just see wind rustling the tops of trees, I see the difficulties the wind may cause on landing if it is blowing from an unfavorable direction or if it is too gusty. Where some might look at snow and think it is beautiful as it covers the ground in white, I see slippery runways and a reduced capability of my airplane to stop quickly. Where there are clouds and thunderstorms, some may look up and see rain and interesting lightning displays, while I see the possibility of turbulence that can tear an airplane apart or windshear that can force an aircraft to hit the ground while it is trying to land. Where some see a hot, sunny day as a good time to relax, I will see that my airplane needs more distance to take off and that it will perform poorly if an engine should fail at a critical moment. The hours of darkness are not necessarily a time to rest. I may be flying all night. Mountains may be beautiful and picturesque, but flying into one means almost certain death for everyone on board.

For the passenger, a destination has meaning in terms of what he will do once he is on the ground. Although pilots look forward to layovers in new places, they remain aware that the most important part of the journey is the process of getting there. The pilot will look at each airport in terms of types of approaches, runways, ATC procedures, hazards, his experience there with the weather.

Now, after 30 years of flying, there are many airports recorded in my logbook. The entries trigger memories. Some more than others. Here a few examples:

Chicago Midway—I have made hundreds of flights into this airport. From the cockpit of a large jet it looks like a small postage stamp surrounded by houses, train tracks, and city streets. This is not an airport that will be forgiving of mistakes. The runways are short. Often there are crosswinds. Cloud cover and reduced visibility can also be factors. The air traffic controllers like to keep the airplanes fast right up to a few miles outside of the Outer Marker for each approach. It is up to the pilot to slow down after that, and it takes skill to get the airplane quickly stabilized on profile at the proper approach speed. You have to be mentally prepared to go-around and try the approach again if everything does not look right as you get close to the landing threshold. Speed and altitude have to be correct. If you make a nice smooth landing here, you go home feeling that you have been just a little bit lucky. Smooth landings are not the real goal at this airport. It is much wiser to get the airplane down and stopped rather than holding the aircraft off the ground to try to get that perfect touchdown. I know of at least two incidents where a jet aircraft landed long and nearly went through the fence at the end of the runway. At home, I have a personal flight simulator set up to fly like my airplane. On days off I occasionally use it to practice landings at Midway. Each landing I evaluate for speed control, profile, and point of touchdown. Of course, in the simulator, I can also allow myself the luxury of judging the smoothness of touchdown, too. So far this practice has served me very well.

237

Flight Simulator on Multiple Screens Using *Wideview*
program by Luciano Napolitano

Los Angeles—This airport has nice long runways. Getting the airplane on the ground and stopped is no problem here. Even the weather is good most of the time. Fog can be a problem in the early morning hours. It usually burns off quickly so that there is enough visibility to make instrument approaches. I actually prefer it if the weather is a little down at this airport, because that means once I have been assigned a particular arrival and instrument approach for a particular runway it will probably not be changed. When the weather is good, the controllers have a tendency to switch runway landing clearances to accommodate a faster flow of traffic.

Many times I have been assigned the arrival to runway 25 Left, on the south side of the airport, only to be recleared by ATC to change over to the arrival to runway 24 Right, which is on the north side of the airport. Most 757 crews find it prudent to set up both arrivals in the flight management computer so as not to have to do a lot of last-minute typing if the arrival clearance gets changed late. On a few occasions, after having been switched from the arrival to 25L to the arrival to 24R, I have been given a last-minute change to land on runway 24L.

In February of 1991, a US Air B737 landing on runway 24L crashed into a Skywest Metroliner that was in position waiting for takeoff clearance on the same runway. The B737 had originally been assigned the arrival for 25L. After starting the arrival, the B737 was then instructed to turn right and intercept the localizer for runway 24R. Finally, once the B737 called the airport in sight, it was cleared to land on 24L. The NTSB attributed the major cause of the accident to the fact that the particular procedures utilized in the tower overburdened the tower controller, and she forgot that she had an aircraft holding in position on 24L when she cleared the B737 to land. The 737 flight crew did not see the other aircraft holding in position until after they were on the ground and it was too late to avoid hitting it. The crew of the Metroliner holding on 24L did not notice that another aircraft had been cleared to land behind them on the same runway.

Orlando—I have made many many trips to Orlando. Normally the weather is very good. On one particular trip that originated in San Juan, Puerto Rico, the weather was not good. As we approached from the southeast, we were in solid IFR conditions and we could see storms around the airport on our radar. Traffic was still being vectored to the final approach course to runway 18R, but it would be only a matter of time before the storms would reach the field. The controllers were trying to deal with a number of aircraft when we called up for our initial vectors. Our instructions took us on a northerly heading where another cluster of cells were visible on the radar. In a few minutes our course would have put us directly into a large cell. We tried to get back to the controller on the radio to tell him that we needed to turn because of our proximity to a storm. The controller was too busy with other aircraft for us to give him our message. I finally used emergency authority and turned the aircraft away from the storm. On his radar scope the controller saw us turning and realized right away why. He gave us a new heading assignment away from the cells and then issued us holding instructions. We were practically on top of the fix when we received the holding clearance. There was no time to enter the information into the FMC to get a graphic display of the holding pattern on the EHSI instrument map display. I reverted to doing it the "old-fashioned way" by tuning in the frequency on the VOR and using the RMI and DME to get established in the hold. Years of flying airplanes with old style instruments helped in that moment. Once established in the hold we followed up by entering the holding pattern into the FMC.

On the radar, it now appeared the storms were moving very close to the airport. We decided it would be prudent to go to St. Petersburg, where the weather was good, and wait until the storms cleared out of the Orlando area.

Detroit—We received a reverser isolation valve fault indication on the left engine as we were climbing out after takeoff. I remembered the Lauda B767 flying out of Bangkok that had an engine go into reverse during cruise, causing it to crash. We throttled back the left engine to idle as a precaution and returned to the field using single-engine landing procedures. It was just an indication problem.

Washington National—I often ask myself why this airport is still open. Close to the south lies Dulles International, a modern, well-equipped airport with several long runways and good approach procedures. Of course, I know why Washington National remains open. It is close to the capitol, and it takes very little time to get to Washington D.C. from this airport. Its proximity to the capitol also means that north of the airport there is nothing but prohibited airspace. For obvious reasons, aircraft are not allowed to take off or land directly over the White House. Approaches to the south runway allow a nice view of the Lincoln Memorial, Jefferson Memorial, the Washington Monument, and the White House for passengers sitting on the left side of the airplane, but the pilots are usually working too hard executing the approach to take much time to enjoy the sights. The normal approach procedures require that aircraft landing to the south must follow an offset final approach course to the airport that avoids the prohibited airspace. Once under the cloud cover, the pilot must make a turn at low altitude, and possibly in low visibility, to line up with the runway. Making the turn can be challenging with a crosswind, and since the runway is not very long, there is not a lot of room to maneuver if the turn is misjudged. The pilot has to be ready for a go-around if he finds he has not executed the turn properly.

Riga, Latvia—My first time in an ex-communist country. The flying procedures were different. We had to use meters instead of feet for altitude. Wind was reported in meters per second, not knots. The controller's knowledge of English was certainly minimal. Our knowledge of Latvian? Zero. Still, we executed the approach and landing without difficulty, and the crew was treated to a few free days to explore the city. I walked around the parks, visited the art museums, and wandered the main market. Consumer goods were not in abundance. The copilot had been here before. He had a

241

Russian girlfriend. She was always asking him for money. It became apparent to me that young Russian women held a precarious place in Latvian society. Once the Russians had ruled. Now Latvia was an independent state. Russian Latvians found it difficult to get work as Latvian became the official language of the country and Russian was gradually discarded. It made me sad to realize that a very beautiful, nicely dressed girl I had seen standing around the shabby downtown market was probably a prostitute with few options to earn a living.

Atlanta—No doubt the worst crisis of my career. It was here that I performed an emergency landing to get medical treatment for passengers who had been injured in an unexpected encounter with severe turbulence over Georgia while en route to Chicago from Aruba. Circumnavigating storms, our aircraft suddenly encountered turbulence that began as a minor rumble and increased in intensity until the whole airplane shook. At the first sign that we might be encountering rough air, Mike Jones, the copilot, turned on the seat belt sign. The air had been perfectly smooth before the first minor rumble had started. Suddenly we were hit with an updraft and then a downdraft that caused two passengers in the back of the airplane who had not fastened their seat belts to be thrown violently against the luggage rack above them. A man suffered a blow to the head, and the other passenger, a woman, received a deep cut on her head that began to bleed profusely, splattering blood on the whole area around her. The whole incident, from the first mild shaking of the airplane to the sudden severe jolt, lasted only 17 seconds. No signs of a storm ahead of us were displayed on the radar, nor did the clouds we were approaching appear particularly menacing in any way. We had taken a turn to go around some clouds that were higher than us miles off to the right, but, apparently, we were unfortunate enough to encounter an isolated column of rapidly rising air.

My first reaction was one of shock, and I thought we had flown through a storm. But there had been nothing depicted ahead of us on the radar, and the only visible buildup was at least 10 miles ahead and off to our right. After the encounter, the flight attendants called up front to state we had serious injuries in back with two people needing immediate medical attention. When I realized we had serious injuries, I admit it took me a few minutes to regain my composure, but we requested an immediate emergency landing at the closest major airport, Atlanta. There followed a hurried descent during which Mike searched for the correct approach plates, we set up the navigation computers for the approach to the airport, and we made arrangements for emergency vehicles and medical personnel to meet us on the ground. ATC was very helpful, quickly giving us the radar vectors and clearances we needed for the descent and the approach.

In spite of the fact I knew we had serious injuries in the cabin, I concentrated on executing a safe approach and landing. After clearing the runway, we were immediately met by the follow-me vehicle we had requested to be waiting, and we were quickly led to the gate, where emergency personnel were standing by to meet us. The injured passengers were quickly taken from the airplane and rushed to a hospital. The rest of the passengers deplaned the aircraft to clear customs.

After the airplane had been emptied of passengers, I went to the back of the aircraft to survey the damage. The sight of the blood on the seats, ceiling and floor made me feel that I never wanted to fly an aircraft again. For the next four days I agonized over the condition of the injured passengers and wanted to give up flying forever. At the end of that time, the hospital released the two patients. They were bandaged and bruised but suffered no broken bones or serious permanent damage.

I felt as if I were in the middle of a bad dream, and I kept asking myself over and over again how this had happened. We had flown through some benign-looking clouds. The kind we go through every day with hardly a bump in the air. Why had we now, instead, been slammed with a severe jolt? Where was all my experience now? And

243

what about all the regular studying I did of procedures and aviation topics? How had all of this failed me? Other line pilots and management pilots offered their moral support. Some related to me their own encounters with unexpected rough air. They emphasized to me that all over the world this happens occasionally, often with more severe injuries than had occurred on our flight.

Retired Captain Charlie Steele, who, long ago, had trained me to fly the B757, and who had been my supervisor for many years, called me on the phone:

"Rich, in my opinion you have always been an excellent professional pilot. You have been doing a great job carrying passengers for over 20 years. I don't want you to lose your confidence over this. You encountered unexpected turbulence. That could have happened to anyone...."

I very much appreciated and needed to hear those encouraging words, spoken as a father would to a son.

The copilot and I had to appear at an investigation to give our account of the event. We were returned to line flying a few days later. It took me months to get over the emotional impact the whole incident had on me. I threw myself harder than ever into studying my manuals, and slowly worked my confidence back up to its previous level. What probably won't surprise you is that I also fell back on my martial arts training to help me rebuild my spirit and avoid a depression. Life goes on after a crisis. We can choose to be part of it or not. My spirit chose life.

San Francisco—During preflight preparations I felt a slight binding in the elevator controls. The mechanics quickly checked the controls and said they felt no binding. I insisted there was a problem, and I decided I wouldn't fly the airplane. I received a message to contact the maintenance control supervisor back at headquarters.

244

"Well, Captain, I am going to have the mechanics run a series of checks on the elevators. If all the checks are satisfactory, will you take the airplane?"

"Not unless you can explain why the controls seem to be binding. I don't think you can always find the answer in a book."

This wasn't the answer he wanted, and I ended up having to speak with the director of operations. The director of operations criticized me for making up my own procedures, and I replied that sometimes that is what we as pilots have to do when established norms don't seem to solve a problem.

We were at a standoff, and management wanted to remove me from the flight and call in another captain. Because I was so insistent, the mechanics actually checked the bearings in the control system to the elevator. They found one to be completely defective. It turned out that not only the bearing on that particular aircraft had to be replaced, but Boeing decided it should be changed on the entire fleet of B757s. Our crew was given a replacement aircraft, and we continued on our assigned flight. The whole incident became referred to as The Princess and the Pea.

When I fly into Madrid I always know that I can look forward to having dinner with friends I met years ago when I was a young man in the Air Force stationed in Toledo, Spain. Going into San Juan, Puerto Rico, one can enjoy the view of Old San Juan as the aircraft approaches Runway 10 from the west. If it is a layover flight, there are plenty of bars, restaurants, and clubs to make the stay entertaining. Flying to Frankfurt, I particularly like the fact that our hotel is in Darmstadt. My great-grandmother was born in this city and grew up there before she emigrated, at age 18, to the United States. In Naples is the restaurant Trattoria, where our whole crew sang songs and danced until the early morning hours. The owner of the restaurant closed the doors to the public at the regular time and made it a private party for all of those dining who wanted to stay. He even rolled out an electronic piano and provided some of the music himself. Of course, the Italian men present made every attempt to romance the flight attendants. I don't remember how successful they were. In Paris we had a similar party later that month.

As I look back on all this—the people, the places, the planes, the many challenges and rewards—I know life has been very good to me. Throughout the history of man, millions have been born enslaved, lived enslaved, and died enslaved. I feel deep gratitude that I was born in a time and place where freedom is cherished and where an individual has the right and opportunity to make choices about how to live his life. I am also thankful for the opportunities I have had to grow as a person. Many times that growth has been accompanied by pain. But life, just like flying, is not only about destinations. What is just as important is how we accomplish the journey we have chosen, and what we learn along the way.

XIX

Beautiful Worlds

Preston, I was not flying on September 11, 2001 when Al Qaeda fanatics hijacked four airliners with the intention of using them as flying bombs. Three of the terrorist teams were successful in reaching their targets. Two planes destroyed the World Trade Center in New York. One airplane crashed into the Pentagon. The fourth airplane crashed into a field in Pennsylvania. Evidence seems to show that the passengers on this flight became aware of their situation and attempted to fight the hijackers. With millions, and in great sadness, I watched over and over again the videos that captured the moments when the airplanes crashed into the Twin Towers of the World Trade Center. And I watched everything that followed.

Once it became apparent that commercial airliners had been deliberately used as weapons of mass destruction, the U.S. government took immediate steps to prevent any other possibly planned hijackings. Air Traffic Control facilities ordered all aircraft to proceed to the nearest suitable airport and land. All commercial air traffic was stopped. Passengers were left stranded all over the country. Initially, only military, police, or emergency aircraft were allowed into the skies.

The first thing I decided, after I recovered from the shock of seeing the destruction caused by the hijackers, was that I would not let any terrorists deter me from doing my job. It seems every other pilot in the country decided the same, because I know of no pilot who quit flying after 9/11 out of fear of future hijackings. Second, an understanding arose among all of us pilots that we would continue flying as long as people wanted air service, and that we would fight to the death if anyone tried to take over our airplanes. This attitude was in sharp contrast to everything we had been taught about hijacking procedures up to that time.

Before 9/11, all U.S. pilots were taught what was called the "Common Strategy." I and thousands of other pilots were indoctrinated year after year in recurrent training classes into thinking that the best way to deal with hijackers was to remain calm and fly them to wherever they wanted to go. We sat through boring videos and listened to security experts tell us all about the undesirability of attempting to overpower hijackers. The possibility of suicidal religious fanatics taking over the airplane and using it as a bomb was never discussed. Even after 9/11 the government resisted any idea that pilots should be armed to be able to defend the cockpit against intruders. That same government, however, has fighter jets standing by to be scrambled in case an aircraft is hijacked by terrorists. Their mission? Intercept the hijacked aircraft and shoot it down before it can reach a major American city.

As soon as flights were resumed, I was assigned a trip. My flight was to begin at Chicago Midway and fly to Seattle. When I reported for duty I expected to find an empty airport and no passengers willing to fly so soon after seeing the images of crashing airplanes on television. Instead, the airport was full of men, women, and children who evidently were not going to allow terrorists to scare them off either. It turned out that my flight was about half full. I felt that was quite a lot of passengers, considering the circumstances. As I watched the passengers boarding our flight, I noticed that there was some tension and apprehension. I realized that taking this flight was a deliberate act of courage for many—possibly all. It also became apparent to me that the group was composed of people from different races and ethnic backgrounds.

Observing the courage of the people boarding the airplane made me feel that I should go back to the cabin and address them face to face once everyone was seated. I don't remember exactly what I said, but it was close to this:

"Ladies and Gentlemen, I am Richard Reynard, and I am your captain on this trip today. Normally I would speak to you from the cockpit, but I felt because of the events of the last few days, you might feel better if I were to come out here and say a few words. I thought perhaps that having just a little closer contact with the person who is flying your airplane today would help to put some of you a little more at ease before the flight.

"We are all sad over what has happened. I wanted to assure all of you that we are planning on a safe flight today. You have seen the increased security procedures. Most of you probably had to stand in line quite a while to be screened before being able to enter the secure portion of the airport. I am aware that many of you may be a little apprehensive. But I am also aware that each of you has made the decision to not be dominated by fear.

"I would like to ask that you look around at your neighbors for a moment. You will notice that we have black people, white people, Latins, Asians, and Native Americans on this airplane. I would guess that quite a few different languages and religions are represented here, too. That's America. It is a place where somehow we have managed to learn enough tolerance to enable people of different races and philosophies to live together and enjoy a level of freedom found in only a few countries. As a nation, we represent an example of how people with different backgrounds can learn to live together. We know we are not perfect, but we do offer, at least, a vision of hope to the world. This is something that those who would attack us will never be able to understand or overcome."

There was a smattering of applause, indicating at least some appreciation for what I had said. I felt that perhaps my comments might have been a little over-patriotic or over-simplified. But my intention had not been to give a balanced discourse on world politics. I was only trying to make my passengers feel better before we began the flight. I learned later that other pilots made similar speeches that day. Some even gave instructions to their passengers on what to do to help defend the airplane if a similar hijacking were to occur. Our flight to Seattle turned out to be smooth and enjoyable.

Going to work every day thinking that somewhere in the world there was a fanatic who would be willing to slit my throat with a box cutter encouraged me to try to understand what these terrorists hoped to accomplish by ruthlessly killing unsuspecting men, women, and children. The fundamentalists who are claiming to represent true Islam are much different from the Muslims I met in Iran and Turkey. Some of those friends invited me into their homes for dinner, where we shared ideas and music together. With other Muslim friends I rode horses, worked on computer programming, or practiced karate. One of the great highlights of my time in Turkey was the joyous Muslim wedding, full of singing and dancing, that I was invited to attend. These were some of my first impressions of Islam. They stand in sharp contrast to the world it seems fundamentalist Muslims wish to create.

If one looks at the "ideal" Muslim society that the extremist Taliban movement has created in Afghanistan, one sees it is just another repressive police state. Here are some of its major characteristics:

— Institution of religious law. To back up their dictates, rulers claim divine authority that cannot be debated or questioned.

— Fostering an atmosphere of intimidation through the use of cruel and appalling punishments such as burying gay people alive, chopping off hands of thieves, and publicly stoning adulterers or unmarried lovers.

— Women confined to their homes and allowed on the streets only if completely covered.

— Women not allowed to work.

— Education of women banned.

— Requiring that houses where women live have the windows painted over.

— No tolerance for any other religions.

— Destruction of ancient Buddhist statues (priceless historical treasures that can never be replaced).

— Young men whipping people in the streets, especially women, for any perceived infraction of laws.

— Banning of music.

— Banning of movies.

— Banning of television programs.

— Banning of toys.

— Banning of kites and paper bags.

If this is what radical Islam is offering to the world, it is a way of life I could never accept. Repressive regimes have appeared and disappeared all through human history. Their Gods or philosophies may differ, but their methods are much the same: Fear and intimidation. Suppression of any opposing views. Their religious leaders make it their duty to expound on what God said and what God meant when He said it. Some warn of "final judgments." Others are not willing to wait for God to make the judgments. Instead, they presume the authority to mete out God's punishments on earth. How can any religious leader dare to claim the right to burn people at the stake, drown them, torture them, bury them alive, or create any other type of suffering in God's name?

It is true that free systems have many problems and are corrupt in many ways. Just because there is freedom in a society does not make it perfect. People can use their freedom in bad ways, and often do. But in a free society at least there exists the hope and possibility of change and evolution toward a better day. In my heart, I have wrestled for years with the concept of religion. I value my spirit, but I've concluded I really don't want anyone to tell me how I should think. This doesn't mean that I don't respect the faiths of others. But for me, personally, I find it preferable to live in a world of conflicting ideas and philosophies.

If one believes doubt is more valuable than faith, where does he receive his moral guidance? I have decided that, for me, above any "-ism," simply a deep respect for freedom and the dignity of the individual is what will lead us to a world of peace and prosperity. For guidance one need look no farther than the Declaration of Human Rights adopted by the United Nations in 1948. I am including a copy of it with this letter for you to look over. The first five articles particularly move me. See if they touch you as they touch me.

Article 1. All human beings are born free and equal in dignity and rights. They are endowed with reason and conscience and should act towards one another in a spirit of brotherhood.

Article 2. Everyone is entitled to all the rights and freedoms set forth in this Declaration, without distinction of any kind, such as race, colour, sex, language, religion, political or other opinion, national or social origin, property, birth or other status....

Article 3. Everyone has the right to life, liberty and security of person.

Article 4. No one shall be held in slavery or servitude; slavery and the slave trade shall be prohibited in all their forms.

Article 5. No one shall be subjected to torture or to cruel, inhuman or degrading treatment or punishment.

Preston, as I've tried to tell you about my life in aviation, more than ever I realize that this career has given me not only a great gift of freedom but also the opportunity to traverse many geographical, psychological, emotional, and philosophical borders. Flying has been a passion for me since the very first time I gently held the controls of an airplane and felt it respond to my touch. Did I like every aspect of this career? No, of course not. No matter what path we choose to follow in life, there will always be things we don't like. We must expect to see our naive misconceptions and fantasies fall away as we gain a more mature relationship with whatever career we wish to follow.

But aviation has forced me to meet challenges. It has taught me to handle responsibility. It has made me find ways to deal with the stress of knowing that I hold hundreds of lives in my hands. It has shown me how to face fear. That doesn't mean I am never afraid. Flying has given me pride. And what is even more important, it has humbled me. Time and again, without mercy, it shows me my flaws and limitations. It has not tempered me into the person I would eventually like to be, yet it has carried me a few steps along the path. It has taught me the importance of not assuming one has all the answers.

With these two letters, Grandson, I have asked you to fly with me. I'm hoping that my journey will help you in some way through your own journey through life. Forgive me, if in my zeal to point out a few of life's pitfalls, I have sounded a little like a flight instructor teaching his student how to fly. But as you fly through life, my wish is that you fly well, with courage, integrity, and generosity of spirit. Try to remember that the freedom of your mind is precious. There will be many who will try to take it from you. Always retain your right to question and to learn. Resist the temptation to accept comforting answers to life's great questions, and your mind will remain free. If your mind remains free, you will be able to tolerate and appreciate that others may think and believe differently from you. Above all, search out your own path. Find the Way that is best for you. But as you search, attempt to do it in love and compassion. Forgive yourself and others for not being perfect. The world has enough hate in it already. There is no need to add to it.

Although I would fight those who would try to harm my loved ones, I hate no one. If I were to die today, the fact that I follow no dogma, no theology, does not worry me. If there is a God, I feel peaceful about meeting Him/Her. In my heart, perhaps I have already done this flying at 35,000 feet.

I love you, Grandson,

Grandpa Reynard

12/22/01

DEFINITIONS AND NOTES

ACCURACY LANDINGS - Training maneuver designed to teach the pilot to be able to land precisely at a spot he chooses if the engine should fail and he cannot restart it. Power is reduced to near idle while in the vicinity of an airport. The pilot must now judge his distance to the point of landing, then maneuver the aircraft so as to touch down no more than 200 feet past the runway threshold.

ADI - ATTITUDE DIRECTOR INDICATOR - An instrument that combines the functions of an ATTITUDE INDICATOR and a FLIGHT DIRECTOR commands on one display. The attitude indicator, or artificial horizon, portion of the instrument provides the pilot with information on the pitch and bank of the aircraft. The flight director commands display the correct amount of pitch and bank required to fly a particular desired trajectory.

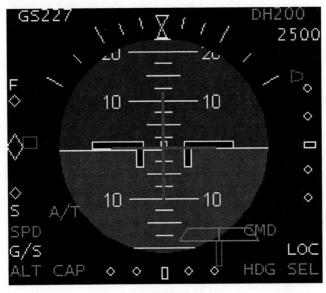

ADI

AILERONS - Control surfaces hinged at the back of the wings, which by deflecting up or down bank the airplane.

AIRLINE TRANSPORT PILOT RATING - The license required of a pilot-in-command who operates large aircraft in commercial operations.

AIRSPEED - Speed of the aircraft relative to the air through which it is moving.

AIRSPEED INDICATOR - Instrument used by the pilot to determine the airspeed of the aircraft. It is usually placed on the instrument panel directly to the left of the ATTITUDE INDICATOR.

AIR START UNIT - A ground unit that is used to provide air for an engine start when the aircraft has an inoperative APU.

AIRWAY - An air route marked by radio navigation aids such as a Very High Frequency Omnirange (VOR) or a Non-Directional Beacon (NDB).

ALTIMETER - An instrument for measuring in feet the height of the airplane above sea level. It is usually placed on the instrument panel directly to the right of the ATTITUDE INDICATOR.

ALTITUDE - The vertical distance from a given reference level (usually sea level) to an aircraft in flight.

ALPA - Airline Pilots Association - Largest pilot union in the United States.

APU - AUXILIARY POWER UNIT - A small turbine engine located in the tail section on the B757 that is used to provide electrical power when the engines are not running and to provide air flow for starting the engines. If the APU is inoperative, electrical power from an electrical cart on the ground is used to power the electrical system until an engine is started and an engine-driven generator becomes available. Also, without an APU, an air cart, or AIR START UNIT, must be used to provide air for engine start.

ASCEND - Climb the aircraft.

ATTITUDE - Position of the airplane relative to the horizon, such as a climbing attitude or descending attitude.

ATTITUDE INDICATOR - Instrument by which the pilot determines if the nose of the aircraft is above or below the horizon and if the wings are banked. The old term for this instrument is the ARTIFICIAL HORIZON. The attitude indicator is usually placed on the instrument panel directly in front of the pilot.

BANK - A flight maneuver in which one wing points toward the ground and the other to the sky. Banking the wings will cause the aircraft to turn.

BRIJJ OUTER COMPASS LOCATOR - A Non-Directional Beacon (NDB) co-located with an OUTER MARKER (OM) about five miles from the runway along the ILS approach path to Runway 28R at San Francisco. Outer Compass Locators (LOMs) are often located along approach paths to runways. They are named with five-letter identifiers. Other typical LOMs are ERMIN, KEDZI, and VEALS.

CEILING - Height above ground of cloud bases.

CHART - An aeronautical map showing information of use to the pilot in going from one place to another. Pilots use one type of chart for visual navigation. They use other types of charts for instrument navigation.

CDU - CONTROL DISPLAY UNIT - Combination of keypad and small computer screen used to input and display flight management

Control Display Unit
Flight Management Computer

computer information. On the B757 there are normally two CDUs and two FMCs.

COURSE - The direction over the earth's surface that an airplane is intended to travel.

CROSSBLEED START - Use of air bled from compressors of a running engine to turn the starter of a non-running engine. Used in situations when no APU is available on the aircraft to provide air for starting of the engines. In this case an air cart is used to provide compressed air to start one engine. The air cart is then usually disconnected, the airplane is pushed back from the gate, and once the aircraft is stopped, power is increased on the operating engine to provide the crossbleed air to start the other engine.

CROSSWIND - Wind blowing from the side, not coinciding with the path of flight.

DEGREE - 1/360 of a circle. Pilots measure their course in degrees. For example: north 360, east 90, south 180, west 270.

DIVE - A steep angle of descent. Airspeed increases rapidly.

DME - DISTANCE MEASURING EQUIPMENT - an indicator in the cockpit that displays the distance of the aicraft from a specific radio navigation aid.

DRIFT - Deviation from a course caused by crosswinds.

EADI - ELECTRONIC ATTITUDE DIRECTOR INDICATOR - See ADI and ATTITUDE INDICATOR.

EGT - EXHAUST GAS TEMPERATURE - Temperature of hot gases leaving the combustion chambers of a jet engine.

EHSI - See HORIZONTAL SITUATION INDICATOR

EICAS - Engine Indication and Crew Alerting System. Two electronic screens on the center instrument panel that display engine pressure ratio (EPR), speed of the three turbines in each engine (N1, N2, N3), fuel flow, oil temperature, oil pressure, and vibration. Warning, caution, or advisory text messages will also be displayed on the screens to alert the crew in case of aircraft system malfunctions.

ELEVATION - The height above sea level of a given land prominence, such as airports, mountains, and so on.

ELEVATORS - Control surfaces hinged to the horizontal stabilizer that control the pitch of the airplane, or the position of the nose of the airplane, relative to the horizon.

EPR - ENGINE PRESSURE RATIO - A measurement of engine power output obtained by comparing the pressure of the air going into the engine to the pressure of the air coming out.

FAK - FIRST AID KIT

FBI - FEDERAL BUREAU OF INVESTIGATION

FIN - A vertical attachment to the tail of an aircraft that provides directional stability. Same as vertical stabilizer.

FAA - FEDERAL AVIATION ADMINISTRATION - U.S. government agency that regulates the use of national airspace. Its many duties include certification of airlines, licensing of pilots, Air Traffic Control, and enforcement of regulations.

FEATHER A PROPELLOR - In the event of an engine failure, to align the blades of a propellor with the direction of flight. Feathering the propellor allows it to create less drag. The aircraft will then perform better with the power available from the remaining operating engine or engines.

FL330 - FLIGHT LEVEL 330. Approximately 33,000 feet.

FLAPS - Hinged or pivoted airfoils forming part of the trailing edge of the wing and used to increase lift at reduced airspeeds.

FLIGHT DIRECTOR - A flight computer which displays command bars on the ADI to indicate to the pilot the proper amount of pitch and bank should be applied to achieve a desired flight path. For example, when flying an ILS approach, the flight director will indicate to the pilot how much bank and pitch change is needed to remain centered on the localizer and steady on the glide slope.

FLIGHT PLAN - A formal written plan of flight showing route, time en route, points of departure and destination, and other pertinent information.

FMC - FLIGHT MANAGEMENT COMPUTER - A special computer on board the aircraft which combines information entered by the pilots through a key pad, information received from several supporting systems, and information stored in its memory. The computer uses the information from these sources to calculate the position of the aircraft along with pitch, roll, and thrust commands required to follow the programmed route and vertical profile. The FMC also sends information to the Electronic Horizontal Situation Indicator (EHSI) so that the pilots may have available a moving map display of the route. Other information pertaining to the flight may be obtained from the FMC such as estimated times over waypoints, wind direction and velocity, fuel remaining at destination, optimum altitude to be flown, and distance to the destination. Supporting systems that provide information to the FMC are the IRS, DME, VOR, ILS, clocks, Fuel Quantity, Fuel Flow, and Air Data Computers.

FRONT (weather) - Boundary of two overlapping air masses. When cold air is advancing on warm air, it is said to be a cold front; warm air advancing on cooler air is a warm front.

263

FUEL FLOW SYSTEM - Sensors and gauges that indicate to the pilots the amount of fuel that is flowing through the fuel system of each engine. This information is also sent to the FMC to be used in its fuel calculations.

FUSELAGE - The streamlined body of an airplane to which are fastened the wings and tail.

GEAR - The understructure of an airplane which supports the airplane. Retractable gear folds up into the airplane in flight. Gear that does not retract is called "fixed."

GLIDE - A motion of the airplane in which the airplane descends using little or no thrust toward the earth's surface.

GO-AROUND - Abandoning an attempt to land. A climb is initiated by applying power, raising the nose of the aircraft, retracting the flaps to create less drag, and raising the landing gear.

GROUND SPEED - Speed of an aircraft over the ground which may be faster or slower than its airspeed depending on the direction of the wind. An aircraft having an airspeed of 100 knots flying into a headwind of 20 knots will have a groundspeed of only 80 knots.

HEADING INDICATOR - Instrument used to determine in which direction the nose of the aircraft is pointing. It is usually located on the instrument panel directly below the ATTITUDE INDICATOR.

HOLDING PATTERN - A racetrack pattern flown over a specified fix while awaiting further ATC instructions to proceed.

HSI - HORIZONTAL SITUATION INDICATOR - Instrument that combines heading information with information from a VOR, an NDB, LOCALIZER, and GLIDE SLOPE. By combining the information otherwise displayed on several instruments, the HSI

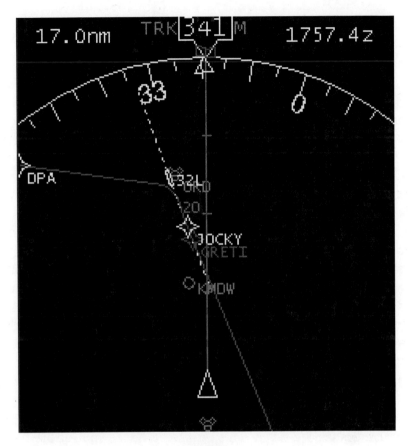

EHSI

allows the pilot to more easily scan his instrument panel to determine two things, namely, whether the aircraft is going in the right direction and what the position of the aircraft is relative to the desired navigation aid. An Electronic HSI (EHSI) may also present a moving map display of the route to the pilot. The HSI is usually placed directly below the ATTITUDE INDICATOR on the instrument panel. On some aircraft, the EHSI may be placed next to the ADI.

HYDRAULIC MOTOR GENERATOR - HMG - A back-up electrical generator of limited capacity used to power the captain's flight instruments and navigation aids, and other critical equipment in the event all power is lost from the left and right AC buses. The HMG can be driven by the left engine-driven hydraulic pump or the right engine-driven hydraulic pump through the PTU.

IFR - INSTRUMENT FLIGHT RULES - Rules pertaining to flights in conditions of visibility below the minimum required for visual flight.

ILS - INSTRUMENT LANDING SYSTEM - A combination of LOCALIZER, GLIDE SLOPE, and MARKER BEACONS associated with a particular runway. The LOCALIZER indicates whether the airplane is left or right of the runway. The GLIDE SLOPE indicates whether it is above or below the proper height for any given distance from the runway. MARKER BEACONS are located along the approach to indicate passing a certain distance from the end of the runway. The OUTER MARKER is usually located about 3 to 5 miles from the end of the runway. The pilot knows he is passing this point by a flashing blue indicator on the instrument panel and an aural beeping tone. The MIDDLE MARKER is located about one-half mile from the end of the runway and passage is indicated by a flashing amber indicator on the instrument panel and an aural beeping tone.

IMC - INSTRUMENT METEOROLOGICAL CONDITIONS - Reduced outside visibility which makes it necessary for the pilot to control the aircraft by reference to the instruments.

INSTRUMENT PANEL - The panel in front of the pilot that contains the instruments that the pilot uses to control the aircraft.

KNOT - A measure of speed, one knot being one nautical mile per hour. One nautical mile is equal to 1.15 statute miles.

IRS - INERTIAL REFERENCE SYSTEM - An electronic device that when properly initialized with a known position starting point uses a laser gyro and accelerometers to provide the following information to other systems on the aircraft such as instruments and the flight navigation computer: Aircraft pitch and bank,vertical speed, ground speed and track, true and magnetic heading, present latitude and longitude, wind speed and direction.

IRU - INERTIAL REFERENCE UNIT - See IRS.

LANDING PATTERN - A set rectangular path around the airport that airplanes follow to land.

LAZY 8 - A very gentle maneuver consisting of a 180-degree turn during which the aircraft climbs and descends, followed by another 180-degree turn during which the aircraft also climbs and descends. Control pressures constantly change during this maneuver.

LIFT - An upward force caused by the rush of air over the wings, supporting the airplane in flight.

LOGBOOK - A permanent record of a pilot's flight experience. A pilot usually logs the type of aircraft flown, origin, destination, duration of flight, time in night and instrument conditions, number of landings, instruction received or given, and any other details of the flight he may wish to record. He may also log time flying a simulator such as when completing one of his periodic checkrides.

LORAN - LONG RANGE NAVIGATION - A navigation system that determines the aircraft position by comparing time intervals between signals received from various low-frequency transmitters. This system is rapidly becoming obsolete as navigation systems based on satellite information are becoming standard equipment in aircraft of all sizes.

MEL - MINIMUM EQUIPMENT LIST - Since many aircraft are equipped with redundant systems, an aircraft may be flown with some components inoperative. The MEL specifies how long and under what conditions an aircraft may be flown with an inoperative component. It may also include certain procedures which pilots and/or maintenance personnel must follow when operating the aircraft that has the inoperative component.

MCP - MODE CONTROL PANEL - A panel located in front of the pilots with several switches and rotating controls that are used to input commands to the autopilots and autothrottles. Commands such as desired speed, altitude to maintain, turn to a heading, climb mode, descent mode, and selection of navigation mode are examples of the type of inputs the pilots may make to the autopilot using the MCP.

MNPS AIRSPACE - MINIMUM NAVIGATION PERFORMANCE SPECIFICATION AIRSPACE - Airspace over the Atlantic Ocean that is very crowded because of the large amount of air traffic between North America and Europe. Flying in this airspace requires adherence to specific procedures, a high degree of navigational accuracy, and special authorization.

NAT - NORTH ATLANTIC TRACK - System of routings for movement of traffic over the North Atlantic airspace between North America and Europe. See MNPS.

NDB - NON-DIRECTIONAL BEACON - A low-frequency radio signal that may be detected by an Automatic Direction Finding (ADF) receiver in the aircraft. The ADF has a needle indicator that points to the station. By comparing how many degrees left or right the needle points with the direction of the aircraft, the pilot can calculate his direction from the station and what course he would have to fly to go to it.

NOTAMS - Notices To Airmen - Supplemental information provided by governing agencies about airways, flight restrictions, airports, and runways that is of a temporary or changing nature.

NTSB - NATIONAL TRANSPORTATION SAFETY BOARD - A government agency whose duties include the investigation of aircraft accidents.

PEDALS - Left and right foot controls in the cockpit by which the pilot controls the action of the rudder.

PIC - PILOT-IN-COMMAND - The pilot who retains the ultimate responsibility for the safe operation of the aircraft.

PTU - POWER TRANSFER UNIT - On the B757, a hydraulic motor-pump which transfers hydraulic power from the right system to the left system. Hydraulic fluid flowing through the right system turns the motor side of the PTU. The rotation of that motor is used to turn a hydraulic pump that uses left hydraulic fluid. In the case of loss of left engine-driven pump hydraulic system pressure, the PTU is used to help power certain items such as landing gear, flaps, leading edge devices, nosewheel steering, and the hydraulic motor generator (HMG).

PYLON 8s - Two points on the ground are selected and the aircraft is flown around them at low altitude in a figure 8 pattern. While doing the maneuver the aircraft is climbed, descended, and banked to keep the pylon lined up with a reference point on the wing.

RADAR VECTORS - Instructions given by an air traffic controller to turn to specific headings. En route controllers often use radar vectors to keep aircraft separated that will be flying at or through the same altitude. Approach controllers use radar vectors to guide the pilot to the final approach course. When he gives his last vector to the pilot, the controller will usually clear the aircraft to complete the approach procedure to the runway.

RAMP - Area outside of airport buildings where airplanes are parked to be serviced or to receive and discharge passengers and cargo.

RMI - RADIO MAGNETIC INDICATOR - Instrument that combines a heading display with needles that will point to a VOR or NDB station. The RMI is normally placed on the instrument panel directly to the left of the HSI.

RUDDER - Control surface hinged to the back of the vertical fin that allows the pilot to control the aircraft around the vertical axis. When the pilot pushes the right rudder pedal, the rudder of the aircraft moves to the right. Air hitting the rudder causes the tail of the aircraft to move to the left and the nose will move to the right. The opposite effect is achieved with the left rudder pedal.

RUNWAY VISUAL RANGE - RVR - Forward visibility available to the pilot measured on a particular runway. It is possible for different runways on the same airport to have different RVR values. A good example would be an airport where fog is covering only part of the field.

RUNWAYS - Runways are named according to their alignment with a magnetic course rounded off to the nearest 10 degrees. The last zero is dropped. For example: Runway 24 is aligned with a course of about 240 degrees. Runway 9 is aligned with a course of 90 degrees, or East. Runway 18 is aligned with a course of 184 degrees, etc. Runway 4L and 4R refer to parallel left and right runways aligned with a northeasterly course.

SLOW FLIGHT - Flying the aircraft closer to the stall speed than normal. At these low speeds the controls are not as responsive and the aircraft is more difficult to control. It is important that a pilot be familiar with the airplane's characteristics at all the speeds at which it is capable of flying. Slow flight is a very valuable maneuver that develops this ability and also helps the pilot recognize the signs that an aircraft is approaching its stall speed.

SPEED BRAKES - Hinged control surfaces located on the upper surface of a wing that are used by the pilot to reduce lift and to increase drag. Speed brakes are used to increase a rate of descent or to slow an aircraft quickly.

STABILIZER - Stationary surfaces normally on the tail of an aircraft that stabilize the airplane around its lateral and horizontal axes.

STALL - Increase of angle of attack to the point where the wing stops producing adequate lift to sustain flight. A wing, to produce lift, requires a certain amount of air flowing by it at the proper angle. In some stalls complete control of the aircraft can be lost unless the proper stall recovery technique is initiated immediately. Stall recovery will always remain an essential part of flight training. All pilots learn to level the wings, add power if available, and lower the nose of the aircraft, which reduces the angle of attack. Also, by practicing stall recovery, a pilot learns to recognize when an aircraft is approaching a stalled condition. By being able to recognize the approach to the stall, he develops the ability to avoid stalls by making the proper corrections before one occurs.

STEEP TURN - A turn in which the angle of bank is 45 degrees or more. A smaller proportion of the total lift of the wing is directed against the force of gravity. Much of the lift now is being used to pull the aircraft in the direction it is banked. To hold altitude in a steep turn, the pilot is faced with an increased workload, as is the airplane. With the wings at a steep angle of bank it is harder to control the pitch, and the pilot feels as if he is being pressed down into his seat. A steep turn of 60 degrees of bank at a constant altitude produces two G's, or twice the force of gravity on the pilot. Developing the skill to execute steep turns smoothly takes practice, but if a pilot is highly skilled with steep turns, all of his flying technique will improve. Most people flying on airliners will never experience a 60-degree bank turn; the most they will ever see will likely be a 30-degree bank. Even that looks like a lot to a passenger looking out the window.

TACHOMETER - Instrument that measures the speed at which an engine crankshaft or propellor is turning. Measured in RPMs (revolutions per minute).

TAIL - The part of the airplane to which the rudder and elevators are attached. The tail has a vertical stabilizer to stabilize movement about its vertical axis and a horizontal stabilizer to stabilize movement about its lateral axis.

TAILDRAGGER - An aircraft that has conventional-type landing gear, such as two main wheels under the wings and a tail wheel under the tail. Because the center of gravity of a taildragger, or conventional gear aircraft, is located rearward of the main wheels, the aircraft is more difficult to taxi, take off, and land than an aircraft with TRICYCLE landing gear.

TOW BAR - Connector between a tow vehicle and an aircraft.

TRICYCLE LANDING GEAR - A type of landing gear in which the main wheels are normally located under the wings and a third wheel is located under the nose of the aircraft. In this configuration the center of gravity is forward of the main wheels, making aircraft control on the ground much more stable than with the older, conventional-type landing gear.

VECTOR - See RADAR VECTOR.

VERTICAL STABILIZER – see FIN.

VISIBILITY - Distance toward the horizon that objects can be seen and recognized. Smoke, haze, fog, and precipitation can hinder visibility.

VOR - VERY HIGH FREQUENCY OMNIRANGE - A high frequency radio aid that sends out signals in 360 degrees of direction. Using a needle called the Course Deviation Indicator and a TO/FROM indicator, the pilot can determine on which radial, or bearing, the aircraft is located. If he can obtain bearing information from two stations he can determine the exact location of the aircraft by seeing where the two bearings intersect.

VOR/DME - A VOR facility associated with Distance Measuring Equipment. A pilot can establish his position easily using a VOR/DME because he can immediately determine his bearing and distance from the station.

VSI - VERTICAL SPEED INDICATOR - Shows the pilot in feet per minute if the aircraft is climbing or descending. It is usually placed to the right of the heading indicator or HSI on the instrument panel.

V SPEEDS
V1 - Takeoff Decision Speed - maximum speed during takeoff that will allow the pilot to stop on the remaining runway in case of a rejected takeoff.
Vr - Rotation Speed - The speed at which the pilot raises the nose up for takeoff.
V2 - Takeoff Safety Speed - Speed at 35 feet AGL assuming engine failure at V1.

WET LEASE - an agreement under which an airline will rent an aircraft from another airline complete with crew for an extended period of time. Under such agreements, the aircraft may even be repainted to fly under the colors of the contracting airline.

WIDEVIEW - Program used to run a home flight simulator on multiple screens designed by Luciano Napolitano. (www.wideview.it)

Appendix

Universal Declaration of Human Rights

On December 10, 1948 the General Assembly of the United Nations adopted and proclaimed the Universal Declaration of Human Rights the full text of which appears in the following pages. Following this historic act the Assembly called upon all Member countries to publicize the text of the Declaration and "to cause it to be disseminated, displayed, read and expounded principally in schools and other educational institutions, without distinction based on the political status of countries or territories."

PREAMBLE

Whereas recognition of the inherent dignity and of the equal and inalienable rights of all members of the human family is the foundation of freedom, justice and peace in the world,

Whereas disregard and contempt for human rights have resulted in barbarous acts which have outraged the conscience of mankind, and the advent of a world in which human beings shall enjoy freedom of speech and belief and freedom from fear and want has been proclaimed as the highest aspiration of the common people,

Whereas it is essential, if man is not to be compelled to have recourse, as a last resort, to rebellion against tyranny and oppression, that human rights should be protected by the rule of law, Whereas it is essential to promote the development of friendly relations between nations,

Whereas the peoples of the United Nations have in the Charter reaffirmed their faith in fundamental human rights, in the dignity and worth of the human person and in the equal rights of men and women and have determined to promote social progress and better standards of life in larger freedom,

Whereas Member States have pledged themselves to achieve, in co-operation with the United Nations, the promotion of universal respect for and observance of human rights and fundamental freedoms,

Whereas a common understanding of these rights and freedoms is of the greatest importance for the full realization of this pledge,

Now, Therefore THE GENERAL ASSEMBLY proclaims THIS UNIVERSAL DECLARATION OF HUMAN RIGHTS as a common standard of achievement for all peoples and all nations, to the end that every individual and every organ of society, keeping this Declaration constantly in mind, shall strive by teaching and education to promote respect for these rights and freedoms and by progressive measures, national and international, to secure their universal and effective recognition and observance, both among the peoples of Member States themselves and among the peoples of territories under their jurisdiction.

Article 1.
All human beings are born free and equal in dignity and rights. They are endowed with reason and conscience and should act towards one another in a spirit of brotherhood.

Article 2.
Everyone is entitled to all the rights and freedoms set forth in this Declaration, without distinction of any kind, such as race, colour, sex, language, religion, political or other opinion, national or social origin, property, birth or other status. Furthermore, no distinction

shall be made on the basis of the political, jurisdictional or international status of the country or territory to which a person belongs, whether it be independent, trust, non-self-governing or under any other limitation of sovereignty.

Article 3.
Everyone has the right to life, liberty and security of person.

Article 4.
No one shall be held in slavery or servitude; slavery and the slave trade shall be prohibited in all their forms.

Article 5.
No one shall be subjected to torture or to cruel, inhuman or degrading treatment or punishment.

Article 6.
Everyone has the right to recognition everywhere as a person before the law.

Article 7.
All are equal before the law and are entitled without any discrimination to equal protection of the law. All are entitled to equal protection against any discrimination in violation of this Declaration and against any incitement to such discrimination.

Article 8.
Everyone has the right to an effective remedy by the competent national tribunals for acts violating the fundamental rights granted him by the constitution or by law.

Article 9.
No one shall be subjected to arbitrary arrest, detention or exile.

Article 10.

Everyone is entitled in full equality to a fair and public hearing by an independent and impartial tribunal, in the determination of his rights and obligations and of any criminal charge against him.

Article 11.

(1) Everyone charged with a penal offence has the right to be presumed innocent until proved guilty according to law in a public trial at which he has had all the guarantees necessary for his defence.

(2) No one shall be held guilty of any penal offence on account of any act or omission which did not constitute a penal offence, under national or international law, at the time when it was committed. Nor shall a heavier penalty be imposed than the one that was applicable at the time the penal offence was committed.

Article 12.

No one shall be subjected to arbitrary interference with his privacy, family, home or correspondence, nor to attacks upon his honour and reputation. Everyone has the right to the protection of the law against such interference or attacks.

Article 13.

(1) Everyone has the right to freedom of movement and residence within the borders of each state.

(2) Everyone has the right to leave any country, including his own, and to return to his country.

Article 14.

(1) Everyone has the right to seek and to enjoy in other countries asylum from persecution.

(2) This right may not be invoked in the case of prosecutions genuinely arising from non-political crimes or from acts contrary to the purposes and principles of the United Nations.

Article 15.
(1) Everyone has the right to a nationality.
(2) No one shall be arbitrarily deprived of his nationality nor denied the right to change his nationality.

Article 16.
(1) Men and women of full age, without any limitation due to race, nationality or religion, have the right to marry and to found a family. They are entitled to equal rights as to marriage, during marriage and at its dissolution.
(2) Marriage shall be entered into only with the free and full consent of the intending spouses.
(3) The family is the natural and fundamental group unit of society and is entitled to protection by society and the State.

Article 17.
(1) Everyone has the right to own property alone as well as in association with others.
(2) No one shall be arbitrarily deprived of his property.

Article 18.
Everyone has the right to freedom of thought, conscience and religion; this right includes freedom to change his religion or belief, and freedom, either alone or in community with others and in public or private, to manifest his religion or belief in teaching, practice, worship and observance.

Article 19.
Everyone has the right to freedom of opinion and expression; this right includes freedom to hold opinions without interference and to seek, receive and impart information and ideas through any media and regardless of frontiers.

Article 20.
(1) Everyone has the right to freedom of peaceful assembly and association.

(2) No one may be compelled to belong to an association.

Article 21.
(1) Everyone has the right to take part in the government of his country, directly or through freely chosen representatives.
(2) Everyone has the right of equal access to public service in his country.
(3) The will of the people shall be the basis of the authority of government; this will shall be expressed in periodic and genuine elections which shall be by universal and equal suffrage and shall be held by secret vote or by equivalent free voting procedures.

Article 22.
Everyone, as a member of society, has the right to social security and is entitled to realization, through national effort and international co-operation and in accordance with the organization and resources of each State, of the economic, social and cultural rights indispensable for his dignity and the free development of his personality.

Article 23.
(1) Everyone has the right to work, to free choice of employment, to just and favourable conditions of work and to protection against unemployment.
(2) Everyone, without any discrimination, has the right to equal pay for equal work.
(3) Everyone who works has the right to just and favourable remuneration ensuring for himself and his family an existence worthy of human dignity, and supplemented, if necessary, by other means of social protection.
(4) Everyone has the right to form and to join trade unions for the protection of his interests.

Article 24.
Everyone has the right to rest and leisure, including reasonable limitation of working hours and periodic holidays with pay.

Article 25.
(1) Everyone has the right to a standard of living adequate for the health and well-being of himself and of his family, including food, clothing, housing and medical care and necessary social services, and the right to security in the event of unemployment, sickness, disability, widowhood, old age or other lack of livelihood in circumstances beyond his control.
(2) Motherhood and childhood are entitled to special care and assistance. All children, whether born in or out of wedlock, shall enjoy the same social protection.

Article 26.
(1) Everyone has the right to education. Education shall be free, at least in the elementary and fundamental stages. Elementary education shall be compulsory. Technical and professional education shall be made generally available and higher education shall be equally accessible to all on the basis of merit.
(2) Education shall be directed to the full development of the human personality and to the strengthening of respect for human rights and fundamental freedoms. It shall promote understanding, tolerance and friendship among all nations, racial or religious groups, and shall further the activities of the United Nations for the maintenance of peace.
(3) Parents have a prior right to choose the kind of education that shall be given to their children.

Article 27.
(1) Everyone has the right freely to participate in the cultural life of the community, to enjoy the arts and to share in scientific advancement and its benefits.
(2) Everyone has the right to the protection of the moral and material interests resulting from any scientific, literary or artistic production of which he is the author.

Article 28.

Everyone is entitled to a social and international order in which the rights and freedoms set forth in this Declaration can be fully realized.

Article 29.

(1) Everyone has duties to the community in which alone the free and full development of his personality is possible.

(2) In the exercise of his rights and freedoms, everyone shall be subject only to such limitations as are determined by law solely for the purpose of securing due recognition and respect for the rights and freedoms of others and of meeting the just requirements of morality, public order and the general welfare in a democratic society.

(3) These rights and freedoms may in no case be exercised contrary to the purposes and principles of the United Nations.

Article 30.

Nothing in this Declaration may be interpreted as implying for any State, group or person any right to engage in any activity or to perform any act aimed at the destruction of any of the rights and freedoms set forth herein.

Credits

Editing

Once again Amy Spungen took over the controls to skillfully guide our flight clear of foggy valleys obscured by incorrect phrasing, beyond dangerous mountains of punctuation marks, and across an ocean of misspelled words. She consistently exercised a high degree of professionalism and attention to grammatical safety to bring us to our destination. Thank you Captain Spungen.

I would also like to thank my wife, Barbara, for the many hours she spent reading the original manuscript. Her questions, insights, and suggestions led to many corrections and changes to the text. Danke, danke. Ich liebe Dich, meine Dame.

Photos

Most of the photographs in this book were located through www.Airliners.net. Many thanks to the editor of Airliners.net, Johan Lundgren, who through his excellent website made it possible for me to easily find the photographs I needed.

Thank you to the photographers from all over the world whose work appears in this book. Their names are included with their photographs.

And special thanks to:

Peter Fagerstrom B757 Front cover photo

Eduard Brantjes B757 Back cover photo

Barbara Rogers Earl Rogers portrait

WWW.AMAZON.COM

Earl Rogers first soloed in 1972. He is type rated in the EMB110, L188, B727, B757/B767, and he has flown extensively as an airline captain in both domestic and international operations for more than 20 years. He currently lives in Chicago and San Miguel de Allende, Mexico.